the

BENEVOLENT LORDS
of
SOMETIMES ISLAND

A NOVEL

by

SCOTT SEMEGRAN

MUTT PRESS

First Edition

Mutt Press
Austin, Texas
https://muttpress.com
info@muttpress.com

ISBN 9781087878645
LCCN 2020909290

Edited by Charlotte Gullick, Brandon R. Wood, and Lori Hoadley
Cover Illustration by Andrew Leeper
Cover Layout by Scott Semegran & Andrew Leeper
Photo of Scott Semegran by Lori Hoadley

Books by Scott Semegran:
The Benevolent Lords of Sometimes Island
To Squeeze a Prairie Dog
Sammie & Budgie
Boys
The Spectacular Simon Burchwood
The Meteoric Rise of Simon Burchwood
Modicum
Mr. Grieves

Find Scott Semegran Online:
https://scottsemegran.com
https://www.goodreads.com/scottsemegran
https://www.twitter.com/scottsemegran
https://www.facebook.com/scottsemegran.writer/
https://www.instagram.com/scott_semegran
https://www.amazon.com/author/scottsemegran
https://www.smashwords.com/profile/view/scottsemegran

"This well-crafted story will appeal to anyone who grew up in the '80s. Fans of *Stand by Me* will also enjoy this trip back in time. Although at times wistful, it's not a purely nostalgic ode to growing up, but a genuine, moving and irresistible meditation on the value of friendship."

— *BlueInk Review* (Starred Review)

"Scott Semegran stretches his literary muscles in this highly accomplished and well-crafted read... a modern classic."

— *Readers' Favorite Book Reviews.* 5 stars.

"A page-turner. With his assured writing, tight plotting, and talent to fill a story with realistic details, Semegran has created another winner... A must read!"

— *The Prairies Book Review.* 5 stars.

"Evocative and compelling... a highly recommended, superb example of psychological twists and interpersonal encounters gone awry."

— *Midwest Book Review*, D. Donovan, Senior Reviewer

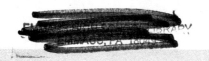

the BENEVOLENT LORDS *of* SOMETIMES ISLAND

A NOVEL

SCOTT SEMEGRAN

For my parents

Michael and Eloise Semegran

Who gave me just enough freedom

As a kid in the 1970s and 80s

To have my own adventures

Table of Contents

"Men do not know how much they are capable of doing till they try, and that we should never give way to despair in any undertaking, however difficult it may seem."

— R. M. Ballantyne, *The Coral Island*

"The thing is—fear can't hold you any more than a dream."

— William Golding, *Lord of the Flies*

"I never had any friends later on like the ones I had when I was twelve. Jesus, did you?"

— Stephen King, *The Body*

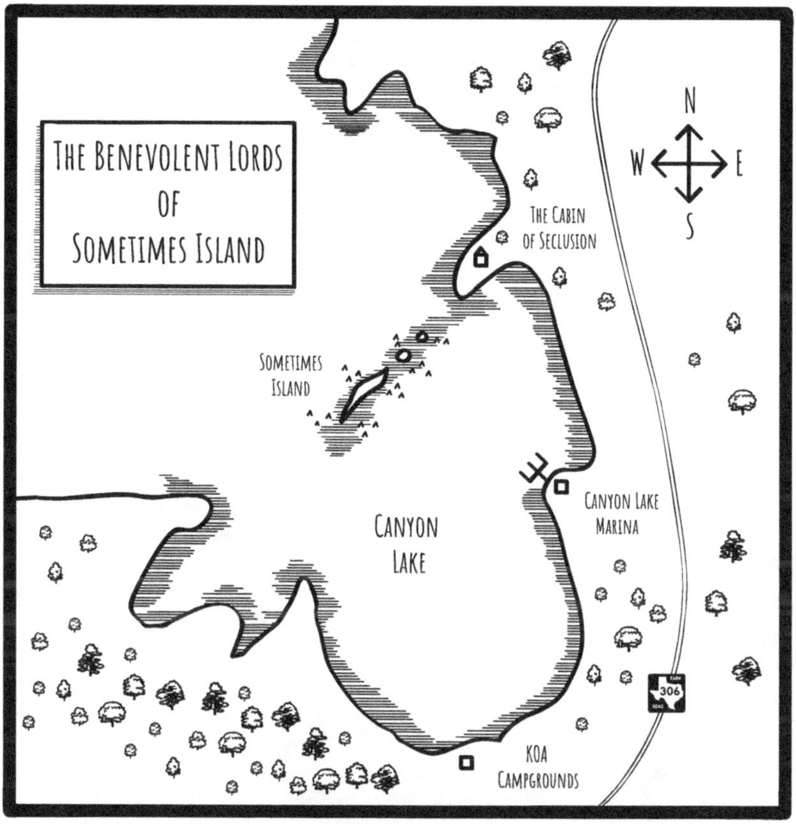

The Benevolent Lords
of
Sometimes Island
N
W
E
S
The Cabin
of Seclusion
Sometimes
Island
Canyon Lake
Marina
Canyon
Lake
306
KOA
Campgrounds

PART I.
Tyranny of the Thousand Oaks Gang

1.

The first time I experienced real, life-threatening danger was in the seventh grade. I may have been in real danger before the seventh grade, but if I was, then I don't remember it. That's the funny thing about memories. Some memories are these delicate, wispy things like dandelion seeds caught in a breeze—maybe sprouting someday, maybe they simply vanish. Other memories are these technicolor, vibrant things filled with music and smells and emotions—powerful and evocative mental cinema. Looking back, a lot of my memories of my friends in the seventh grade are living, vibrant things. I didn't need danger to make these memories of my friends stick in my brain. But there was once this remarkable time with them that you won't believe. When I finally tell you the whole story, you'll most likely say, *Nah! That didn't happen.* But it did. It really did.

Before I tell you about the time me and my friends got ourselves into some real danger when we were in middle school, first let me explain about myself and where I grew up. My name is William Flynn. I'm from a little suburban town outside of San Antonio, Texas called Converse. This town's sensibility was more strip mall than metropolis, but it did have the basic necessities for middle school kids: a dollar cinema (cheap flicks and all-you-can-eat popcorn), an arcade (with our faves *Donkey Kong* and *Joust*), a comic book store (Marvel titles more than DC), a skating rink, plenty of convenience stores, and the like. What more could a kid want? Back then, my parents called me Billy—a nickname that referred to my uncle who died during the Vietnam War—but I preferred my real name, William (even more so since Bloody Billy came into my life, but more on that later). My birth parents divorced when I was a baby, so I grew up mostly with my mom, Pam, and her new husband, Steve. He was a nice enough guy, although mostly quiet when it came to me. He loved my mom very much. That was obvious by the way he kissed and hugged her. I don't think he cared for me too much since he rarely acknowledged my presence back then, not even with a pat on the shoulder.

Anyway, the middle school in Converse, Texas that I attended was called Franklin D. Roosevelt Middle School—a better president I couldn't think of for a school moniker. Funny thing was, it was rare to have a school in the South named after a Northerner like Roosevelt, especially a liberal do-gooder like F. D. R. Most of the schools in and around San Antonio were named after Confederate war heroes like Robert E. Lee or Jefferson Davis. Don't ask me why. It's just an observation. But fortunately for me and my friends, we went to Franklin D. Roosevelt Middle School (Now, don't get me wrong, the name was great, but the outside looked more like a state penitentiary than an institution of learning). Most of the kids had a parent who worked at the nearby Air Force Base: Randolph. And because F. D. R. had students whose families were from all over the United States, the kids were all the possible shades of human beings, from pale white to middling brown to dark black. In the mid-1980s, it must've been a rare thing having a school population like that in Texas. Looking back, I can't imagine my childhood any other way. It's where I made my best friends, my posse, *mis compadres*. Their names were Randy Moss, Brian Johnson, and Miguel Gonzalez.

We were thick as thieves, as they say, or four peas in a pod, or whatever you want to call a tight crew of close friends. We did everything together, and when we weren't together, we made plans to meet up. We usually met after school in the wooded area behind F. D. R., a path cutting through the oak, pecan, and cedar trees that led the students home to the surrounding neighborhoods like Thousand Oaks or Hidden Oaks. As you rode your bike down the path, a small clearing appeared deep in the wooded area, and there was always some extra sporting equipment and metal bleachers lying around, left there by school district workers after football or baseball games. And on this day—the day that would be remembered as the day the real danger seeped into our lives—it was hot as blazes as Randy and I rode our BMX bicycles to the clearing to meet Brian and Miguel. It was the second to last week of school and even though it was technically still spring, it felt like summer had already arrived. The end of school always exuded the promise of fun. Summer couldn't come fast enough.

When Randy and I reached the clearing, we jumped from our bikes (BMX style with handlebar pads) and watched the riderless metal steeds careen into the surrounding brush. It was our unique way of dismounting our trusty rides. The sight of our bikes stabbing the bushes, then falling over, always made us laugh.

"Bullseye!" Randy cheered.

"Two points!" I belted out.

Randy hopped on the bottom bench of some metal bleachers. He was the tallest and burliest of the four of us—almost to the point of looking more like a grown man than a middle school-aged boy, his t-shirt and shorts fitting more snugly than they did when his mother bought them last fall—and standing on the metal bench made him appear gigantic, his hulking frame jutting up toward the sky, his red hair closely cropped on his square, freckled head. No one messed with Randy, not even high schoolers, and I enjoyed the security that came from standing next to such a massive friend. But little did they know that good ol' Randy was really a softy under that burly exterior. He rarely started trouble anymore like he did in elementary school. He mostly just wanted to make his friends laugh.

"I got some new jokes," he said, his hands on his hips, one foot tapping the metal bench. "Want to hear 'em?"

"Yeah, I want to hear 'em." I sat in the grass, his attentive audience of one. "We got time before Brian and Miguel show up."

"All right, let's see," he said, his eyes rolling up to scan the mental list of fresh jokes he'd been compiling throughout the day, instead of listening to his teachers. He carried a copy of *Truly Tasteless Jokes* by Blanche Knott in his back pocket and studied it like the Bible as well as copies of *Mad Magazine* and *Cracked* that he kept in his backpack. He couldn't get enough of these sources of juvenile jokes, puns, and riddles. "Did you hear about the monster with five legs?"

"No," I replied. "What about him?"

"They say his trousers fit him like a glove!" he said, punctuating his joke by extending his arms toward me, as if to say *Ta-da!*

I always burst into laughter when listening to Randy and his joke routines. He was just so enthusiastic about it, even if the jokes weren't all that funny. I loved that about him: his enthusiasm. Sometimes, a little enthusiasm will go a long way.

"I got a million of 'em," he quipped, a smirk on his face, confident in his new juvenile material. "Want to hear more?"

A rustling in the bushes behind us caught our attention and we both looked with curiosity, searching for what may be creeping around us. Not seeing anything, Randy said, "Must be a stupid squirrel."

"Yeah," I agreed.

"Now, where were we?"

But before he could continue, Brian and Miguel's bikes appeared riderless and crashed into the brush behind the metal bleachers. Randy's audience of one turned instantly to three.

"Got some new jokes?" Brian said, dropping next to me.

"I could use a laugh," Miguel chimed in.

"I'm here all night," Randy said, smirking. "I'm just getting warmed up. What took you guys so long?"

Brian sighed, then thumbed in Miguel's direction. "He had to whiz. Took *forever*!"

"I drank two cans of Big Red in seventh period. I had to go bad!" Miguel lamented. "I almost peed my pants."

"That would've been unfortunate," Brian said, patting his shiny, auburn Afro back into its original shape, then dusting shards of grass from his jeans. He was lanky like Miguel and me, but with longer, sinewy arms that reminded me of a praying mantis, and possessed a bright, toothy smile that was impenetrable to the sugary snacks we constantly ate. I don't know how we were so thin because we ate everything in sight like four trash compactors. I'm not joking. It seemed only Randy's mass consumption of junk food metabolized into muscle. The rest of us had black holes for stomachs where Twinkies, soda, and potato chips disappeared into another dimension.

"It would've been embarrassing!" Miguel was serious. The potential for embarrassment was to be avoided at almost all costs, especially in middle school. Miguel's earnest disposition was matched only by his studious fashion sense, which that day was Izod shirt and khaki shorts, an outfit closer to a uniform than what the rest of us wore. His curly mane always neatly cut and styled, the result of his father's militaristic routine of visiting the Randolph Air Force Base barber shop every three weeks.

Randy watched the three of us from his metal perch, unamused by the interruption to his comedy routine. His spotlight was dimming with every passing minute that Brian and Miguel bickered.

"Guys," he said. "You're holding up my show. I worked all afternoon on this routine."

"Go on!" I said.

But before he could continue, we were joined by a solemn crew emerging from the brush, tall high-schoolers who we knew all too well: The Thousand Oaks Gang. Led by "Bloody" Billy Callahan, the high school bruisers surrounded the metal bleachers while Randy hopped down to stand in-between us and the thugs. Bloody Billy was one of the few people not intimidated by Randy's over-sized stature.

"We want to hear more," Bloody Billy hissed, setting his backpack on the ground, then cracking his knuckles as he slowly approached our group. "I love jokes."

"Fuck you!" Randy barked. The Thousand Oaks Gang all chuckled. "We didn't ask you to join us."

"Really?" Bloody Billy stopped in place and looked around. "I wasn't aware that this was private property."

Billy Callahan—known as Bloody Billy for his propensity for profuse nose bleeds while fist fighting—was a lurking presence to the fearful middle-schoolers of F. D. R. Like the Boogie Man, his notoriety had only grown exponentially with time, and some middle-schoolers even whispered that he had failed several times and was quickly approaching 21-years of age, a perpetual senior at the neighboring Robert E. Lee High School. And although Randy certainly wasn't scared of Bloody Billy, we didn't want him brawling with the mean leader and his ruthless cronies. Bloody Billy was a reedy giant with fists like boulders and veins in his neck the size of water hoses, wearing a fascist uniform of tight-fitting jeans and a black Iron Maiden t-shirt. He even fit the part of lead singer for a heavy metal band—his shaggy, shoulder-length brown hair and square, stubbly jawline were perfect for a front man—albeit a lousy cover band at best. To make matters worse, Miguel's older brother, Rogelio, was a member of the Thousand Oaks Gang and Bloody Billy's main crony. Don't ask me why. His unerring allegiance to Bloody Billy was a constant thorn in our sides. He was the spitting image of Miguel except taller and his face gaunt with an insidious quality that I can only liken to an angry possum. But whenever Rogelio saw his little brother, he seemed to float to the back of the angry rabble like a ghost. Maybe he felt guilty for being a part of the gang that liked to rough us up. Maybe, but I doubted it. Randy stood his ground.

"Leave us alone," he said.

"But I want to hear your jokes, fuck stick—"

"Hey!" a husky voice called out behind us.

A security guard fast approached on a teetering golf cart, waving a flashlight in one hand while driving the cart with the other. When I turned around to see what Bloody Billy and his gang were going to do, they were already running down the path at full speed.

"Come on!" Randy commanded, and he darted for the surrounding brush. Brian and Miguel followed him in, and so did I as best I could with my gimp leg, after scooping up the backpack that Bloody Billy abandoned. I mean, there it was literally right before me—bright maroon with black shoulder straps and heavy metal band patches glued on—begging to be picked up. I didn't even think about it; I just grabbed it.

The security guard followed the gang of high-schoolers down the path, being that the gravel and dirt trail was an easier route for the golf cart to negotiate than off-roading in the woods, skidding in the leaves and mud after us middle-schoolers. We dove into a dank culvert and waited for the commotion to pass.

As we sat inside the culvert, panting and wheezing, we snickered at our predicament. It wasn't unusual for us to be chased by a security guard or a gang of high-schoolers, but every time it happened, it was still a big surprise. The inside of the culvert smelled like mildew, wet dog, and turds, but it was better than being beaten to a pulp by the Thousand Oaks Gang. A persistent dripping of water echoed from the other end of our hideout.

"That was close," I said, panting.

"Yep," Randy agreed, breathing heavily. "Say, did you hear the one about the dyslexic Satanist?" Nobody even tried to answer. Just panting all around. "He sold his soul to Santa."

"Very funny," Brian said, trying hard to catch his breath. "William, whose backpack you got?"

I shrugged, then sat the backpack in my lap.

"I think it's Billy's. It sure is heavy," I said.

"Open it," Miguel said. "Let's see what's inside."

I unceremoniously unzipped the backpack and pulled out its contents. In my hand was a large, clear bag of skunky vegetation that was most likely marijuana, although we didn't know for sure, having never been around marijuana, but certainly hearing about it. Underneath that in the backpack, thousands of dollars in various denominations of paper bills, some wadded, some rolled, and some just loose.

"Oh shit!" Randy said, his proclamation echoing.

Yep. What he said.

2.

What would you do if you found a bag filled with money? I imagine most people would fantasize about what they would do with all of it. Maybe they'd daydream about buying a fancy car (Italian sports car, fine leather seats). Maybe they'd imagine shopping for some fancy clothes (Nike tennis shoes, double-breasted suits). But the four of us—huddled and scared in that stinky culvert—we didn't discuss any grand plans after I unzipped that backpack. All we could think about was how to escape. We knew, without a doubt, that if Bloody Billy found out we had his backpack, then he and his gang would pulverize us. And we didn't want to get pulverized. So, when all the commotion above ground calmed down and all we could hear was the wind rustling the leaves across the dry grass and the exposed roots of the ever-watching trees, we quietly crawled out of the culvert to retrieve our fallen bikes. But rather than go the typical way home along that path, we cut through the wooded area to find a different street to ride home. We figured the Thousand Oaks Gang was leading the security guard on a wild goose chase through the neighborhood and would most likely come back as soon as Billy discovered he didn't have his backpack. We wanted to be long gone by then.

Brian suggested we ride to his house being that his family lived in Hidden Oaks, instead of Thousand Oaks like the rest of us, as well as most of the Thousand Oaks Gang. That seemed like a pretty good idea.

"Besides," he added, "It's Taco Thursday at my house. You guys hungry?"

Even better.

The prospect of food was always convincing, and Brian was a persuasive host. He patted his auburn Afro some more, a habit that never ceased to boggle my mind since his hair never seemed to move or be out of the desired shape, no matter what he did. I always secretly admired his hair's fortitude and resistance to change. It was his suave helmet, for sure.

We followed Brian to his house, a massive, brick two-story monstrosity of luxury we all dubbed The Mansion, being that it was larger than the rest of our families' more modest homes over in Thousand Oaks, and whose manicured lawn deemed it country club worthy. Brian's parents were like The Huxtables incarnate, the well to-do fictional family lead by actors Bill Cosby and Phylicia Rashad on the NBC sitcom, *The Cosby Show*. Brian's dad was a doctor—an oncologist more specifically—and his mother was a lawyer (what her specialty was, I didn't know). And, if you can imagine that powerful TV couple, then you know exactly what Brian's parents looked like: successful, amiable, and authentically African-American. We rode our bikes up the long driveway that snaked around The Mansion where a detached, three-car garage sat, with a winding cobblestone walkway slithering through the pristine, Bermuda grass to the house. We tossed our bikes on the ground like we always did and followed Brian in the back door. Inside, the smell of delicious food greeted us and we took our dirty shoes off in the boot room (which was almost the size of my family's living room, just saying) and lined them up against the wall, as Brian's mother had instructed us many times. I peeled Bloody Billy's backpack off my sweaty back and held it at arm's length. A stench clung to it like an apparition, a stinky reminder of the illicit package inside, underneath the adhered patches with band names like Judas Priest and AC / DC. I remember thinking to myself, *I don't want this anymore.*

"What do I do with *this*?" I said to everyone, and to no one.

"Just hang it there," Brian said nonchalantly, pointing to a brass coat rack attached to the wall.

"OK," I said, glad to be free of the smelly backpack.

"Ugh, it stinks," Miguel griped. He pinched his nose, then swatted at the air with his other hand, but the stench was cloying. The only thing to do was walk away.

We followed Brian to the kitchen where his parents were happily preparing dinner. At that moment, we caught them slow dancing to a song by the Commodores. Brian was not pleased with their show of affection for each other.

"Mom! Dad!" he said, turning his head with disgust.

"Sorry, son," his dad lamented. "It's our wedding song."

His mother pulled away and dusted herself off, as if particles of her husband's love and affection clung to her denim apron. She shook her head as she snickered at her son's protestations. Whenever I was at Brian's house, his parents were always clinging to each other, their love too strong to be contained by decorum. To be honest, I thought it was sweet. But I don't blame Brian. What kid likes to see his or her parents necking, especially when their friends are around? Totally disgusting.

"Do your friends want to stay for dinner?" his mother said, frying succulent ground beef in a gourmet pan on a fancy restaurant-style stove. "It's Taco Thursday."

"Yeah!" we collectively replied. Who would turn down free homemade tacos?

We grabbed some leather stools and sat around the massive island which took up valuable real estate in the middle of the kitchen—its shiny, glistening granite top cool under our sweaty forearms. The smell of dinner cooking was intoxicating: ground beef frying, beans stewing, and tortillas warming in a large skillet. Brian's father, who preferred to be called Mr. Johnson, beamed as he stood next to the island, his fists pressing against his hips, his growling belly pressing against his cashmere cardigan. He still wore his pants from work and looked like a super hero in repose, a few droplets of red on the front of his pants, which could've either been blood or ketchup. It was hard to tell.

"I know Brian has been busy writing letters to congressmen for a recommendation for Eagle Scout. What have you boys been up to?" he said.

Brian feigned embarrassment.

"Dad!" he protested.

"What?! I'm proud of you, son," he said, winking at his boy. "William, what keeps you busy?"

"Oh," I started, a little embarrassed. I didn't like to be the center of attention. "Just working on art. And writing."

"That's wonderful!" Mr. Johnson bellowed. "Art and writing are good for the soul." He turned to Randy. "What about you?"

Randy's face lit up. Unlike myself, Randy loved the attention, and took any and every opportunity to talk about himself.

"I've been working on my comedy act."

"Comedy act? You mean *jokes*?"

"Yeah, jokes."

"Like Richard Pryor? You hear that, honey?!" he called out while thumbing at Randy. She continued without looking at us, pushing the ground beef around in the pan with a spatula. "Randy wants to be like Richard Pryor!"

"Well," Randy said, sheepishly rubbing the back of his neck. "No one's like Richard Pryor."

"That's true," Brian's dad agreed. "He's an original. Tell me a joke then. Wha' cha got?"

Randy looked at the three of us, sort of perplexed, as if his brain was riffling through all the jokes he'd been consuming, and all the other functions his brain controlled seized up like an automobile engine after burning off all its lubricating oil. Then his face lit up.

"What did Helen Keller's parents do to punish her for swearing?"

"I don't know," Brian's dad said. "This better be good!"

"Washed her *hands* with soap," he said, then extended his own hands as if to say *Ta-da!*

Brian's dad burst out laughing, a loud, booming laugh that shook the kitchen like thunder.

"That's good. I like your enthusiasm, too." Then he turned to Miguel. "What about you?"

"Me?" Miguel said, pointing at his chest, the upturned collar of his shirt an added bit of emphasis to his surprise.

"Yeah, you. I'm not talking to anyone else," he said, chuckling.

"I've been studying ancient rulers."

"Ancient rulers? Ya mean, like Napoleon?"

And with this question, Miguel's face lit up. "Yes, but more like the difference between benevolent and malevolent rulers in history. I'm curious as to why the rulers of history chose to go down one path or the other. Very fascinating."

"Really?" Brian's dad replied. He was caught off guard a bit. "Seems a little heady."

"Yeah," Miguel quipped, smirking. "Heady."

"Well, I'd offer you boys some brewskies, but I wouldn't want to offend your parents. So, how about some *root* beers?"

"Yeah!" we answered.

He pulled four cans of Barq's Root Beer from the giant Amana refrigerator.

"Now, you boys keep up these fine hobbies and don't get yourselves into any trouble messing around with drugs or anything like that."

When he said the word *drugs*—drawing out the 'u' in a throaty uh sound—we cocked our heads back and looked at each other, a little surprised at even the mention of the word, as if he knew what we discovered earlier in the backpack of

Bloody Billy while huddled in the culvert, the same stinky backpack hanging on the wall in the boot room.

"Dad?!" Brian said. "You *can't* be serious right now?"

Mrs. Johnson agreed with her son's lament. "Leave them alone, dear." At which time, she turned the stove off, poured the ground beef into a serving bowl, then placed it on the island with the rest of the taco fixings. "You boys eat up now."

The four of us and Mr. Johnson made ourselves decadent tacos, piling beef, shredded lettuce, and mounds of cheese on top. It seemed to please Mrs. Johnson that we all were enjoying a meal together. She lovingly watched us without fixing herself a plate, probably still on the *Elizabeth Taylor Diet* or something (she was always boasting about starving herself with one strange diet or another in 1986).

"Dear?" she said to her husband. "You should invite Brian's friends to join us this weekend."

"This weekend?" he said, his mouth already filled with food and bits of beef showering the island.

"Ya know? *Camping*?"

"Yes! Camping," he stammered, deliberately chewing the rest of the food before continuing. "Good idea. Would you boys like to join us camping? We're driving the camper up to Canyon Lake for the weekend. It's nice to get away from civilization for a few days. You boys don't need to bring a thing 'cept yourselves. What do you say?"

"Yeah, guys," Brian continued, finally pleased with something his parents said. "It'll be fun! Plus, I can show you all the stuff I've been learning for my Eagle Scout."

The three of us were generally agreeable, except I was worried about asking my parents. Sometimes, they could put a damper on things, especially if it was anything I considered to be fun. They could be real sourpusses. Randy could sense my reluctance and he already knew what I was reluctant about.

"It'll be fine," he said, putting his hand on my back. "Tell them we're all going."

"All right."

"Yeah," Miguel chimed in.

"All right, all right," I said. "I'll ask them as soon as I get home."

When we finished eating, it was getting late. I thanked Brian's parents for feeding us, which they agreed was simply the right thing to do, and said goodbye to my friends. I went into the boot room to retrieve my shoes and was reminded about the backpack from its lingering stench. As I slipped on my shoes, Randy appeared next to me. It seemed he also remembered the backpack—including the illicit items it contained inside—and was curious what I was going to do with it.

"I don't know. Put it in my room somewhere," I answered.

Randy nodded. Most people would've been suspicious with a friend running off with a backpack full of money, but not Randy. We trusted each other. We had an unspoken bond. And stashing the backpack in my room seemed to be just as plausible an idea as any other.

"Cool. See ya tomorrow!" he said, then bolted back to the kitchen, probably for some dessert.

I took the back-way home, just in case any of the Thousand Oaks Gang was out and about. The back way consisted of a short ride to the end of Brian's street which turned into a cul-de-sac. A handy cutout for a yet-to-be-laid cement driveway for a future custom home was the portal to a wooded area that separated Hidden Oaks from Thousand Oaks, and I rode my bike through it as fast as I could. I didn't see anyone from the Thousand Oaks Gang on the way, which was quite a relief, although I could hear the bellowing exhaust of their sports cars somewhere in the distance. That sound was a frightening reminder that they could appear at any second to terrorize us.

When I got to my house (tinier and simpler compared to The Mansion that Brian's family owned), I tossed my bike into the unkempt grass next to the broken lawn mower by the back door, and ran inside. But instead of greeting my parents in the kitchen—where they were finishing their own dinner of Hamburger Helper accompanied with iceberg lettuce salad and cherry Kool-Aid—I went straight to my room and closed the door. It was my sanctuary and I knew my mother wouldn't come in. The décor was pretty much unchanged from my early elementary school years and I liked it that way. On the floor were my precious possessions: Micronauts action figures, Hot Wheels race cars, Star Wars action figures and vehicles, Evel Knievel doll and motorcycle, Shogun Warriors in various sizes, and a pile of Legos intermixed from various sets. My art supplies were spread across the floor as well and, as I scurried to my desk to find a screwdriver, I stepped over the various markers and coloring pencils strewn on the dingy shag carpet as well as my latest obsession: coloring the black and white pages of a pocket book copy of *The Amazing Spider-Man.*

"Billy!" my mother called from the kitchen. Remember, she liked to call me Billy even though I preferred being called by my real name: William.

"Yeah, mom?" I replied. "What is it?"

I opened the top desk drawer and found a flathead screwdriver. "Yes!" I enthusiastically whispered to myself.

"Are you going to eat with us?" my mom called out.

"Be right there!"

With the screwdriver in hand, I opened my closet, shoved the hanging clothes to one side, which revealed what I was looking for: a metal plumbing vent. I unscrewed the vent cover from the dry wall and set it on the carpeted floor. Inside the gaping, rectangular hole in the wall, I could see plumbing pipes and pine wood studs connected with cob webs, dead bugs clinging to the white strands like Christmas ornaments. I quickly shoved the stinky backpack into the gaping hole, propped the vent cover back over it, and screwed it back to the wall. Satisfied with the hiding place, I slid the hanging clothes back and closed my closet doors.

My mother continued to call from the kitchen. "We made cheesy Hamburger Helper. Your favorite!"

"I said I'll be right there!"

I put the screwdriver back in the desk drawer, then joined my parents at the dinner table in the kitchen. At their insistence, I ate a huge helping of Hamburger Helper, then had mint chocolate chip ice cream for dessert. I didn't mention a word about the Thousand Oaks Gang but the knowledge of what I was hiding in my room gnawed at my insides. I hated the idea that my mother might snoop around in my room the next day while I was at school, so I thought of better ways of concealing what was hidden in the wall of my closet—maybe stacking some dirty clothes in front of the plumbing vent or piling up sets of toys and boardgames—while finishing the last of my dessert.

3.

The next day during lunch, the F. D. R. cafeteria was abuzz. Summer was around the corner and all the kids were chattering about their vacation plans with their families over lukewarm tray lunches (Salisbury steak with mashed potatoes or pepperoni pizza with corn) and brown sack lunches. The smell of bleach and reheated meat products always mixed into a noxious aroma that permeated the walls of the loud and raucous cafeteria, along with the stench of teenage hormones and body odor. My three best friends and I chattered, too, about our camping trip that night with Brian's parents. Brian wanted to make some things clear about his parents and their unique set of rules for camping, mostly that there really weren't any rules except to respect their "alone time." It seemed his mom and dad were looking forward to this trip just as much as we were.

"They like to *reconnect* on these camping trips," Brian said. "And when I say reconnect, I really mean *hump.*"

"Ewww!" we all agreed. The idea of discovering Brian's parents in the throes of passion was terrifying to our young minds. I think we would've preferred traipsing across fresh roadkill to viewing any of our parents *doing it.*

"But on the other hand," Brian continued. "That also means we can do whatever we want! Just remember, when my dad says, *if the camper is a rockin'*..., then you know what he's talking about. Don't say I didn't warn you."

"That's disgusting but 10-4!" I said, then pointed at a desirable lunch item in front of Brian. "I'll trade you my Capri Sun for your Little Debbie cake."

"Duh!" Brian agreed. That was a good trade between us.

"I don't think I can go," Miguel said. "My mom said she doesn't want me to miss church."

"What's missing *one* Sunday at church gonna do?" I said, unwrapping the Little Debbie cake, then shoving it whole into my mouth, which didn't impede my ability to communicate. "How many-thh have yoouu missed-thh? None-thh?!" Spittle and Little Debbie bits rained on my friends as they attempted to swat them away.

"She just hates us cause we're not Catholic," Randy said. "She's a Protestant-hater."

"Yeah," Miguel agreed. "That, too."

"Don't worry, Miguel," I said, swallowing the last of the cake, remnants of icing coating my lips. "I'll call her and convince her. Or Randy will. Your parents always listen to him."

Randy nodded. "No problemo, dude."

"I don't know," Miguel said. He slowly bit into his peanut butter and jelly sandwich. "She's wicked serious about church."

"I'm serious, too," I said, patting him on the back. After Miguel meekly smiled, I turned to Randy. "Your mom is cool with it, right?"

"Yeah, she's cool with it. Anything to give her some *alone* time. She's still pretty sore at my dad."

Randy's mom finally kicked Randy's dad out, his abusive ways cracking fissures through their marriage that made their rocky relationship untenable. He moved into a tiny, studio apartment in Universal City (the next tiny town just west of Converse) and she changed the locks to the house as soon as she could, filing a restraining order with the Bexar County family court soon after. Although Randy didn't see his dad much, his lurking presence hung over the house like a dark thundering cloud. Any chance for a respite from parenting was good news for Randy's mother.

"Great! My folks are cool with it, so it looks like we're all in."

"B-I-N-G-O and camping was our game-O!" Randy belted out in his best high-pitched Michael Jackson imitation, which of course made us all laugh, prompting him to jump up and rhythmically thrust his hips back and forth like the King of Pop would have if he was dancing in a dark alley somewhere on a Hollywood set. Randy loved the attention from us so much, it was ridiculous. And when we were done laughing, Randy leaned over to me, cupping his hand to his mouth.

"Hey, what did you do with the backpack?"

Yes—the backpack. It was so easy to forget once it was out of sight and hidden in the wall in my bedroom closet, like a carefully buried treasure on a remote beach in the Caribbean. But before I could answer, Miguel started waving his hands all over the place and shushed us. The color drained from his face and it looked like he had seen a ghost, or even something worse.

"My brother is coming over," he said, terrified.

"Damn!" I said, refusing to look, as if ignoring Miguel's older brother Rogelio would simply make him disappear.

The lunch table shook when he plopped in the spot next to Miguel, putting his younger brother in a headlock so fast that Miguel couldn't defend himself. He tried to wriggle from Rogelio's firm arm clamp, but couldn't. Miguel also tried to yell, but his voice was muffled and sounded like his protestations were coming from under smothering pillows. Rogelio dug into his little brother's scalp with the knuckles of his right hand, dispensing a vicious noogie.

"Leave him alone!" Randy demanded, almost standing, which made Rogelio dig deeper into Miguel's skull. The pain poor Miguel felt was audible through squeaks and pants.

"You can't tell me what to do with my own little brother," Rogelio said, squeezing Miguel's head tighter, then releasing him. Miguel's hair stood on end as if statically shocked and his face flared bright red. He was mortified.

"What was that for?!" Miguel said. His brother laughed.

"I know you have Billy's backpack, turd breath," Rogelio said. He shot a penetrating stare. Miguel looked away.

"I don't have it," Miguel said. "None of my friends do."

"Mmm hmm," Rogelio said. He slowly rose to his feet. "If you give it back to me by the end of the day, then nothing will happen to you or your so-called friends."

He swatted his little brother's sack lunch to the floor, the remainder of his lunch sliding across the tile. He stepped on a bag of Fritos when he walked away, leaving quickly before any of F. D. R.'s faculty or security staff noticed his presence, all of whom did their best to keep the Thousand Oaks Gang off campus, even if it was practically impossible. I felt bad for Miguel. I could never figure out how two completely different boys—opposite in every shape, way, and form—could come from the same womb. Miguel was the nicest guy and his brother was—to put it bluntly—a real dick.

"I was finished with lunch anyway," Miguel cracked, then smirked. We all snickered.

"Yeah!" we all chimed in, and as a sign of solidarity, the rest of us tossed our sack lunches on the floor, too.

"He's gonna get his someday," I told Miguel, but he returned a look like that premonition would never come to fruition.

"Doubt it," he said. "As much as we go to church, you'd think God would've punished him by now."

I couldn't argue with that logic.

After school, we rode our bikes over to Brian's house, a little worried that we might get accosted by Bloody Billy, Rogelio, and the rest of the Thousand Oaks Gang on the way, but we didn't see them. But that didn't make the bike ride any less tense. Once we got to The Mansion and went inside, I demanded that Miguel call his mother, so I could talk to her.

"She's just gonna say no," he said, reluctantly dialing his home number into the phone mounted on the wall in the kitchen, then handing the phone receiver over. It had a ridiculously long phone cord that coiled to the floor, an added feature that Mrs. Johnson insisted her husband install. You'd think with all their money that she'd want a newfangled cordless phone, but she feared the wireless devices would give her family brain tumors, and opted for a ten-foot, old-fashioned cord instead. Even though her husband was an oncologist and insisted the cordless phones wouldn't cause brain tumors, she still preferred a corded phone.

"She won't say no to me," I said slyly, a smirk sliding across my face. "I know how to talk to the *ladies*."

Miguel cackled at the notion that his mother would fall for my supposed cool demeanor, but as soon as she answered the phone, I laid it on thick. She eventually said yes, to Miguel's utter surprise. When I hung up the phone, Miguel's jaw practically hit the floor.

"Told ya," I said, wiping my hands together as if ridding them of the dust of his dubiousness.

"Amazing!"

As we milled about in the kitchen, raiding the refrigerator and pantries, Mr. Johnson shuffled in with a large Igloo cooler in hand, knocking kids out of the way as he approached the refrigerator.

"You boys take your backpacks outside to the camper while I fill this cooler with sodas and ice. Throw your stuff in the back. Go on! Get!" He set the cooler on the floor in front of the fridge, popped the top, and tossed soda cans inside from the refrigerator. He then pulled the ice bin from the freezer and dumped all the ice in there. "T-minus 20! I want to get to the campground before dark!"

We scurried outside.

All of us packed our backpacks the night before. (Although he claimed his mother would still say no, Miguel even had his backpack. Sometimes he spoke like a pessimist, but his actions usually screamed optimism.) We had the few necessities we'd need for the weekend: a pair of shorts (which we would practically spend the entire weekend wearing), a ball cap, a spare pair of underwear, a spare t-shirt, sandals, a tooth brush, and a towel that we could use as both a pillow and to dry ourselves. Brian's parents were providing the rest.

Mr. Johnson soon came outside to find us all standing around the camper, but instead of throwing our backpacks in the back like he demanded, we stood in the driveway with our backpacks in our hands, facing the street, staring at something quite unexpected.

"What the *heck* are you boys doing?" he said, setting the cooler on the ground. When he stood back up, he discovered what we were all looking at, standing at the end of the driveway in the street: The Thousand Oaks Gang. Bloody Billy and a few of his stooges leaned against a white `82 Camaro parked at the curb closest to the driveway. Rogelio and a few others stood around a black `84 Mustang across the street. Both cars idled, their engines gurgling. Mr. Johnson pushed through our petrified group, then stood at front. He turned to examine our faces, then turned back to the gang in the street.

"What the heck?" he said, then called out. "What do you—"

Billy raised his arm in the air, lassoed a circle with his index finger, then hopped in his Camaro, the rest of his stooges following. The two muscle cars screeched across the asphalt street, then were out of sight. Mr. Johnson turned to us, a sour look on his face.

"Are you boys causing trouble?" he snapped.

"Us?!" Brian said. "Why do you think we're the ones causing trouble?"

"'Cause you look guilty, that's why. Come on, now! Let's get the camper loaded up. It'll be dark soon." Mr. Johnson squatted to lift the cooler, then struggled to pick it up. Randy and I helped him lift it while he bemoaned his back troubles. "Sucks getting old," he said.

We put the cooler in the back of the camper, then he went inside to retrieve his wife. We placed our backpacks in the camper, a 1986 Volkswagen Westfalia model, the one where the roof would prop up at a 45-degree angle when released, a deeper color of lollipop blue I hadn't seen on any vehicle. Brian's dad was very proud of that camper—buying it new from the Volkswagen dealer earlier that spring—although it didn't have enough seats for all of us. His parents would occupy the two front seats, while three of us took the back-bench seat, which left Brian free-range on the floor. He didn't seem to mind, though. In fact, I think he preferred the precarious place, an element of danger in being the one sitting loose while the camper delivered us to the lake.

"Does anyone have to whiz before we go? Miguel?" Brian said, giving Miguel the stink eye.

"Why me?" Miguel replied, a look of surprise on his face.

"Because you always need to whiz!"

"I already went," he replied, satisfied with his attentiveness, adjusting the neck hole in his t-shirt as if straightening a tie.

"Mmm hmm," Brian hummed, still skeptical.

We jumped in the camper and continued to wait for Brian's parents. Randy looked distressed as he turned to look at the street, the smell of burnt tires and car exhaust still in the air.

"I don't think they're ever gonna leave us alone until they get that backpack back. Are they?"

A quiet profundity consumed the group, as if Randy's observation had a dismal answer we all didn't want to confess was true.

"Probably," I said.

"So why don't we just give it back to them?" Randy said.

"You think we should?"

"Better than being hunted like dogs."

"But they really don't know I have it. And if they do think I have it, they don't know where I hid it."

It was a quandary, for sure, one without an immediate answer, certainly one that wouldn't be answered at that moment as Brian's parents approached.

"Let's call a meeting tonight at the campground," Brian said. "When my folks want alone time."

He leaned to the side door to slide it closed. Brian's parents hopped in the front and his dad turned around to face us.

"Everybody ready?" he said.

"Yeah!" we cheered.

"Then we're off!"

He pressed the button to the garage door remote control clipped to the visor above his head, then turned the key to crank the engine. And soon we were off, heading to the campground on the shore of Canyon Lake, about a thirty-minute drive. As we pulled away from the neighborhood, I turned and watched the road retreat behind us through the rear window, hoping Bloody Billy's white `82 Camaro would not appear unexpectedly and follow us to the lake.

4.

Before we go on, I must admit that I forgot to mention something. Earlier, I said that middle school was the time in my life when I first experienced real danger, but I failed to recall a time in my life during elementary school when, in fact, I also experienced something quite dangerous. Sorry I didn't mention it earlier, but that's how it goes with memories sometimes. They can appear and disappear in your mind like fireflies dancing across your front lawn on a warm spring night. But as I was telling you this story about me and my friends in middle school and the danger we would get ourselves into, I remembered something important. It might shed a little light on why I was so tight with my friends.

You see, Randy Moss and I weren't always friends. There was a time when he was my sworn enemy. In the third grade, Randy was the school bully. He pushed, shoved, punched, and menaced most everyone at Crestridge Elementary School, boys and girls alike. He was pretty angry and I didn't know why. Nobody did. Everyone knew to just stay away from him or else you'd get thrashed. In the third grade, he was a mean son of a bitch. There's really no nicer way to put it.

But one day, I grew tired of his bullying and decided to do something about it. I hawked a gun from my mother's nightstand—a 25-caliber American Derringer pistol—and stashed it in my *Star Wars* lunchbox before school. When it was time for recess, I moved the gun to my pants pocket and meant to teach Randy a lesson real good on the playground. Instead, Randy knocked me to the ground, then he was sent to the principal's office by my teacher, Ms. Brookshire. Dejected, I went home after school and retreated to the treehouse in my backyard. To my surprise, Randy appeared in the wooded area behind my house. He waved a wilted gesture of surrender, then climbed up in the treehouse. Turns out, Randy's dad was *his* bully, evident by his bruised jaw. He confessed that he really wanted to be friends and was sorry for being a jerk to me. We've been best friends ever since.

That is not all. There is more to this story. While our rivalry did turn to friendship that day in the treehouse, I forgot that the gun was still in my pants pocket while we abdicated our rivalry. When my mother called us to come to dinner, we cavalierly jumped to the ground from the treehouse. When my feet hit the earth, the gun discharged, sending a bullet through my thigh. My mother was shocked, as was Randy. Neither of them knew I had a gun in my pocket and I had forgotten all about it, as young kids are prone to do about important matters. Nor would either of them have suspected that a quiet boy like me was capable of the amount of rage required to sneak a gun to school and shoot a classmate as revenge for daily bullying. Thankfully, everything turned out all right. Obviously, I didn't die since I'm telling you this story now. But from that point on, once I healed, I walked with a limp, the bullet having torn through my thigh muscles and nicking the iliotibial band in such a way that it shriveled. Isn't it funny how a poor decision can alter your life in such a way? It could've been much worse. I could've died, or Randy could've been hurt, too.

A friendship grew from a dangerous situation, yet Randy always felt guilty about it. I think he felt that his bullying was the reason my leg got hurt from the gunshot. He always marveled that the bullet that went through my leg was really meant for him. I think as we grew older, Randy became more and more protective, like he was trying to make up not only for bullying me in the third grade, but for mistreating me so badly that I wanted to bring a gun to school and shoot him. Pretty crazy, huh? Threats of violence like that change a person, even a blockhead bully in elementary school. He must have realized that his life could have been over, quickly extinguished by a bullet from a 25-caliber American Derringer pistol that was originally intended for my mother to use to protect our home. But this incident in the third grade, as scary as it sounds, was nothing compared to what was going to happen to us in middle school. Real danger was waiting for us across the placid waters of Canyon Lake. I'll get to that soon enough.

You may also be wondering, if I met Randy in the third grade, then when did we become friends with Miguel Gonzalez and Brian Johnson and add them to our tight-knit group? Randy and I met Miguel in the fifth grade. Turns out, Miguel's father was in the military—the Air Force to be exact—and stationed at Randolph Air Force Base, just right outside of Converse, relocating there in the middle of the school year from Edwards Air Force Base in California. Miguel's family moved into a small, three-bedroom house in Thousand Oaks, not too far from Randy's house and mine. Our teacher, Mr. Head, introduced Miguel to Randy and me after class one day because Miguel told him that he liked Marvel Comics (*The Amazing Spider-Man*, *The Uncanny X-Men*, *The Fantastic Four*) which—of course—Randy and I did, too. Mr. Head had confiscated dozens upon dozens of our comic books and knew our devotion to them. He thought we'd all make good friends, which made us skeptical of each other. A grownup putting kids together—a despised teacher even—wasn't how kids became friends! But the funny thing was, once the three of us started talking about comic books—particularly when Miguel went on and on about how much he loved the malevolent ruler and super villain Dr. Doom and how his metal suit was superior to Iron Man's—our friendship was sealed. Weird how that happens. Plus, once Miguel learned about our love of all things *Star Wars*, then the three of us became inseparable. We loved everything about Miguel except his older brother, Rogelio, who was a royal douche bag, even back then. We could never figure out how two brothers who were so different in every way came out of the same mother.

We met Brian a year later in the sixth grade during P. E. Since he lived in Hidden Oaks and Randy, Miguel, and I lived in Thousand Oaks, Brian was from a different elementary school: Dwight D. Eisenhower Elementary School. Both elementary schools fed into F. D. R. Middle School. When our P. E. teacher seemed less than thrilled to monitor our activities (a bad attitude I would realize years later was engendered by constant hangovers and low self-esteem), he made the class play Dodge Ball. And the sixth graders *hated* playing Dodge Ball because the eighth graders would absolutely destroy them. One day during a particularly vicious game, I got pegged in the face by an overenthusiastic eighth grader who was gleefully performing his school-sanctioned bullying. I hit the parquet floor like a sack of potatoes. Lights out. But once I opened my eyes, I discovered I was being taken care of by Brian who, I learned while he sat with me at the side of the gym, was an expert in C. P. R., the Heimlich Maneuver, and a number of other medical procedures he offered to perform on me, valuable lessons he learned while in the Boy Scouts, in hopes of being a doctor one day like his father. After Randy and Miguel were demolished during the game, they crawled over to where I lay with Brian. As all middle schoolers learn while sitting with each other for brief periods of time, we had a lot more in common than we thought. Turns out, Brian loved Marvel Comics, too. His favorite character was Doctor Strange, who served as the sorcerer supreme in the Marvel Universe, but was also a doctor—a surgeon more precisely—just like his namesake. Of course, we became fast friends. Turns out, Brian didn't like *Star Wars*, though. He preferred silly movies like *Real Genius* starring Val Kilmer to sci-fi movies. What a weirdo.

Once we were friends, we were inseparable. I don't know if it was divine intervention, teacher intervention, or just damned pure luck, but it's funny how your friends in middle school can be some of the most influential friends of your life. To this day, I still think quite fondly of the adventures and troubles we got ourselves into. It's pretty remarkable that none of us lost any fingers, toes, eyeballs, or testicles. And like I said before, real danger was waiting for us in the seventh grade. I wouldn't have wanted to experience it with anyone else besides Randy Moss, Brian Johnson, and Miguel Gonzalez.

5.

On the way north on I-35, then west on FM 306, the sun began its descent behind the evening clouds, casting pastel reflections across the sky and earth as we headed to the campgrounds, giving our road trip the slightest hint of divinity and otherworldliness. Huddled together in the back of the camper—serenaded by the wail of the rear-mounted engine nestled beneath the back bench that three of us sat on—we listened to a cassette of various pop songs on a tape player that Randy ganked from his mom (ganking was our slang for stealing). The black rectangle emblazoned with the Sony logo finished with chrome paint was a small, one-speaker, battery-operated player she bought at K-mart, so she could listen to motivational speakers on tape, but never did. Brian's parents exchanged goo-goo eyes in the front of the camper. They insisted on listening to Lionel Richie or Barry White albums on the camper's cassette player which, to our younger ears, was appalling. Stereo wars between parents and kids weren't unusual—the generational gap on full display through vastly different musical tastes—but Brian's parents didn't seem to mind that we didn't want to enjoy the music of their "love." We preferred the kinky music of Prince or the raunchy crooning of Robert Palmer to the sultry R & B that Brian's parents enjoyed. If we felt especially giddy or goofy, then we'd play Art of Noise or Peter Gabriel, artsy stuff Brian's parents wouldn't be caught dead listening to.

Playing our own music in the back allowed them to enjoy theirs in the front without interruption and provided us with some cover, along with the rowdy engine, for our important conversation about our shared conundrum: girls. We marveled that Cindy Hammond's breasts were much larger than they were the year before and that Kathy McDonald smelled more like a grandmother than a middle-schooler. I would later discover why her alluring scent reminded us of an octogenarian when I helped clean out my own grandmother's house soon after she passed away. On her dresser sat a bottle of Chanel No. 22 and when I popped the top and curiously sniffed it, the scent awakened memories of standing next to Kathy McDonald in line for a school assembly and secretly inhaling the air between us, as if we were sharing an intimate moment, even though we were just waiting to listen to the principal of F. D. R. go on about pep rallies and the dwindling supply of chocolate milk. Memories can do that, though; they can transplant all five senses into our brains like some sort of metaphysical incantation. Weird, huh?

Anyway, as we whispered and snickered about girls in the back, the asphalt route of FM 306 loped over and through the Texas Hill Country, eventually leading the Volkswagen camper to the KOA campgrounds: our destination for the weekend. Mr. Johnson turned onto the gravel drive that led to the campgrounds, pebbles crunching underneath the tires and occasionally clinking against the underside of the wheel wells. A small, triangular, wood shack with a single window guarded the entrance with a striped guardrail—the kind with reflective orange and white paint that would tilt up with a flick of a switch—and when the camper stopped next to the shack, we peeked out the side window to see who manned the station. To our surprise, a beautiful teenaged girl occupied the entry post, looking bored and annoyed at the same time, but still beautiful nonetheless. With a red KOA t-shirt stretched over her large bosom and tucked into khaki shorts, her sparkling green eyes were complimented by a mound of curly, strawberry blond hair cinched in the back into a long ponytail of ringlets. We gawked at her from behind the side window curtain. When she asked Mr. Johnson if he had a reservation, she noticed our eight eyes peering, which seemed to please her. A smirk blossomed on her face.

"She sees us!" Brian blurted, then slid the curtain shut.

"What are you doing?" Randy said, his eyes penetrating through irritated slits. Brian shrugged. "We *want* her to see us, doofus."

"Yeah," I agreed. "And she looks way older than us, like 16 or something."

"Maybe 17," Miguel added. "A full-grown *woman*."

Mrs. Johnson chuckled from her vantage point in the front seat, knowing full-well that our juvenile observations were way off the mark. Mr. Johnson paid the young woman, asked a few questions (where to go, times for things, the usual arrival-information mumbo jumbo), then asked her what her name was.

"Victoria," she answered.

"Her name is *Victoria*," Randy cooed. She was casting a spell over us without even trying.

"I'll come find you if I need anything, Victoria," Mr. Johnson said. Mrs. Johnson patted his arm, as if pleased with his resourcefulness. He smiled at her, then turned back to Victoria.

"I'm sending someone over to your spot to help you, actually," she said, picking up a phone and dialing.

"Sounds good."

The gate raised and he drove into the campground. Brian slid the curtain back open and we looked at the other families setting up tents or propping up canopies on the sides of their campers in their designated sites—cement slabs floating on a sea of grass. There were camp fires blazing within rings of stone and BBQ grills exhaling smoke. Kids chased each other with pop guns or sticks, while their parents watched from folding chairs, beers in hand insulated with neon Koozies. And through the trunks and sturdy branches of the watchful oak and pecan trees that surrounded the campground, the waters of Canyon Lake glistened and shimmied in the light of the setting sun. Without warning, the camper jerked back and forth—the result of Mr. Johnson driving the Volkswagen Westfalia onto our cement pad—and when he slammed on the brakes to park, the three of us sitting on the rear bench toppled on top of Brian.

"Get off me!" he cried. "I can't breathe!"

"Sorry, dude," I said, pushing myself from the heap. "We didn't fall on you on purpose."

Mr. Johnson chuckled as he pulled the camper's emergency brake. As he was getting out, he stopped to commandeer our attention. "Brian, get the tent from the back and show your friends how to put it up."

"Yes, sir," Brian told him, then slid open the side door. "Come on, guys!"

Quickly lifting the rear hatch, Brian pulled the tent out while we helped him since it was large and heavy. We set the long, canvas package in the grass and Brian unfastened a series of snaps and ties, allowing us to pull the tent out. Brian, being that he was a Boy Scout, was well-versed in the ways of camping and survival, and patiently showed us how to prop up and secure the tent to the ground that we'd be sleeping in the next two nights. Although not self-explanatory, it didn't seem too difficult to setup. We had a canvas home constructed in less than ten minutes.

As we hammered the stakes into the ground to secure the tent, as Brian directed, I noticed Victoria approaching our camp site. Randy elbowed me in the ribs—whistling through his pursed lips while he jabbed me—and when I turned to him with an annoyed look, he tilted his head in the direction of our approaching guest. He didn't need to do that, though. You couldn't miss her coming from a mile away.

Victoria walked past without even looking at us and found Mr. Johnson. She said something to him we couldn't understand, although it seemed authoritative enough, then he followed her behind the camper. A moment later, they reemerged, and Mr. Johnson shook her hand, looking pleased. Then all of a sudden, she approached us. She examined our handy work and nodded.

"Looks like someone knows how to secure a tent," she said, sliding her hands in the back pockets of her jeans, then rocking to and fro on her heels.

Brian jumped up. "I showed 'em. I'll be an Eagle Scout soon."

"I can see that. Nice work."

"Thanks!" he said, flustered from her compliment.

"Me and my boyfriend usually hang down by the water after the office closes at nine o'clock. We roast marshmallows and stuff. Watch for shooting stars. You know? Hang out."

"You're inviting *us*?" Randy said, befuddled. For such a big and intimidating looking guy, he sure could reveal his weaknesses quickly.

"We like to meet other kids around our age. Make new friends. It gets boring working all day long."

"Around *your* age?" Randy said. She had obviously mesmerized him something bad.

Victoria laughed. "Nine o'clock. Be there or be square."

She walked off. We watched her get back in the triangle shack by the entrance. When we were sure she was inside, we teased Randy.

"Around *YOUR* age?" Miguel whined, mimicking Randy's surprise. Randy's face turned red with embarrassment, knowing that his internal monologue was audible for the rest of us to hear. It was a humorous revelation.

"Ha ha," Randy bemoaned. "Very funny."

"Just kidding." Miguel patted him on the back.

Mrs. Johnson examined our work with the tent, then offered her motherly approval to Brian. "You know where to find us, if you need us."

"Yeah, I know. In the camper," Brian said. "Hey mom?"

"Yes, dear?"

"Victoria, the girl that works here, she asked us to meet her and her boyfriend down by the lake to roast marshmallows and stuff. Can we go?"

"Sure," she said, then her face contorted into a look of concern. "But stay away from the water. You know you can't swim."

"Can't swim?!" I exclaimed, slapping my forehead. "But aren't you in the Boy Scouts?"

"Yeah," he replied, a befuddled look on his face like his deepest, darkest secret had been unwittingly revealed by his callous mother.

"What if you have to rescue a bunny from a brook or something?"

"I guess the bunny's gonna drown," he quipped.

We all laughed, but not his mother. "It's all fun and games until *you* fall in the water. Mind your mother."

"Yes, ma'am," Brian answered.

"You boys be good," she said to the rest of us, wagging an indignant finger. Then she climbed into the camper and slid the side door closed. In a matter of seconds, *Sweet Love* by Anita Baker played inside the camper, causing strange looks and raised eyebrows from my friends. *When the camper's a rockin'...*

For an hour or so, we sat inside our tent while the tarp of night slowly laid atop the campgrounds. Randy, Miguel, and I played a couple of rote games of *Uno* while Brian flipped through his pocket-sized *Boy Scouts Survival Guide*—obviously taking notes for how to survive in case we needed him to step it up and lead our ragtag group of friends in a do-or-die situation—then we made our way down to the water along a crushed granite pathway around nine o'clock to meet

Victoria and her mysterious boyfriend. As we walked, I fell behind a bit, because my limp made it hard for me to keep up with my friends sometimes. I looked back at the Volkswagen camper to see the lights inside go out. I knew Brian's parents wouldn't miss us. The path led to a picnic area that nestled the shore of Canyon Lake, with a silhouette of a couple lounging on top of a table at the far end, who I could only assume was Victoria and her boyfriend. I sped up to catch my friends. The rising moon's visage reflected in the smooth waters of the lake. Occasional ripples from straggler insects stitched the surface and the nipping, floating turtles pursued them, accompanied by the smell of the surrounding trees and fires from the campground. The funny thing about early summer nights in Texas back then was that they weren't much cooler than the summer days—just darker and still. Randy and I peeled off our t-shirts, then slung them over our shoulders. Victoria called to us.

She introduced us to her boyfriend. "This is Tony."

Slender with shaggy, long, cinnamon brown hair and stick-thin arms, he wore ragged blue jeans and a yellow t-shirt with the words Canyon Lake Marina and a silhouette of a motor boat on the front. He extended his large, bony hand to me for a shake. "How's it going?"

On the table was a pack of Camel cigarettes, a lighter, and two bottles of Lone Star beer.

"Great," I said. I gave him a firm handshake. "Where are the marshmallows?"

Tony chuckled, then he tilted his head up to gander at Randy's tall stature. He seemed a little miffed when he commented to Victoria. "I thought you said these were some *younger* kids."

"They are," she said.

"Riiight," he said, then extended his hand to Randy. "Dude's a giant."

"I'll be fourteen in the fall," Randy quipped, crushing Tony's hand with his massive, meaty mitt. Tony shook the pain out of his hand, then extended it to Brian and Miguel for a slap, which they did.

"Nice meeting you boys," Tony said.

I looked out across the lake at a structure that appeared to be floating in the water with Christmas lights strewn along the top at one side.

Tony cleared his throat. "That's the marina where I work. My parents own it."

"And my parents own the campground," Victoria added. "That's how we met."

"Nice love story," Miguel said. Brian elbowed his ribs, then shushed him. "Hey!"

"If you guys want to rent a motor boat, then come by tomorrow morning. I'll set you up."

"That sounds coooool," I said, turning to my three friends for approval. Brian returned a sagging disapproval. "Except Brian can't swim."

"That's all right," Randy said. "We got life jackets. No sweat!"

"Coooool," I repeated.

Brian didn't seem convinced. But rather than talk about it, he walked closer to the lake, picked up a flat rock, then flung it side-armed, the small projectile skipping across the water. It hopped once, twice, three times, then plunked on the fourth, quickly sinking in the black water. Miguel joined him soon after, skipping another rock across the water. I looked up at Randy to see if he also wanted to skip rocks, but his attention was elsewhere, somewhere far across the lake.

"What's that over there?" Randy said, then he pointed to the object of his attention.

Tony and Victoria looked in the direction he was pointing.

"Oh, that's the abandoned Meyer lake house," he said, peering at the dilapidated bungalow that sat on a piece of land that jutted out into the lake, a tiny peninsula across from the marina on the other side of the bay. Tony smiled slyly. "Vicky and I go over there sometimes."

"Don't tell them *that*!" she said, then shoved her boyfriend in the chest. She crossed her arms to defend herself from his apologetic touch. "Don't even touch me!"

"Sorry, babe! I didn't think you'd mind me saying so."

"That's *private*," she whispered, then sighed.

"I'm sorry, babe," Tony said, gently patting her arm, a gesture she reluctantly allowed him to perform. Then he turned to us. "If you guys come by the marina tomorrow, I can take you over there in a boat. Just don't tell anyone that I'm taking you there. I could get in trouble."

"Why's that?" Randy said.

"It's private property," Tony replied. "And they say it's unsafe, but it doesn't seem unsafe to me. I just don't want my parents on my ass about it. That's all."

"That sounds coooool," I said. "I wanna go."

"Me too," Randy chimed in.

"Great, just come by in the morning," Tony said, then he twisted off the cap to one of the bottles of beer. With a snap of his fingers, the bottle cap flew ten feet to an aluminum trash can, then clinked on the side down to the grass. "Almost made it."

"It must be fun working out here at the campground and the marina," I said, rocking on my feet from heel to toe, then back and forth some more in a repetitive motion that felt like a dance.

"I guess," Victoria said. "It's kind of a drag working for my parents sometimes."

"Except *after* work," Tony said, clucking his tongue, then placing his hand softly on Victoria's arm, a move that must've elicited a positive response at some point before, but at that moment sent Victoria into repellent throes of discomfort and irritation.

"I said, *don't* touch me!"

"Come on, babe! I've been looking forward to being with you all day!"

Victoria stood her ground for a moment or two, then turned to reveal that her act of rebellion was just a tease. She wasn't really mad at her boyfriend. She smirked, then kissed him on the cheek. Tony breathed a sigh of relief.

He took a swig from his beer, then offered it to me and Randy. "Want a swig?"

Randy and I looked at each other, then shook our heads. A swig of disgusting beer was the last thing on our minds.

"They're good boys, unlike you," Victoria teased, then she leaned in to kiss her boyfriend again.

But rather than stand around and watch them make out, Randy and I walked over to where Brian and Miguel were enjoying their game of rock skipping on the shore. Randy and I gathered a few flat rocks of our own, then took turns skipping rocks across the glassy water, laughing when it seemed our rocks were whizzing by unsuspecting moths and mosquitoes, cheering when one of our rocks surpassed the others with its delicate skips and plunking demise. Every time a rock sunk at the end of its dance, the reflection of the moon on the water exploded across the retreating ripples, along with the laughing and cheering from my friends and our two new friends: Tony and Victoria.

6.

Later that night, after we all fell asleep in our tent, I had a vivid dream about a flea infestation. I was standing in a nondescript yard with a sea of St. Augustine grass around me and various things you'd find around someone's house (BBQ grill, lawn furniture, yard gnomes). I didn't know whose yard it was, and I was scratching and scratching my arms and legs, but nothing relieved my suffering. It was one of those kind of dreams—nightmare, actually—that seemed to go on forever in a continual loop of misery, just scratching and scratching with no relief. Then, I awoke in the morning to my hands scratching my face, my skin irritated and swollen under my fingertips as my nails raked across inflamed bumps. Shafts of sunlight stabbed through the seams of the tent. Lying next to me was Miguel and as my eyes shifted into focus, I noticed tiny black dots all over his face, black dots within larger red splotches. Surprised, I sat up and peered around. The tent was infested with mosquitos, allowed in through an unzipped tent flap which fluttered in the morning breeze. I panicked and cried out, startling my sleeping friends.

"Mosquitos!"

Shooting up from under their blankets, my three friends discovered squadrons of flying bloodsuckers buzzing around our heads, dozens of which stuck landings to our faces, feasting on our blood. Arm-swatting and hand-slapping commenced as we bolted out of the tent in search of a clearing, all of us screaming at the unexpected infestation. The campground was mostly still in the morning light, so our screams ripped through the air like shrieks from banshees.

"Who didn't zip the tent flap?" Brian said, looking frantically at each of us, his head swiveling back and forth as his stiff hands repeatedly stabbed the air in front of him for emphasis. "We were supposed to zip it shut!"

But we were all too busy to answer, instead swatting the remainder of the mosquito squadrons. Our gang wasn't into the blame game, anyway. What was done was done, and we weren't about to look for blame when assigning blame wasn't going to do us any good. Mrs. Johnson heard us squawking, though. She burst out of the camper—her hair and sleep clothes askew—to find out what was going on.

"Why are you boys yelling out here so early in the morning? Don't you know that people are still *sleeping*?" She immediately saw our faces—puffy, inflamed, and splotched with mosquito bites—then burst out laughing. "Why, you boys were somebody's dinner last night. Let me get the calamine lotion from the first aid kit."

She climbed inside the camper and rummaged in a cabinet for the first aid kit. Mr. Johnson woke up and asked what was going on—his head peeking out the side door—but she told him not to worry about it before hopping out of the camper, so she could mend our splotchy faces.

"I'll fix you boys up. Hold still," she said, unscrewing the top off the calamine lotion tube, then she commenced to dab Brian's face first with a cotton ball soaked with the pink lotion, leaving large pink blobs over each mosquito bite. She jabbed quickly as she covered all the bites, then moved onto Miguel, Randy, then me. When she was done, we all looked like pink polka-dotted, shirtless, sad clowns. "That oughtta do!"

"Thanks, ma," Brian said. We all thanked her as well.

"What are you boys wanting to do today?"

"We were thinking of going for a hike or something," Brian said.

"That sounds fun. Just stay away from the water. You hear me?" She wagged her indignant finger at us again. She really liked doing that.

"Yes, ma'am," we all grumbled.

"Hungry?" she added. We all agreed we were. "I'll get you some breakfast."

Back in the camper, she shoved some things in a shopping bag (Pop Tarts, granola bars, bags of chips), then tossed it to Brian.

"You boys be good," she said, smirking as she examined our polka-dotted faces, then slid the camper door shut.

Brian looked into the bag, then shrugged. The rest of us shrugged, too.

"Let's go down to the picnic tables by the water and eat," I suggested. We all agreed that was a good idea, so we quickly retrieved our shirts and shoes from the tent—swatting at any remaining kamikaze mosquitoes in that dome of terror—and walked down the path to the picnic tables. As we weaved through the camp sites to get to the lake, the other camping families were milling about as well, some campfires still barely smoldering while BBQ pits wheezed their last bits of smoke from the seams of their lids. Once we reached the picnic area by the shore, we marveled at the size of the lake, its surface still except for one early morning ski boat and trailing slalom skier slicing through the water, their wake extending back to the marina. Brian reached into the shopping bag, then tossed the Pop Tarts and other snacks on the nearest picnic table.

"Breakfast is served," he said, then snickered.

We ripped open the silver packaging and devoured our processed pastries, nut bars, and chips. We didn't have discerning palates and strawberry Pop Tarts were just as good as any other breakfast, requiring minimal effort except to shove them in our hungry faces. When we were done, we put the wrappers in the shopping bag, then noticed Brian looking at something off in the distance, his attention piqued. We all turned to see who he was looking at: Victoria.

"She's already working," he said, watching her in the triangle shack accepting payments and directing campers to camp sites, a line of cars, vans, and trucks with trailers snaking down the gravel driveway to the farm road. "Let's go see when she gets off work."

We hoofed it over there and when we reached the shack, I eagerly knocked on the back door. Victoria popped her head out, obviously flustered.

"What do you want? I'm working," she said, not even happy to see us, then returned a queer look. "What's up with your *faces*?"

"We were attacked by mosquitoes," I said meekly.

"You look ridiculous," she said.

"When do you get off work?" Brian said.

"After five. But you can go bug Tony at the marina right now. He can take you out in a boat if you want. I'm really busy."

"Sounds cool!" I chirped, but she didn't acknowledge my exclamation. She just rolled her eyes, then slammed the door.

"Real smooth," Randy said, then slugged my arm. "Let's go to the marina. Come on!"

He put his arm around Brian and the two skipped down the path toward the marina like elementary school kids. Miguel's head sagged as he stood next to me, his shoulders radiating dejection.

"*Somos pendejos*," Miguel muttered, his propensity to curse in Spanish whenever girls offered their displeasure in our presence. He would repeat the things his father would angrily say, but in his own adolescent way. When other boys called us things like geeks or nerds or pussies—an occurrence as prevalent as the sun going up then down—the name-calling didn't seem to faze Miguel. But a pretty girl's verbal displeasure was different. It was his Kryptonite. It was a pride crusher.

"Come on, man. Don't worry about it. Let's go have fun," I told him, putting my arm around his shoulders.

"All right," he said. "But I'm washing this stuff off first."

He tore into a full sprint to the water, kneeling on the pebbly shore and flushing the pink dots from his face the best he could with the cool water. I knelt next to him and did the same, streams of pink splattering the lake's surface. We both dried our faces on the front of our t-shirts as we made our way to the marina, pleased we were no longer speckled with pink dots.

The path led us to a wood sign that spelled out Canyon Lake Marina in large, block letters, a colorful hand-painted map of the area also on the sign. A long, wooden pier stretched out onto the lake from behind the sign, leading to a structure floating on the water which housed the office as well as a convenience store and tackle shop. Randy and Brian waved from the entrance of the store, having already trekked across the pier, then went inside. We followed them.

Inside, the store smelled of mildew, compost, and coffee. There were a couple of rows of shelves in the middle containing everything boaters would need like a variety of snacks, boating accessories, and first-aid supplies. Along the walls, an assortment of drink coolers with sodas, beer, and water stood on one side and tackle / worm station stood along the other wall (which is why the smell of compost was in the air). And in one corner manning a counter stood Tony, wearing white shorts and a blue Izod-styled shirt, except with a monogrammed sail boat on the breast instead of a little alligator; the back of his shirt said Canyon Lake Marina in bold, yellow lettering. It was apparent he was in a better mood than Victoria, as he yucked it up with Randy and Brian while sipping coffee, pointing at the spots on their faces and laughing. I was glad Miguel and I washed our faces. A percolator and paper cups sat on the counter and Tony offered some coffee to us for free. We demurred.

"You got any Big Red or Dr. Pepper?" Randy said, patting his shorts to see if he had any money. He didn't, and rarely did.

"I have some cash," I offered, then plucked a Velcro wallet from my shorts pocket. Inside it, I pulled a wad of twenties out, to the surprise of my friends and Tony. "Lawn mowing money."

Not remotely the truth, it was a wad of bills I secretly pulled from Bloody Billy's backpack before we left home for the lake, but didn't tell any of my friends about it.

"Money bags," Tony quipped. We grabbed some sodas from the coolers and I paid Tony for them. "What are you guys doing today?"

"I don't know," I said. "Just hangin'. Got any suggestions?"

"I got nothing to do. I could give you all a boat tour, if you pay for gas."

"Deal!" I said, and plopped a twenty on the counter. But when I looked at my friends, I expected them to be pleased, yet they weren't, particularly Brian.

"I can't go because I can't swim," he said. "My momma would kill me if she found out I went with y'all."

I thought this realization would throw cold water on our prospects for fun, but Tony seemed to have all the answers. He was good like that.

"No worries, my man!" he said, then pulled a box from under the counter and set it on top. "I have plenty of life vests. Plus, I'm an excellent swimmer. I wouldn't let anything happen to you."

"I don't know," Brian mumbled. He looked at the three of us for advice. We all wanted to go and didn't want to leave him out. "Are you sure?"

"Sure as I've ever been."

Brian didn't mull it over too long. I certainly would have expected him to decline going out on that boat, but he didn't. In fact, he seemed happy to appease us. His face lit up, as if this tiny decision was a life-changing affirmation, one that would alter the trajectory of our lives. That wasn't too far from the truth. "All right!"

"Good deal!" Tony said, taking my twenty and stuffing it in his shorts pocket. "You wait here while I gas up the boat."

We guzzled our sodas inside the store while watching Tony from a window as he filled the outboard motor of a fishing boat with gasoline from a can. The boat was made of aluminum and tied to the marina with a white, nylon rope. It had three rows of wooden benches inside, just enough for the five of us—two of us per row, then Tony in the back to steer. And even though Brian was going to wear a life vest, he still looked nervous as hell. I think his fear of not being able to swim consumed him more than we realized, or maybe it was the fear of his mother's wrath. Randy, Miguel, and I were all capable swimmers, but I think we took it for granted that our parents forced us to swim in the neighborhood pool at an early age. Brian's parents must've dropped the ball on the swimming lessons. I remember later Brian telling me something like Black people didn't learn to swim for a reason, but the reason he gave didn't make too much sense because we were all friends and his parents were so well-off. He tried to explain that it was because of racism and the lack of community pools in Black neighborhoods. But Brian's family didn't live in a Black neighborhood, so it seemed like a lame excuse to me. Anyway, I helped Brain secure the vest and told him everything would be all right. Tony called to us, so we went out there and stood next to the boat. He was already down in it. He raised his hand to help us in. Calling the boat a nautical vessel would be a stretch, considering there were just as many bolts and rivets rolling around in the bottom of it down by his feet than there were holding it together; sunken ship to-be was more like it.

"Come down," he said, then helped us get into the rickety water craft. Once we were all seated, he pulled the starter cord to the motor—which was secured to the boat on a rotten two-by-four pine plank with an adhesive that looked like dried orange shaving cream—and it roared to life. "Here we go!"

Tony steered slowly through a row of covered motor boats, all docked and waiting for their owners. Once past the end of the row of boats, he slowly weaved through an array of anchored sailboats which peppered the bay. I looked back at Tony and he winked confidently, then I looked at my friends, all of whom had big smiles on their faces, except for Brian. He gripped the side of the fishing boat like his life depended on it. Once we passed the last anchored sail boat and a row of buoys delineating the edge of the marinas domain (there were even signs on the buoys declaring that boaters keep their speeds low), Tony fully throttled the motor. The front of the boat tilted up as we flew across the bay toward the other side.

I'll never forget that feeling of first riding in a boat as it glided across the top of lake water, occasionally catching air from waves or the wakes of other boats, the motor belching smoke and screaming from the back. I could see some fish in the water attempting to swim away from the hull of the boat and birds flew in the sky above, as if following us to wherever we were going. There is a freedom and otherworldliness to cruising across a large body of water in a motor boat, your balls vibrating in your seat while the wind whips through your hair. It's a magnificent feeling.

When we reached the other side of the bay, Tony let off the throttle and the boat eased to a gurgling crawl. We floated slowly to a rickety pier that looked like it was 100-years old and had seen better days, maybe before the Second World War. When the boat nudged the pier, Tony tossed a loop of rope over a post to secure the boat, then cut the motor.

Brian didn't look amused.

"We're not getting out, are we?" he said, still gripping the side of the boat.

"Nah, just wanted to show you something." He pointed up an embankment. At the top sat an old lake house, one that was in a similar state to the pier; its construction of withered wood, rusty nails, in pathetic squalor that was just sad to witness. I would later learn that the lake house was a classic bungalow built in an arts and craft style, with two dormer windows perched on the roof, and a large veranda at the front that wrapped around one side. It probably was magnificent at some point in its history, just not at this moment. It was a dilapidated house that would've been perfect in a scary movie from the 1950s or modeled for an illustrated haunted house in an episode of *Scooby-Doo.* "That's the old Meyer lake house I told you about yesterday. Up there."

We peered up at the wilted lake house, and I couldn't help but see the potential in such an abandoned place like this. All it needed was a little love, just like Linus declared when he first saw Charlie Brown's sad, sagging Christmas twig of a tree. If Superman had his Fortress of Solitude, then Spider-Man should have his Cabin of Seclusion. And if not Spider-Man, then why not four friends from Converse, Texas? To me, at that moment, it looked like it would make a fantastic hideout, but I didn't say it out loud while we sat in the motor boat.

"Have you ever been up there?" I said, examining the lake house, then looking curiously back at Tony.

A sly smirk slid across his face. "I've taken Vicky up there. You know? To *make out.*"

"That sounds coooool," I said. Tony nodded an agreement. "You like to call her Vicky?"

"Yup," he said, then clucked his tongue.

"And how do you get up there? From here?" I continued, looking at the rickety pier, then back at Tony, who now appeared taken aback by my inquisition.

"Actually," he said, thumbing over his right shoulder. "I drive up the road back there behind those trees. There's a gate at the driveway to the property. It looks like it's locked with a chain, but the chain doesn't actually have a lock. I just put the chain back the way it was when we leave."

"Interesting," I said. "So, do you think it's safe to go up there?"

My three friends were growing impatient with my interrogation at this point. Brian looked like he was going to throw up. Miguel was in a trance of boredom; floating on the water wasn't his thing. And Randy, he was interested in something different than the old lake house, looking some place not so far away, just across the bay from where we floated in the water.

"What's that over there?" Randy said. We all turned, and he pointed at an island way out in the mouth of the bay, a slender bit of land that jutted sharply up out of the water with a row of trees on top. "That *island.* Is that what that is?"

"Yeah," Tony said. A deflated sigh slipped from his mouth. "That's Sometimes Island. Can't go on it, though. Your boat would get ripped apart from the jagged rocks that surround it under the water if you tried to land near it."

"Sometimes Island. That's a weird name," Miguel added, perking up. "Why *Sometimes*?"

"Let's put it this way," Tony began, taking the loop of rope off the rotten wood post, then pushing the boat away from the pier. "In the old days, the level of the lake used to go up and down quite a bit, so sometimes the island was there, and sometimes it wasn't. That's how it got the name of Sometimes Island. Nowadays, the level of the lake is pretty steady, and the island is visible most of the time, but we still call it Sometimes Island."

"Makes sense," Randy said, and he quickly changed the subject. "How fast can this boat go?"

"It can go faster than you think. Wanna see?"

A look of distressed washed over Brian's face as his swollen hands continued to grip the side of the boat. He stammered to protest, but Randy interjected.

"Yeah, I wanna see!"

Without asking Brian if he was OK with it, Tony pulled the starter cord and the boat roared to life. He fully throttled the motor, the boat quickly picking up speed, and the front of it tilting upward again as we flew across the glassy surface of the lake. We quickly approached Sometimes Island and the information Tony just shared with us rushed through my mind. I thought of the jagged rocks just underneath the water's surface, ripping through the hull of our boat as we went over them, sending all of us into the air, then splashing into the cold water.

"AYY-YAA-AAAH!" Brian screamed, as the boat got closer and closer to the island.

"Yee haw!" Randy called out.

Tony turned the boat to the right while Sometimes Island flew past us on our left, the buoys demarking an imaginary line that boaters shouldn't cross without certain disaster, coming close but not quite hitting the side of our boat. I could hear Tony laughing behind us as he steered out into the open water at the center of Canyon Lake. Of course, he wasn't going to steer the boat over those rocks. Why would he do something like that and risk his job and the lives of four middle-schoolers?

But for one brief moment, it almost seemed like he would. Brian huffed and puffed his anxiety out from deep in his chest. I patted him on the back as we cruised across the lake to the other side for more places of interest to investigate on our lake tour.

7.

After a couple of hours on the water, we spent the rest of the day on land—to the satisfaction of Brian and Miguel; me and Randy not so much—doing the type of fun things most kids expect to do on a camping trip. We played a rowdy game of horseshoes down by the picnic area in a grassy patch next to the picnic tables. Randy was the winner, of course. Then we hiked around in the wooded area southwest of the campgrounds, hoping to find something worth bringing back to the camp to show Brian's parents and keep as mementos. We did find an old, weather-beaten copy of *Playboy* and a couple of unopened cans of Pearl lager beer, but figured they probably belonged to Tony and didn't want to defile his hidden stash. We even shot at a few empty beer cans that we lined up on a tree stump with a BB gun Miguel ganked from his older brother, Rogelio, but we only were able to shoot it about a dozen times with the amount of BBs it already had in it because Miguel didn't bring the canister of extra BBs to reload it. Pretty lame, if you'd asked me, but it was still fun for a brief moment nonetheless. We felt like rebels out there in the woods with a ganked BB gun, even if we really couldn't hurt most living things with that poor excuse for a pistol. Plus, possessing Rogelio's personal property was an additional thrill for all of us. After shooting the beer cans, Brian showed us his remarkable talent for tying various knots, all of which he would need to exhibit whenever he finally took his Eagle Scout test, the date of which remained mysterious. He always reminded us that he was going out for it, but never seemed to tell us exactly when it would happen. The thrill of preparing for the illustrious Eagle Scout designation seemed almost more exciting than finally receiving it in some ways. Funny how things are like that for you when you're in middle school, right?

Once the sun started to set, we hoofed it back to the campgrounds and sat around a campfire Mr. Johnson made for us. We ate a chili dinner that Mrs. Johnson heated up from cans of Wolf Brand Chili with beans, then listened to a spirited debate between his parents—instigated by Mr. Johnson, of course—about whether Texas chili should contain beans in its recipe or not. He claimed that Texas chili should never be made with beans; it should be simmered with beef and spices only. Mrs. Johnson didn't have any ax to grind or skin in this game; she admitted to not even reading the labels on the cans when she bought them at the grocery store, a simple act she wished she had done to avoid such a silly argument with her *obnoxious* husband (her words, not mine). Mr. Johnson huffed as he dug out then flung the beans over his shoulder with his spoon. We concluded dinner with roasted marshmallows and s'mores for dessert, a finer meal we couldn't have wished for.

When it was time to hit the hay, Mrs. Johnson reminded us to zip the tent closed this time, unless we wanted our faces to be the meals for a new batch of hungry mosquitoes. We immediately zipped the flap shut after being reminded of this unfortunate incident from the night before.

My three friends seemed to doze off rather quickly as I lay on my blanket on the ground, my towel rolled up under my head as a pillow, and their phlegmy snores interrupting my drowsiness. Through the din of their gurgled inhalations and wheezy exhalations, I could hear an owl hooting somewhere, its unwavering rhythmic call telling me that it knew I was in the tent listening to it, hoping I would give it clues as to where its next meal would be scurrying to. *Hoo huh hoo, hoo huh hoo.*

I marveled at its tranquil song until it finally serenaded me to sleep.

The next morning, Brian's mother woke us by quickly unzipping the tent flap and tossing Pop Tarts inside, her go-to breakfast for the trip. We were pleased to see that our faces were not chewed into hamburger by mosquitoes, but having our breakfast tossed at us was not a pleasant way to wake up. She commented about *not* wanting to see us without our clothes on, a curious statement that baffled us while we ate our second breakfast of strawberry Pop Tarts.

"What does she mean: *naked?*" Randy quizzed Brian, who was too embarrassed to respond and quickly stuffed his mouth with breakfast pastry, a simple yet effective ruse so he wouldn't have to offer an answer. Miguel and I snickered.

After we finished our breakfast, Mr. Johnson instructed us to take down our tent, pack it up, then put it in the back of the camper along with all our belongings. While we dismantled the tent (actually, while the three of us watched Brian dismantle the tent), I noticed Victoria walking over, so I elbowed Randy, who then elbowed Miguel. Brian didn't notice, being that he was too busy with the tent. She stood in front of us, a clipboard in one hand, and a can of Dr. Pepper in the other.

"You guys leaving?" she said, then took a swig from her soda.

"Unfortunately," I said. "We have school tomorrow. It's our last week."

"Bummer," she said, then took another swig. "Maybe you will come back later this summer."

"Maybe," I said.

"Hopefully!" Randy blurted, barely containing his excitement. It was embarrassingly obvious he liked Victoria, even though she had a boyfriend. Randy wasn't good at playing it cool. "May-be..." He awkwardly ran his fingers through his hair, then looked out at the lake. Victoria rolled her eyes, then read something on her clipboard.

"We'll probably come back," Brian said. "My parents love coming here."

"Cool," Victoria said, then jumped with surprise. "Oh yeah, Tony wanted me to let him know when you guys were leaving. He has something for you."

"For us?" I said, surprised.

"Yeah. Hold on." She reached for her back pocket and pulled out a walkie-talkie. She squeezed a red button on the side. "They're getting ready to leave."

A few seconds of awkward silence passed before Tony answered.

"Be right there," he said, his voice muffled and staticky. "10-4."

"You don't have to say that. You know?"

"All right," he said meekly. "Tell them I'll be right over."

"He'll be right over," she repeated to us, then slid the walkie-talkie back in her rear pocket. "Is your dad around?" she asked Brian. "I have a receipt for him."

Brian popped his head up from dismantling the tent.

"Yeah, he's by the camper," he said, thumbing over his shoulder, then sneering at us. "Are you guys gonna help me or *what?*"

The three of us laughed that it took him so long to notice. Victoria went to find Mr. Johnson while we helped our friend. It was the least we could do for Brian, for hosting such a fun weekend. He attempted to explain the puzzle of putting the tent back into its bag, but it was useless. We didn't get it, and just watched him do it. Eventually, we saw Tony trotting over from the marina. He panted from the trek, standing in front of us with his hands on his hips.

"Heading out, huh?" he said.

"Yeah," we all said in unison, dejected.

"Bummer," he said, echoing Victoria's sentiment. "If you guys want to come back, then give me a ring," he said, then handed each of us a business card. On the card, it said, *Canyon Lake Marina*, along with the address, phone number, and his name handwritten at the bottom in blue, ballpoint ink.

The four of us looked at the business cards, a little stumped as what to do with them. I don't think any of us had been handed business cards before, and it seemed I was the only kid with a wallet. I instinctively pulled it out and placed the card in there; the others just held onto their cards.

"Will do," I said, putting my wallet back in my pocket, feeling slightly more sophisticated than my other three friends.

"I could even come pick you up, if your parents are too busy and all," he said, the suggestion mystifying us. Never had an older teenager offered to give us a ride before. "It gets boring out here sometimes."

He stood there—rocking back and forth on his heels and the balls of his feet—when Victoria came back over, having given Mr. Johnson the receipt for their stay.

"Check ya later," Tony said, draping his arm across Victoria's shoulder.

"Later," I said.

Tony and Victoria walked away.

"*Later!*" Miguel mimicked, his voice higher pitched and more annoying than mine. I elbowed him in the ribs, then the three of us helped Brian finish packing the tent so we could all go home.

The ride back to Converse was quieter and sullener than the ride to the lake a couple of days before. The trip home after a vacation can be like that, like a hangover after a night of partying and overindulging alcohol. Brian's parents were noticeably quieter. Their Texas chili argument had dampened their amorous mood. Brian and Miguel lay on the camper floor—dehydrated and dozing off—while Randy and I occupied the rear bench. Randy leaned against the window, his towel rolled up as his pillow on the foggy glass. Out my window, I watched dark grey storm clouds gather on the distant horizon, slowly consuming the mimeograph blue sky as they grew in strength. For the first time in a few days, I thought of the backpack I stashed behind the vent in my bedroom closet and the wads of money and marijuana inside it. Kids have a way of forgetting about things like this—illicit things that would keep any normal adult up late at night—and I wasn't any different than most kids. Even when I pulled the wad of twenties from my pocket to pay for the gas for the boat ride, I didn't as much as ponder the idea of the backpack hidden in my room or what would happen if Bloody Billy found out I had it. And why would I? I was having fun with my friends. The thing furthest from my mind was what Bloody Billy would or wouldn't do to me or my friends concerning his backpack.

But as the storm clouds muted the sunny afternoon—bringing an ominous and palpable feeling of dread—my exhausted mind turned inward and I was consumed with what Bloody Billy might do to us (to me!). All the dreadful things I had heard about the Thousand Oaks Gang seemed at that moment to not be just horrible rumors, but possible consequences for being so stupid. *What would they do to us?* I thought. *Wait for us after school so they could beat us up? Follow us home like they did to Brian's house and beat up our parents?* The oppressive dread coming across the horizon with the storm clouds was now inside my chest and consuming my heart, choking out the mirthful feelings from the last couple of days and replacing them with grief and regret. What I didn't notice was Randy watching me.

"Hey," he said, sitting up, rubbing both eyes with his rolling fists, then setting his towel on his lap. "You OK?"

"I was just thinking about the... backpack," I said, my voice trailing off. My gaze returned to the dark clouds. The light blue sky was mostly gone, retreating behind some green and granite-colored hills way off in the distance.

"Oh," he said, his posture stiffening. A sigh escaped between his pursed lips. "*That.*"

"Yeah," I replied, still looking out the window. "Maybe we should give it back to them."

"No way, man. If we give it back, then they will *know* we took it. They'll beat the shit out of us." He sighed again. "I mean, I'm tough, but I'm not *that* tough to take them all on."

"I know," I said, depressed even more. The predicament I was in became more and more apparent with every passing minute, second, even nanosecond. It was excruciating. "I guess I'm just worried. That's all."

"Worried? Worried about what? Screw those guys. *Screw* the Thousand Oaks Gang."

His response caught me a little off guard and I turned to him to see that he didn't look miffed at all. In fact, he looked quite pleased, happy even. It was weird.

"But—"

"No buts," he said. "Nevermind what I said before. Fuck those guys. What's the worst they can do?"

Whenever Randy cussed, it sent an energy through me like static electricity, a quick shock then a tingly sensation throughout my body. It was rare that any of us said the "F" word, so the profane pronouncement carried more weight than the usual blustery, meeker curse words. He was serious, and meant it.

"They could beat us up."

"Maybe, if they can catch us. Good luck with that. We haul ass on our bikes, plus we can go off-road. They can't go off-road in their sports cars. They'd bust an axle."

"True," I said, chuckling at the idea of Bloody Billy ditching his white Camaro in a patch of mud while trying to catch us through the woods after school. It was a really funny day dream.

"Yeah, *screw* the Thousand Oaks Gang," Brian said from the floor. He sat up and smiled.

"Screw them," Miguel agreed, also sitting up.

I thought they were sleeping on the floor, but they must have been quietly listening. Hearing the three of my friends rebel against the Thousand Oaks Gang was a sign of solidarity that I needed—that I wanted, even. We had power when we stood together, even when it seemed like the odds were stacked against us.

"Yeah," I said. "Fuck 'em!" I clenched a defiant fist.

"Boys!" Mrs. Johnson said from the front seat. Her sudden interjection startled us. "Watch the *language!*"

We clamped our mouths tight, repressing laughter into snickers, although Mrs. Johnson didn't think it was so funny. Her eyes blazed her contempt for foul language back at us.

"I can't believe what I am hearing from your innocent mouths. It's disgusting!" She turned around and looked out the windshield, obviously peeved. "I'd tell your father to pull over so we could leave you by the side of the road. Too bad there's a storm comin'. It saved your hides."

Even though the storm was upon us, the storm clouds around my heart evaporated. Being with my friends would do that. They could ease my worries and my fears. A good group of friends can do that for anyone. A good group of friends is the best medicine for whatever ails you. And Randy changed the course of our conversation the best he knew how: with jokes.

"Hey, guys. Guys! Did you hear about the man who drank five gallons of tea?"

Randy waited briefly for us to answer, even though he knew we wouldn't. It was part of his shtick. We leaned toward Randy, eagerly waiting for the punchline.

"He drowned in his *tepee!*"

We all laughed and laughed, and Randy brazenly continued his routine, telling dumb jokes that got us all in better spirits. Even Brian's parents perked up. It made the ride home more enjoyable, despite the rain. Not all storms are depressing. Sometimes, they just make things a little dark before they pass.

8.

The last week of school was supposed to be a joyous time for all the students and teachers of Franklin D. Roosevelt Middle School. While the teachers were daydreaming of cruise ship vacations in the Caribbean or road trips to Port Aransas for weekend beach vacations, the students were chattering about their own summer plans. Many bragged about going to a water park in New Braunfels called Schlitterbahn (a silly sounding name which means slippery road in German, a nod to the German heritage of the region of Texas) to ride the infamous water slides, or even tubing down the frigid water of nearby Guadalupe River. Others confessed of their desire to visit AstroWorld in Houston, so they could ride the mind-bending *Greezed Lightnin'*—a coaster that flew forward then backward through a single vertical loop—or take the equally long trip to Six Flags Over Texas in Dallas for a gut-twisting ride on the *Texas Chute Out*, a 225-foot-tall parachute-drop ride. Both rides were guaranteed—it was rumored—to make a kid hurl chunks, which was the perfect dare for any of the students at F. D. R., most of which wanted to come back to school in the fall with bragging rights of barf-free coaster rides or free-fall drops. The only kids not enjoying this final week of school were Randy, Miguel, Brian, and I. We spent that last week—like idiots—running for our lives or riding our bikes for our lives to be more precise, rather than making summer plans. How could we have been so stupid as to agree to keep Bloody Billy's backpack hidden in my closet?

Every day after school during that last week, we took the Thousand Oaks Gang on a variety of wild-goose chases through the wooded areas surrounding the Thousand Oaks and Hidden Oaks neighborhoods or rode our bikes down the cement ditches—coursing through our neighborhoods like a concrete circulatory system—to escape their souped-up sports cars. We even hid in the local fire station—pretending our impromptu visit was a trip down memory lane when our third-grade elementary class visited for a field trip—by convincing the station captain that we really, *really* wanted to examine the top of the fire engines for educational purposes. But when Thursday came around, Bloody Billy and the Thousand Oaks Gang had our number. We had grown cocky as the week closed and decided that we could evade them anywhere and anytime, even stopping at a 7-Eleven after school for Slurpees, Cheetos, and candy. The 7-Eleven was a popular hangout for the middle-schoolers and the Thousand Oaks Gang patiently waited outside by the bike rack, which was parked around the side of the building and out of sight from the front windows. So, when we came outside, already drunk with a sugar buzz from 24-ounce Slurpees and mouthfuls of gummy bears, they ambushed us, dragging us around to the back of the building. Without mincing words, they beat the crap out of us. I literally only remember pushing the glass door open for Randy, Miguel, and Brian, then someone grabbing my arm and dragging me behind the building. By the time I figured out who was dragging me—and not knowing what happened to my friends, although I could hear them screaming—I witnessed a firework display that was unparalleled in my experience, before or since. When the fireworks dissipated and the ringing in my ears stopped, I remember looking up at Bloody Billy from the hot asphalt.

He looked pissed, really pissed. He cracked his knuckles which were covered in blood (I assumed it was my blood). "I know you have it. You better tell me where it is before you get a beating that is worse than any nightmare."

Now, the saying "he was beaten senseless" is a cliché, but there is quite a bit of truth in it. Because even though Billy was talking to me, he might as well have been speaking to a rock. I could hear his words, but my brain couldn't parse any of my thoughts into a cogent answer. In fact, all I could think about was where my Slurpee had gone (I was enjoying it immensely when he snatched me, and I still had the taste of it in my mouth) and that the asphalt underneath me was very hot, searing the skin of my forearms and lower back. I should've just told him that the backpack was hidden behind a plumbing vent in my closet, and that he could drive me home and I would simply get it for him, but I didn't do that. I just babbled senselessly.

"I'm gonna count to three," he growled, grabbing my t-shirt at the neck hole, then pulled me closer. His breath smelled of Big Macs and cigarettes. "And if you don't tell me where it is, then it's lights out. You got that, dickhead?"

"It's... it's—"

"Where is it?" he hissed, clinching the material of my shirt tighter in his fist.

"It's hot. The ground... it's hot," I told him, recoiling from his rancid breath, and hoping to avoid more beatings.

I watched him raise his other fist, ready to pound me, when the convenience store clerk yelled something about calling the cops and that we were going to get arrested for loitering or trespassing or a ruckus or something to that effect. Billy released my shirt, and he and his cronies were gone as fast as they came, like teenage apparitions, jumping in their muscle cars then peeling away. My friends helped me to my feet, so we could hop on our bikes and escape, too. We all were rattled from the sneak attack. Miguel looked the worst with a swollen left eye. Randy and Brian seemed fine if not at least shaken up, their hair tussled and sprinkled with blades of grass and dirt.

"Let's get out of here!" Randy demanded, and we couldn't have agreed with him more.

We mounted our BMX bikes, then rode away. We heard a police siren but never confirmed if it was going to the convenience store or coming for us. Once we were deep within Hidden Oaks, we stopped for a breather at the neighborhood park next to the jungle gym. That's when Miguel's black eye introduced itself to the rest of us. It looked like a purple explosion on his pale face.

"Dude!" I said, a little horrified. "They got you good."

"Speak for yourself," he quipped. "You should see *your* face."

With the tips of the fingers on my right hand, I carefully touched the tender area around my right eye, the place where a subterranean pain lingered. Just the slightest bit of pressure shot bolts of pain to my brain. Randy nodded an agreement.

"You OK?" he said to me. He winced. "It looks painful."

"It's not," I said, fibbing a bit. It hurt pretty bad actually, like my eye socket had been bashed repeatedly with a rubber mallet, and the bone and tissue around my eye pulverized to expose the delicate nerves in my face.

"Maybe we should just give Bloody Billy his backpack back. He's gonna keep after us until we do," Brian said, exasperated. He was still panting from the bike ride.

"Maybe," I said, a little angry now. "I'll think about it."

"You do that," Miguel said, turning his handlebars. "I gotta get home. I've had enough excitement for today. Besides, my mom is gonna kill me when she sees my face."

"Later, dude," I said. Then he rode his bike home.

"I gotta go, too," Brian said. He still had bits of grass and asphalt pebbles stuck in his shortly cropped Afro. "I have a longer ride than you guys. I need to be home before dark."

"It won't be dark for three hours," Randy said, baffled.

"Yeah, I know. Later dudes," he said, then he rode away.

Randy sighed. "Sorry I didn't protect you. Their sneak attack was good."

"You don't have to protect me from *everything*," I snapped, my pride bruised as much as my eye, as I watched two little kids—a brother and sister maybe—approaching the jungle gym from the sidewalk.

"I know," he said. "But it doesn't hurt to try. You OK to ride home?"

He held out his hand for the Secret Crestridge Elementary School Handshake, a fraternal ritual we had performed since becoming friends in the third grade. It was a salutation we mostly performed between the two of us. Brian and Miguel knew of the Secret Crestridge Handshake, but rarely performed the ritual themselves, the significance of it for Randy and I was lost on our other two friends. We performed the secret handshake flawlessly, and it did make me feel a little better.

"Yeah, I'm OK."

"Cool. See you tomorrow. Last day of school, you know?"

"Later, dude," I said, then watched him ride away.

The two little kids scaled the jungle gym, then peered from the top like frail birds, shaking a bit and their round eyes wide open. They looked upon me with horror. My damaged eye was probably much worse than I knew, so I decided to skedaddle and head home before they started screaming or something.

The ride home was uneventful, although not without its moments. I didn't see Bloody Billy and his crew of miscreants, but I could hear their hot rods wailing through the neighborhood somewhere not too far away, maybe back at the 7-Eleven where they left us on the hot asphalt, or maybe tearing through the parking lot at school hoping to find us again and give us a second round of beatings. When I finally got home, I tossed my bike in the grass and quickly ran inside, making sure not to talk to my parents or let them see my face. My mother heard me come in the back door and called from the kitchen, but I ignored her. I snuck to my room, closed the door, then locked it. I slid down the door to the floor, my back to it, relieved to be in the sanctity of my room. It was like my own hidden lair.

My mother quietly rapped on my door with her knuckle. "Billy? Why don't you come to the table for dinner?"

"I'm not hungry," I replied, then sighed. I hated when she called me Billy so much. "I like to be called William, mom."

An awkward silence. "Will you open the door?" she said, then rapped once more.

"I don't feel good, mom. OK?"

She waited a while before responding. "Is there anything I can bring you that would make you feel better?"

"A Hot Pocket," I told her.

She said OK, then retreated to the kitchen. I was relieved to finally be alone. I knew it would take her ten minutes or so to complete my snack request and that was time I used to reflect on everything that had happened to me and my friends ever since I noticed the backpack on the ground, then grabbed it while we escaped from the Thousand Oaks Gang and the middle school security guard the week before. For a while, it seemed fun—daring even—to be in possession of something that belonged to the evil gang and their leader. But as time wore on and the reality of what could happen to me and my friends became painfully clear (my face was throbbing at this point and my eye sealed shut), I wasn't sure I wanted to keep the charade going.

Maybe we should just give Bloody Billy his backpack back. He's gonna keep after us until we do, Brian said earlier. And maybe he was right, the more I thought about it. But there was also a rebellious part of me that didn't want to do that because... well, I just didn't want to. Stupid, right? I never said I was a genius back then. Who is a genius in the seventh grade? There was a sense of power I gained from possessing the backpack and giving it back to Bloody Billy seemed to me like giving up that power, like surrendering, like accepting that he could push us around whenever he wanted to. But I also wasn't sure that keeping it was the best idea, either. I sat on the floor and gently touched the sore spot on my face as I pondered what to do.

I noticed my pocket book copy of *The Amazing Spider-Man* in the middle of the floor amongst my art supplies and doodles. I scooched over and picked it up, then flipped through it, examining the pages with my good eye. In issue #5, Spider-Man battled Doctor Doom. (Remember, he was Miguel's favorite Marvel character) A lot of the action in this issue happened within an abandoned factory where Doctor Doom performed his evil experiments. His factory was surrounded by a small lake and Spider-Man fell into the water when he narrowly escaped the grasp of Doom. This got me thinking about Doctor Doom's castle, Castle Doom, back in the country he lorded over, the fictional Latveria, and how it was surrounded by a churning mote that protected the castle from intruders. And the more I thought about the various bodies of water near Doom's factory and lair, the more I thought about how nice it would be if my friends and I had our own lair, our own Castle Doom, our own Fortress of Solitude (like Superman had), or our own place of seclusion—a place to escape from the menace of the Thousand Oaks Gang.

Then my mother rapped on the door again, startling me.

"Billy?" she said. "I have your Hot Pocket."

I was really annoyed she kept calling me that stupid nickname. "Can you leave it by the door, Pam? I'll get it in a minute."

"Honey? Are you all right? Can I come in?" she persisted.

"Mom, I'm not dressed. Come back later, please."

There was a long, uncomfortable silence, although I could sense the wheels of worry turning in her mind. I could even sense her putting her ear to my door to see if she could hear any audible clues but couldn't. I kept as quiet and still as possible.

"OK," she said finally. I heard her setting the Hot Pocket on the carpet outside of my door, then walking away.

The "I'm not dressed" trick always worked. With my back to my door, I slid down it to sit on the floor. I imagined what our summer would be like, being chased all over by the Thousand Oaks Gang, in constant fear that they would run us over while we rode our bikes, or jumped out of bushes or from the backs of buildings to beat us up, and this thought of a cruel summer kicked my imagination into overdrive. *What can we do?* I thought. *Where could we go?*

And then—just like that—it hit me.

The Cabin of Seclusion, I thought to myself. *We could have our own* Cabin of Seclusion.

An image of the abandoned cabin on Canyon Lake appeared in my mind—the old Meyer lake house—as if I was again sitting in the motor boat in the water, with Tony in the back and my friends sitting around me. Although this time in my mind, we were all nodding as if in agreement that this poor excuse for a vacation home was the place to go for solitude, our Cabin of Seclusion, our escape from the gang that wanted to hurt us every day after school.

And I knew how to make it happen. I pulled my wallet from my back pocket and rifled through it, until I found what I was looking for: a business card. I pulled it out and turned it over, finding the telephone number. Then I lunged for the telephone I had on my desk. One of the only things I had in my room that you could consider *fancy* was a crème-colored, slimline telephone. Now, I didn't have my own telephone number—a level of fanciness that none of my friends had except for Brian—but having a telephone in my room as a kid was a level of fancy that kept me above the gaggle of ordinary middle-schoolers without telephones or hi-fi stereos or even 13-inch TVs in their bedrooms, for that matter. Anyway, I dialed the number on the card and the line rang and rang. After seven or eight rings, an answering machine picked up.

"Thank you for calling Canyon Lake Marina. We're away from the phone right now, probably putting gas in a boat or helping a sailboat anchor in the bay. But don't worry. Leave your name and telephone number and someone will call you back shortly. Thanks for calling. Bye now!" the answering machine said, then beeped.

I hung up the phone, read the business card again, then turned it over. Tony had written his name in blue ballpoint ink, surrounded by doodles of boats and birds. It was kind of funny. I picked up my phone, then dialed the number again.

Someone answered. "Hello. Tony speaking."

I was nervous that he wouldn't remember who I was and the greeting clung to my tongue like a glob of peanut butter.

"Hello?!" he said into his hand receiver. I could hear rustling, like the receiver was being covered by a shirt or jacket, then some muffled, indecipherable yelling. Then quiet. I hesitated before speaking.

"Tony? Hey, it's me, William. I was camping with my friends last weekend and you took us for a boat ride. Remember?"

The line was silent for a couple of seconds, except for a bit of static. "Yeah, man! I remember you guys. How's it hanging? I didn't think I'd ever hear back from you."

"It's going OK. Listen, I have an idea. If I gave you some money, then would you be able to come pick us up and take us back to the lake?"

"Pick you up? Where do you live again? If it's not too far, then I might be able to."

This sounded promising. "I live in Converse."

"Converse? That's not far at all. How much money you got?"

I wasn't prepared for this next step in the bargaining process. In fact, I was strolling through this conversation completely on a whim. I hadn't really thought it through before dialing. All I had been thinking about was telling Tony my brilliant idea of giving me and my friends a ride back to Canyon Lake, so we could make the abandoned lake house our Cabin of Seclusion. It seemed like such a great idea before I actually picked up the phone to call Tony. I gambled on a random answer.

"One hundred bucks," I said, meekly.

"*One hundred buckaroos*?! Is that what you said?"

"Yeah."

"Fuck yeah I'll come get you guys! I'd do almost anything for a hundred bucks. When do you want me to pick you up?"

I gave Tony Miguel's home address—for some reason that sounded better than giving him *my* home address—and told him to pick us up the next day at five thirty. I asked him if he had a ride big enough for him and the four of us and he told me about his 1982 Ford Bronco XLT and how it could hold all of us as well as a cooler of beer and a hot babe like Victoria to boot.

"That sounds coooool. Are you bringing Victoria, too?"

"No way! Why would I do that?" he said, scoffing at my question. "Then she'll want me to share the hundred bucks. And I'm not doing *that*."

"Got it. So, I'll see you tomorrow then?"

"Wait! Do you want me to reserve a site for you at the campgrounds?"

"No," I said. "We're not staying at the campgrounds."

"Then where are you staying? You can't stay at my house. My parents would freak."

"Well..." I said, biting my lip, then taking a deep breath. I was winging it really good. "We're going to stay at the abandoned lake house. The one across the bay you showed us."

"Wait! The Meyer lake house?"

"Yeah," I said, worried he would say no. The silence on the other end of the line was unbearable and seemed to last for an eternity. Worry can do that—stretching time into a suffer fest. But he didn't say no. In fact, his reaction wasn't what my seventh-grade brain expected.

"Fucking *awesome*! Yeah, I'll pick you up tomorrow at five thirty. Don't forget to bring bug spray or you'll get eaten alive."

"Wait, what?!"

And that's how it all began: the real, life-threatening danger. It's easy to look back years later and know that this wasn't a very well-thought-out plan. There wasn't even a minimal resemblance to a plan. Mostly, it was just a fart of an idea that popped in my mind while flipping through a Spider-Man comic book. It seemed doable to my seventh-grade brain. But sometimes, that's how things happen. There have been marriages planned with just as much foresight. There have been babies created with even less foresight. How did I know that this impromptu trip to the lake would affect the rest of our lives? I had no idea what would happen to us out there on Canyon Lake.

After I hung up the phone, I cracked open my bedroom door and grabbed the Hot Pocket. It was still warm sitting there on the carpet. I gobbled it down as fast as I could, then thought about what I was going to tell my friends the next day at school.

9.

I couldn't wait to see my friends during lunch and tell them about my plan to escape to our Cabin of Seclusion. Fortunately, I was able to get out of my house before my mom saw my face, being that I woke up earlier than usual, showered quickly, pulled a Texas Rangers baseball cap low over my brow, and wore a pair of neon-colored sunglasses I won the previous summer playing a game of ring toss at AstroWorld, to disguise the galaxy of broken blood vessels around my right eye. It was a thoughtful disguise, although I couldn't wear the cap or sunglasses during class. Stupid dress code. The minute I took them off in school, anyone and everyone who saw my face gasped (the girls, the teachers) or chuckled (the boys, the coaches). It got to be pretty irritating, especially since it didn't hurt much anymore. It seemed everyone was making a big deal about nothing. But isn't that what all middle school kids do anyway?

Miguel had a much better disguise than I did. He wore an eye patch from a pirate costume he had stashed in his closet—one he wore in elementary school and kept around in case he ever needed it. He was resourceful like that. When I finally sat down with my friends in the cafeteria, Randy and Brian didn't seem to care much about Miguel's disguise; they were too busy stuffing their faces. I marveled at Miguel's ingenuity and gumption.

"I've just been telling everyone it's National Pirate Day," he quipped as he nibbled on his peanut butter and jelly sandwich.

"And that *worked*?" I marveled.

"Yep!" he said, then raised a hand with his index finger crooked, imitating a pirate's metal claw. "Yar!"

We all laughed. That was pretty funny and ingenious, and made me wish I had thought of it. My black eye was still exposed and garnered unwanted attention. Usually, my presence at school was ghostly; no one except for my friends hardly looked at or interacted with me. Not even my limp made me special, except for the occasional *poor kid* stares from the popular kids, but I had gotten used to that which was more irritating than anything else. Having your face beaten to a pulp certainly changes that dynamic, like pouring a bottle of ink on a ghost. I became exposed.

"What's the plan this weekend?" Randy said, then taking a Little Debbie cupcake from his brown sack lunch. He always ate dessert first. Always. And this was his second cupcake. He shoved the entire thing into his mouth and slowly chewed, almost as if he was letting it absorb into his tongue rather than chew and swallow it. He mumbled with his mouth full, bits of cupcake and spittle showering the table. "We should-thh all hang out-thh."

"You guys could come to my house and spend the night," Brian said. "My mom seems to like you guys more lately. Said you were a good influence or something."

"Little does she know!" Randy quipped. "Sucker."

We all laughed.

"Wait!" I said, taking a deep breath, then exhaling slowly, preparing myself for what I wanted to tell them. "I have a better idea."

All three of my friends stopped chewing, then set their curious gazes on me.

"Since it seems the Thousand Oaks Gang aren't going to let things lie, I have a proposal. I know a place where we could go where they won't find us, and we could take the backpack out there and hide it. They'd never, ever guess where it was then."

"But don't you think they'd still bother us?" Miguel said. "They're relentless, bordering on insane. I mean, look at our faces."

He lifted the eye patch, then tilted it upwards, revealing the nebula of burst capillaries around his eye. The three of us winced.

"Yeah. Well, they can only bother us for so long. Eventually, they'll lose interest and look somewhere else."

"You mean, hide it like treasure?" Brian said. Just the sound of that intriguing idea perked him up. "Sounds very interesting."

"Where is this place?" Randy said.

"I call it *The Cabin of Seclusion*," I said with a satisfied grin. "On Canyon Lake."

"You mean, like the Fortress of Solitude?" Miguel interjected, leaning forward with both hands flat on the table. "Or even better—like a lair?"

"Yeah," I said, taking a bite from a Pop Tart I brought from home for lunch. Frosted cherry this time instead of strawberry: my favorite flavor. "Yeah, but like I said, more like a Cabin of Seclusion. Remember that abandoned lake house Tony showed us last weekend?"

My three friends looked at each other. They all seemed to land on the same memory at the same time and nodded an epiphanic agreement.

"I called Tony last night and asked him to pick us up today at Miguel's house at five thirty."

"Why my house?!" Miguel said.

"It's better than mine. My mom would know something was up if a guy in a Bronco showed up. Anyway, I told him I'd pay him a hundred bucks to pick us up and take us out there. He said it was cool."

"A hundred bucks?!" Randy said, his eyes wide with disbelief. "Where did you get one hundred—" He stammered, then realized exactly where I got one hundred bucks from. A smirk slid across his face.

"But why go out there?" Brian said.

"Because we can. Because Tony said he'd drive us out there. Because I have the money to pay him. And because..."

I looked at each of my friends as they looked back at me. They were a little clueless. They didn't see the potential in the Cabin of Seclusion that I did. But they soon would.

"Because no one goes there. It's abandoned. But *we* could make it into something. It can be our hideout where no one bullies us, where we can be free to be ourselves. No bullies, no parents—"

"No food! What a nightmare!" Miguel said.

I patted him on the shoulder to calm him down.

"That's what the money is for: food, drinks, candy. Right?"

"Riiight," they all said in unison. The potential in the cabin was becoming clearer and clearer.

"And when we're ready to come back home, we'll bury the 'treasure.' No one will know where it is, except us."

"Can I bury it?!" Brian called out. "I wanna!"

"Sure, dude," I agreed. "You can bury it."

A self-satisfied look appeared on Brian's face as he gnawed on a Fruit Roll-Up. He was already thinking of his burying technique, I could tell.

"Wait!" Miguel said. "What do we tell our parents? We can't just tell them a high-schooler we hardly know is picking us up in a Bronco and taking us to an abandoned lake house on the lake for the weekend. They'll freak out!"

I was prepared for this quandary. I had been thinking it through the entire morning in class and while I was sitting in the cafeteria with my friends. I had the perfect plan.

"So, this is what we do. Me, Randy, and Miguel. We tell our parents we're spending both nights at Brian's house this weekend. They'll immediately believe that."

"Yup," Randy concurred. "It's true. They would."

"Then Brian, you tell your parents that you're spending the night at Randy's for the weekend. His mom is always on dates anyways, so even if they get a wild hair and try to call, she won't be home."

"Hey!" Randy said, as if mentioning his mom on dates was some precious secret not to be revealed to the rest of us with parents that were still married.

"That's..." Brian started. He tilted his head back, rolled his eyes into the back of his head, then bellowed to the ceiling, his arms shooting upwards into a victorious V. "That's genius!"

"Yup. It's fool proof," I said, pleased with myself. It really was a good plan, at least in my mind at the time. "So, all we gotta do is go home after school, pack some clothes and shit, then meet at Miguel's by five thirty. We'll just tell Miguel's parents we're meeting there so we can go to Brian's house together. Cool?"

I placed my hand out above the table and waited for my friends to place theirs on mine. One by one, they emphatically stacked them. Once our hands were all together—our collective sign of unity levitating above the table—we all said, "Cool!"

"Now," I began, pulling the second cherry frosted Pop Tart from my backpack. "Who wants to trade me something for *this*?"

***

The bike ride home after school was tense, but I didn't see Bloody Billy or any of his cronies on the way. Nobody followed me in a car or waited in the park behind some shrubbery, which was a relief. But it did intensify their mysterious ways in my mind. Their ominous presence in the neighborhoods sent shivers down my spine. Their random appearances gave them a mythological quality like sightings of Sasquatch or *Chupacabra.* But fortunately, their absence after school on this day gave me a little bit of a reprieve.

When I got home, I completely forgot about my black eye. So, when I saw my mother in the kitchen, I wasn't prepared for her bloodcurdling scream. It scared the crap out of me.

"Oh my god!" she cried. Her mouth stretched into a disbelieving O as she approached me with both of her hands out. She quickly cradled my face. "What happened to my adorable baby?!"

I squirmed from her grasp. "It's nothing mom. *Really.*"

"Did you get into a fight?" she continued.

"I wouldn't call it a fight."

"Who did this to you? Let me get some Neosporin."

My mother bolted for the master bathroom and I took her absence as my cue to duck in my bedroom and lock the door. The first aid supplies under her vanity sink were in disarray, so I knew I had a few minutes to pack my backpack and get a couple of important items. I flung my closet door open and pushed my hanging clothes to the side. I knelt in front of the plumbing vent where I hid Bloody Billy's backpack and unscrewed it from the wall with a screwdriver I left in my closet. And there it still was—undisturbed inside the gaping cavity in the wall—in the same place from the last time I pulled it out and stealthily took a small handful of bills. I tossed the backpack on my bed, then knelt back down in front of the opening for one more thing. I navigated my hand into the wall, then downward to the cement floor—touching the splintery wood bits, crunchy dead bugs, and stray insulation poofs—where I had one more hidden item: my mom's 25-caliber American Derringer pistol.

I pulled the gun out and wiped the dust off it. As I examined it, my mother called from her bathroom.

"Billy, you doing OK?!" she cried out. That damn nickname.

"Yeah mom!" I replied.

"Should I take you to the emergency room?!"

"No, mom. Really!"

"I'm still looking for the Neosporin. Be right there!"

I held the small pistol in the palm of my hand and remembered the day I accidentally shot myself in the leg, when my mother and Randy accompanied me to the emergency room at the hospital. My mother was so distraught and wracked with guilt. She believed at the time that it was her fault that I shot myself, even though she had nothing to do with it. I mean, it was *her* pistol, but I took it without her knowledge. So, after I recovered from the wound, she asked my step-dad, Steve, to get rid of the pistol. He promised her he would, but he never did. He was a gun enthusiast, like many men in Texas, and even though his step-kid had shot himself, Steve probably didn't feel that was a good enough reason to get rid of a perfectly good gun. I'm not really sure of what his rationale was for not keeping his promise, but I found the pistol a couple of years later in the garage on a metal shelf behind some cleaning supplies. Steve never, ever did any cleaning, so he probably just forgot about it. But when I found it—having gone out there in search of bleach because my mother insisted I look in the garage—all I could think about was keeping it for myself. It caused me so much pain that keeping it made me feel like I had power over it. I know that's kind of stupid, but that's what I thought at the time. So, I hid it in my closet.

My mother called out once more. "Found it! Be right there."

I knew I only had a minute or so before she came knocking. I pushed the hanging clothes back and closed my closet door, quickly shoved the pistol and some clothes in Bloody Billy's backpack, along with a towel and my *Spider-Man* pocket book, and put my ball cap and sunglasses back on by the time my mother started banging on my bedroom door. I flung my school backpack underneath the bed. I wouldn't need it.

"Let me put some medicine on your face, sweetheart. Please!"

I opened the door to find her prepared to apply Neosporin, her hand up and a finger extended, covered in the clear, medicinal gel.

"Mom, I gotta go. I'm spending the night at Brian's house this weekend."

I tried to move past her, but she trapped me with her other arm.

"Let me just put this on," she said, with an aggrieved look. The guilt she emitted crushed me.

"Fine," I said. Acquiescing, I tilted my sunglasses up, so she could gently apply the gooey medicine, which appeased her.

"Thank you, dear." She smiled, then patted me lovingly on both shoulders. "Be good then."

"Yes, mom!" I said, kissing her cheek, then running out of the house.

I rode as fast as I could to Miguel's house, then tossed my bike in the grass next to my other friends' bikes. Inside, Brian was sitting at the breakfast table with Miguel, trying to convince Miguel's parents—his father stout and hairy like an armadillo and his mother dainty and demure like a hummingbird—to let Miguel spend the night at his house, but I could see that they weren't convinced. Miguel used to always tell us he felt his parents were racist and that they didn't like Black people. Of course, we never wanted to believe that, but the mounting evidence was convincing. I looked at Randy. He was leaning against the wall behind them—his arms crossed and looking bored—and I tilted my head as if to say, *You convince them.* He nodded and interrupted Brian. Once Randy began his well-thought-out argument, Miguel's parents seemed to give in, and also proved that what Miguel was trying to tell us about them being racist was maybe a little true.

As I watched my friends and Miguel's parents work it out, I had a realization that maybe I should try to call Tony and tell him to meet us down the street instead of in front of Miguel's house. I didn't want his appearance to blow our scheme. So, I tapped Miguel on the shoulder and asked him to come to his room. I think he realized that Randy had things covered, so he came with me.

In his bedroom, I picked up his telephone and dialed the number on the business card that Tony had given me. The phone seemed to ring forever. When someone finally answered and I asked to speak to Tony, the voice on the other end said he wasn't there, which I figured might be the case. A digital clock with red numbers in Miguel's room flashed it was 5:28.

"We should go wait outside," I said. "We don't want your parents to see Tony's Bronco."

"OK," Miguel replied.

He grabbed his back pack and we went back to the kitchen. We said goodbye to Miguel's parents and left before they could change their minds. In the front yard, we waited in the shade under a large ash tree. Brian read the time aloud from his Casio digital wristwatch.

"Five thirty-five. You sure he's coming?" he said to me.

"Pretty sure. I called the marina and they said he wasn't there."

"He could be anywhere," Brian quipped.

But just as he said this, a Bronco that I could only assume was Tony's barreled toward us. As it got closer, I came out from under the tree and pointed to the Bronco, then pointed to the other end of the street. I motioned for my friends to follow me down there to the stop sign, which was four houses down.

As we trotted down the street, Randy put both of his hands on my shoulders and leaned closer from behind me to say, "This is going to be awesome!"

"I know."

The cream-colored Bronco passed us, then screeched to a stop at the corner. The engine farted out plumes of smoke and ribbons of steam from the tailpipe as it idled. It was a mean-looking ride with matte black wheels, burly bumpers, and chrome running boards for getting in the cab. When we got next to the Bronco, I could see Tony inside smoking a cigarette. He leaned over to turn the crank to roll down the passenger side window.

"What's up, ass bandits?" he said, then sat back up in the driver seat. Cigarette smoke was exiting every orifice in his head. Once the smoke cleared and he got a good look at my face and Miguel's face, the cigarette fell from his mouth into his lap. "Dude?! What happened to your—"

It's amazing how fast a cigarette can burn through a pair of jeans, particularly in the groin area. Tony squealed then swatted at his jeans, trying to extinguish the cigarette. He quickly found it and tossed it out his window.

He breathed a sigh of relief. "What happened? You guys get in a scrap?"

"Yeah," I said, sheepishly.

A smirk slid across Tony's face. "You little dudes are... BAD ASSES!" he said, punctuated by a finger snap.

We chuckled, pleased with Tony's adulation, although skeptical we were in anyway bad asses.

"Come on and get in," Tony commanded, then opened the door with the inside handle.

I got in the front seat. Brian and Miguel got in the back seat and Randy got in the way back, sitting on the floor.

Once everyone was in and we closed the doors, Tony said to me, "I hope you cold-cocked whoever gave you that black eye."

"I got in a good one."

"Good. Got the gas money?"

I pulled the hundred bucks from my pocket and slapped it in his hand. He flashed his teeth through a sly grin.

"Let's do this shit!" he said.

He stomped on the accelerator and the rear wheels of the Bronco burned a long, steaming skid mark as we tore through the intersection. I looked over at Tony—a new cigarette wedged between his clinched teeth and his hands gripping the steering wheel like he was twisting a wily snake to death—then I turned back to look at my friends. We all knew we were on our way to something adventurous and exciting. We just didn't know what we were getting ourselves into. But I will say this. Real danger was waiting for me and my friends on Canyon Lake.

PART II.
Escape to the Cabin of Seclusion

10.

I often look back at my time in middle school like it was a dream. It certainly seems like a dream sometimes. That's what happens when you get older and your past zooms away into history, like looking at your younger self shrinking in the rear-view mirror of a speeding car. When thinking back, I marvel at the freedom my friends and I had, at the audacity we had. We definitely took it for granted. Nowadays in our evermore connected world, we seem to have less freedom and less courage. I mean, on the one hand, we—the human race—have more information at our disposal than we've ever had before. But on the other, our constant desire to tell the world what we're doing at every given moment and our willingness to allow our devices to monitor our every move means we've given up our anonymity, and in doing so, some of our freedom and adventurousness. But in 1986, once we left our homes and the watchful eyes of our parents, there was no one watching us or tracking us or telling us what to do. We were free to do whatever we wanted, as long as we didn't get caught by our parents or were home when we said we'd be home. Good times indeed.

I distinctly remember a couple of things about Tony's Bronco. 1) The inside of the cab smelled like cigarettes, mildew, stale beer, and sunbaked vinyl. It smelled like punk rock. To me, it smelled like the summer of 1986. And 2) the Bronco rattled like it was about to catastrophically fall apart.

Every time Tony drove over a bump or crevice, it felt and sounded like the Bronco was going to explode, but it never did. Something magically held it together like divine intervention, or just pure luck—which is also a form of magic. And Tony kept on gripping that steering wheel tightly as if letting it go would lead to the end of us all. The Bronco must have been a beast to drive, but you wouldn't have known that by Tony's demeanor. He looked free as a bird behind that steering wheel. He oozed satisfaction while he played *Let It Be* by The Replacements on the cassette deck and drove us north on I-35, the cab filled with smoke and our hearts filled with joy.

We asked our older teenaged chauffer all kinds of questions about the lake and the lake house and the campgrounds and his job at the marina and, of course, Victoria. Once we arrived at the mysteries of love and the opposite sex, our questions revealed our naivete. Many of the tidbits of information we had acquired from our moron acquaintances about girls were more like tropes of science fiction than reality and, after a while, Tony couldn't help but laugh.

"Where did you guys learn this *shit*?" he said, placing another cigarette between his teeth, then pressing the car lighter button. "None of you have been with a girl, have you?"

He looked at me, then the rest of my friends in the rearview mirror. Our silence was our acknowledgment. When the car lighter popped up, he pulled it from the dash and lit his cigarette—the fiery orange center of the lighter singeing the end of his smoke—then quickly inserted it back.

"Don't you boys worry. I'll tell you the truth about women this weekend."

"Great!" I said, looking out the window at the passing businesses and ranch homes along the access road of I-35. There was a lot more to marvel at along the interstate on the way to FM 306 than you would think. There was a junkyard, a classic car museum, and an oddball attraction with the tantalizing name of Snake Farm. But none of these things were as exciting as the prospect of learning about girls—the TRUTH about girls—from an older teenager that was as cool and bad ass as Tony. "We can't be men without the knowledge. Right?"

"Riiight," Tony drawled, then chuckled. Smoke seeped out of his clenched teeth like a dragon's exhalations.

"How long til we get there?" Randy called out from the back of the Bronco. "I need to stretch my legs soon. It's cramped back here."

"Oh, maybe twenty minutes. What are you guys going to do about food?" Tony said, turning to me. He leaned a bit closer and lowered his voice slightly as if to whisper a secret. "It doesn't look like you brought any supplies with you."

"Supplies?"

He straightened himself back up in his seat, then took a long drag from his cigarette. A huge plume of smoke erupted from his mouth and escaped the cab through the small triangular window in the driver side door.

"What are you going to live on? Fresh air and lake water?"

I was miffed. "Is there a grocery store near the lake house?" I said, a little worried now. None of my friends mentioned bringing food and drinks. That would've been the smart thing to do.

"Nope, no grocery stores near the lake house."

"Oh. Man."

"But you can buy food at the marina, if you have money."

"I got lots of money!" I said, then plopped Bloody Billy's backpack on my lap. I began to unzip it, but Tony interrupted me.

"The only thing is, if you want to sneak up to the lake house, then it's probably best you don't go into the marina, just so no one sees you."

"That's coooool," I said, unzipping the backpack.

"So, give me some cash and tell me what you want. I'll buy it for you."

At this point, I pulled the backpack apart, exposing the bills inside. I lifted it slightly when Tony turned to me. Once he saw the money in the backpack, his eyes opened wide in astonishment.

"Shit, little dude!" he said, the cigarette in his mouth twitching up and down. "That's a lot of lawnmowing green."

I zipped the backpack shut and set it back down between my feet on the floorboard. It also pleased me that I now attained a level of cool that Tony realized he hadn't reached. He knew a lot more about girls than I did, but I had a load of cash that he could only have dreamed about. Touché, as the French say.

Brian leaned in from the back seat. "We ganked it actually."

"Shhh!" I hissed, then took a deep breath. "More like, found it."

"If you call taking it from the Thousand Oaks Gang *finding* it." Brian leaned back into his seat, flopping his arms in his lap. He looked to Miguel to chime in.

"We... uh, appropriated the money from a malevolent assemblage to a benevolent collective."

"Yeah, what he said," I told Tony, then wiping my hands together as if dusting them. "Appropria-ma-tated."

Miguel and Brian snickered at my mispronunciation, but it didn't hurt my feelings. I was still feeling powerfully proud.

"I won't ask any questions—for now. So, it seems you got the bread to buy food. I'll stop at the marina."

Soon enough, we exited I-35 for FM 306 and headed west toward Canyon Lake. In about fifteen minutes or so, we arrived at Canyon Lake Marina while the curtain of night slowly descended around the lake. Tony parked his Bronco in a dark gravel area past the parking lot, partially surrounded by shrubs and cedar trees, then killed the engine.

"You guys stay here. I'll be back," he said, then jumped out, slamming the door behind him.

We all turned and watched Tony cross the wooden pier to the marina, then disappear inside the store. It was painfully quiet now that the Bronco was slumbering. There was no one around or any cars in the parking lot. The night sky was ink brush black, still, and clear, speckled with stars and the occasional flashing lights of airplanes or satellites. The only signs of life were the fluorescent glow inside the marina store and several illuminated specks on anchored sailboats dotted across the bay like fireflies bobbing across a field of shimmering black ripples.

With four middle-schoolers stowed away in a Bronco, it wouldn't be quiet for long.

"What do you think our parents would do if they found out we were here?" Miguel quizzed us.

I shushed him. "Keep it down."

"Why? No one's around."

"Still," I insisted.

"They won't find out," Randy whispered. "We have a solid alibi."

"Solid as a rock," Brian sang, imitating the chorus of the R&B hit song by Ashford & Simpson. We all giggled.

"Why'd you show Tony the money?" Randy said, climbing into the back seat from the trunk area and plopping in between Brian and Miguel. He elbowed them for more room.

"I don't know. Just seemed right. He is helping us, you know?"

"Yeah."

"I don't know what made me do it. I just did. Sorry."

"It's OK," Randy said. He endearingly shoved the back of my head, which surprised me.

"Hey!" I said. "Why'd you do that?"

"I don't know. Just seemed right," he replied.

"Jerk."

"He's coming," Brian said.

We watched Tony cross the pier back to dry land, then walk over to the Bronco, his feet crunching on gravel. In his arms were two brown grocery bags full of food. He hopped back in the Bronco, giving one bag to me and the other to Randy in the back seat.

"Got you covered for at least a day and a half," he said, then started the slumbering Bronco. "Easy street."

He put the Bronco in reverse and slowly backed it into the parking lot from the dark, gravel area.

"Did anybody ask questions?" I said, setting the grocery bag filled with junk food in my lap, while I fastened my seatbelt.

"Nope," he said, putting the Bronco in drive and pulling out onto the farm road. "No one was inside. My dad must be out in the bay helping an anchored sailboat or something. Not unusual."

"Ah," I replied. "Coooool."

Tony drove the Bronco a short way up the dark farm road, then turned left onto a gravel one that took us into the wooded area surrounding the lake. The cab of the Bronco rattled as he maneuvered along the prehistoric drive. We could see glimpses of boat lights flashing between the trees and the surface of the lake reflecting the moon's soft glow. In front of us, it was dark and all we could see were two shafts of headlight beams stabbing forward, occasional tree trunks appearing then disappearing again into darkness. We soon arrived at a gate where Tony parked the Bronco, then got out. Leaving his door open, I watched him walk over to the metal gate and, just like he said before, unwrap a chain securing it to a metal pole. But there wasn't a padlock on the chain. After unwrapping it, he pushed the gate open, and hopped back in.

"Be there in a jiffy," he said, as he drove through the gate and parked on the other side. He jumped back out and repeated the fake security scheme, then got back into the Bronco. "The lake house is just up there."

He drove the Bronco up a short gravel drive, then over a clearing of wild grass, parking behind the old Meyer lake house. Its dark silhouette loomed large.

"We're here," he said, killing the engine. "Shangri-La."

He grabbed a flash light from the glove box—although he didn't turn it on—and we followed him with all our stuff (backpacks, grocery bags, and all) along a path to the side of the house. On the side door was a padlock but it was not locked. He lifted it from the rusty metal latch and easily opened the door, hanging the padlock on the latch hasp. Inside, he turned on the flashlight and directed Randy and I to the kitchen.

"Set the bags in there," he said, lighting our way with a flash of his light. Randy and I did as he asked, stomping through the dark house and quickly setting the bags on the first counter we could find, then came back to the group.

We all stood in a large open area in the middle of the lake house—the ancient floor boards underneath us creaking—and could see out into the bay through an array of grimy windows on the other side of the room. Tony turned the flashlight off.

"I recommend not using the flash light much at night in here. You don't want to bring unwanted attention to yourself. I have a camping lantern in the Bronco along with a few other things you might need. Stay here. I'll be right back."

While he fetched the lantern, the four of us stepped over to the wall of windows and peered outside. The phosphorescent lake had a magical quality that mesmerized us.

"Coooool," I said.

My friends agreed. The lake's incantation was interrupted by the stomping feet of our chauffeur. In one hand glowed a camping lantern, its light much more subdued compared to the bright beam of the flashlight. He gripped a bottle of beer in the other hand. We met him back in the middle of the room.

He lifted the lantern closer to his face—its soft glow casting eerie shadows under his brow and nose, a lit cigarette between his clinched teeth. "Which one of you ass bandits knows a scary ghost story?"

11.

We setup camp on the floor in the middle of the house, then played games (Uno, Black jack) and told stories (some scary, mostly funny) late into the night. Tony brought in a couple of sleeping bags that he kept under the backseat in his Bronco for him and Victoria, and said we could use them that night. But if he decided to bring Victoria with him the next night, then we'd have to give up the sleeping bags, which made perfect sense to us. We set the lantern on the floor and gathered around it—the five of us, two unfurled sleeping bags, our backpacks, and all our groceries. We dumped the food and drinks out on the floor like pirate booty, all our supplies spread out for the taking: mostly junk food and soda. Then we played the game *Rock-paper-scissors* to see who would get the privilege of sleeping in the sleeping bags. Randy and Brian won. Miguel and I got the consolation prize: the hard wood floor. Tony would eventually be going home, but said he would come back the next day on a motor boat with more supplies. He had work early in the morning and didn't want his parents knowing he was over here.

We quickly learned why Tony asked if we knew any ghost stories—the old lake house was an ideal setting for scary tales to be told. The house seemed ancient with its pier and beam construction, creaky wood floors, drafty spider-webbed rafters, and grimy windows. Except for what we brought with us inside, the lake house was completely empty apart from some old hinges, knobs, and tools randomly strewn about on the floor in various rooms. With every gust of wind or invisible shift of the earth, the lake house creaked, squeaked, and cracked its disapproval, sometimes even rumbling like an acidic, upset stomach. The house smelled of dried wood, mildew, mold, and death. Maybe there was a dead rat or possum under the floorboards—having slowly died, then rotted alone in the silty bed below the house—but we never cared to look, preferring to just ignore the smell the best we could.

Miguel was the first to tell a scary story, opting for his father's favorite *Chupacabra* tale, the one he had told me before but the others hadn't heard yet, where his neighbors mistook a rabid stray dog for the mythical Mexican beast, and asked his father to catch it. Since he was in the military, the neighbors assumed he was qualified to catch a rabid animal, even though he wasn't more qualified to do it than any of them. He reluctantly accepted the job and was bit by the dog on the arm, requiring him to get twenty rabies shots in his stomach.

"Boy! Was he mad at the neighbors for making him catch that dog!" Miguel said, flopping his thin arms across his gut while belly laughing, the shadows from his skinny limbs dancing on the drafty ceiling and cob-webbed rafters. "It was hilarious!"

"That's a classic," I said, patting Miguel on the shoulder for a story well-told—even though I had heard it a million times, it never got old—then turned to Tony. "How long has this house been empty?"

"The Meyer lake house? Shit. A long time," he said, taking a swig from his beer, then sucking a deep drag from his cigarette. He blew large rings of smoke, the shimmying circles drifting up to the rafters, then disintegrating on impact. We gawked at this parlor trick, even though the smell was hard to take. None of us liked the smell of cigarette smoke or being around smokers, particularly Randy and me. Our fathers and my step-dad were all heavy smokers—two packs-a-day kind of guys. We'd inhaled enough second-hand smoke in our young lives that we'd probably develop lung cancer as grandpas (still a way to go for that). Tony continued. "Maybe twenty years."

"Twenty years!" we all said in unison. It seemed inconceivable that such a cool place would be uninhabited for so long.

"Maybe longer. Ever since I can remember. My dad once told me that the Meyer family were pretty wealthy in the olden days and that they had made a bunch of oil money in the 1890s or something like that. They were like Texan Rockefellers or some shit," he said, then guzzled the last of his beer, wiping his mouth with his forearm. He burped prolifically, which of course made the rest of us bust out laughing. Tony grinned. "But then, the shit hit the fan."

"What happened?" Randy said, sitting up. We loved these type of stories; most boys do from my experience.

"Yeah?" Miguel added. "What happened?"

We all leaned in to hear Tony's story. Brian offered me a hunk of beef jerky, which I willingly accepted, then gnawed on it.

"Well, you see, the top of the food chain in the Meyer family back then—in the oil money days—was Griffin and Mary Meyer. They made a shit ton of money, then they built this vacation lake house out here on Canyon Lake, looking for quieter times during the hot summer months. And not only did they have a shit ton of money, but they had a shit ton of kids, too. Nine of 'em to be exact."

"*Nine* kids?!" I said, astonished. "They must have been *doing it* like rabbits!"

"I guess you could say that," Tony said, chuckling. "Anyway, all the kids grew to love this place as you can imagine, growing up here in their summer months. So, when Griffin and Mary finally both kicked the bucket, which I heard happened within hours of each other, those nine bastards fought tooth and nail over this lake house—"

Tony stopped, interrupted by a sound outside. He turned his head to get a better listen, raising an index finger to his lips. Then we all heard the bird song: *Hoo huh hoo, hoo huh hoo.* A smirk spread across his face.

"That's an owl!" he whispered, speaking quietly.

We could barely contain our excitement, but Tony did his best to keep us quiet, pressing the air down with both hands, a sterner indication to hush. We all listened as time went by—what felt like twenty or thirty excruciating seconds—when the owl sang again: *Hoo huh hoo.* It was a marvelous avian chant.

"Pretty cool, huh?" he whispered some more. "He's probably stalking a mouse or something."

"So coooool," I said, and my friends agreed.

"As I was saying," Tony said, leaning back on his elbows, his legs splayed out in front of him, not interested in the owl anymore. "Those kids have been fighting over this lake house ever since. At least that's what I've been told. Family business can get messy, especially with a bunch of assholes in your family."

This observation resonated with me, and probably Randy, too. My parents' divorce left deep scars on my soul, and Randy was in the throes of his parents' own ugly separation. Eventually, his parents' divorce would get uglier while we were in high school, a particularly rough time in Randy's young life. But at least we had each other to lean on back then. Divorce eviscerated our nuclear families. I eventually learned that my step-dad Steve was a much better husband for my mother than my birth father, but I wasn't aware of that as a kid. What kid is aware of this type of thing? All I knew was that family business was messy.

"Families can suck," I replied.

"Yup," Randy added, then popping his lips.

"Not all families are bad," Brian said. "Mine's pretty good."

"You're lucky," Randy said.

Tony must have sensed the dour direction our conversation veered into, so he sat up. "Say, tell me more about this backpack filled with money you found."

"Well, like I said earlier, I found it. The Thousand Oaks Gang—"

"*Thousand Oaks Gang*?!" Tony laughed, like that moniker was the funniest thing in the world. "What a stupid name!"

"Yeah," I agreed. "It is kinda stupid. Our neighborhood is called Thousand Oaks and most of these jerks live in Thousand Oaks, so I guess it's a convenient name and all."

"Seems right," Tony said, lighting another cigarette, sucking it to life, blowing a grey cumulous, nicotine cloud into the rafters. "Continue."

"We were hanging out after school when they surrounded us. We thought they were gonna pound us, but then a security guard chased us all away. And when I started to run, the backpack was just there on the ground. I didn't even think about it. I just grabbed it."

"Then while we were hiding underground, he opened it. It was filled with money and weed," Miguel added.

"Wait a minute—" Tony interrupted. "Did you say *weed*?"

"Yup," Miguel said, pleased with himself.

"What are you going to do with it?" Tony said, turning to me.

"I don't know. It's at the bottom of the bag. Want it?"

Tony froze, paralyzed with excitement from his good fortune.

"Fuck yeah, I want it!"

I grabbed the backpack, which was sitting on the floor behind me, and unzipped it. I dug through its contents—paper bills, other sheets of paper, empty potato chip bags, and even felt the cold metal of the 25-caliber American Derringer pistol—then pulled out the stinky bag of marijuana. I gladly handed it to Tony.

"Here ya go. You deserve it."

"Thanks, little dude!"

"No problem," I replied. "Glad to start getting rid of some of this stuff. They've been hounding us hard for this backpack. They even beat us up behind the 7-Eleven. I guess that's why I thought it would be good if we came out here to escape. Maybe even bury the money—"

"Like pirate treasure!" Brian blurted. "I'm gonna bury it good."

We all laughed. Brian's enthusiasm for burying treasure was a little ridiculous, yet endearing.

"They don't know you're out here?" Tony said, sucking more on his cigarette.

"I doubt it," I said. "I don't know how they would know we're way out here."

"Yeah, improbable," Tony said. He picked up the sack of marijuana and pressed it against his face, taking a deep whiff. A satisfied look appeared on his face, as if just the scent of it intoxicated him. "But I will say one thing. If they ever did find you out here, and I'm not saying they would..."

Tony stood up with the bag of weed and walked to the kitchen. His shadow danced against the wall, then stretched up to the rafters.

He continued. "*But* if they ever did. Don't try to get away from them across the water. You'll probably drown."

"Drown?!" I cried out.

"Yeah," he said, opening a kitchen drawer and setting the bag of marijuana inside. He closed the drawer and walked back over to where we were. He stood there, his hands on his hips. "Lots of hydrilla underwater. Your feet could get tangled and you could drown. Or there are sharp rocks just under the surface around this part of the bay. Just sayin'."

"Good to know," Brian said, as if filing this bit of information away in his Boy Scout brain for another day, just in case of an emergency.

I looked up at Tony, who was still standing and looked as if he was ready to leave. "You're not staying here with us?"

"Nah, I gotta get home. I have work early in the morning. But I'll come back over in the fishing boat around eight or so. Give me some green so I can buy you more stuff."

He extended his hand. I rifled through the backpack and pulled out a wad of cash—not even counting it—then crammed it into his hand.

"Gnarly," he said, shoving it in his pocket. "Good night, ass bandits. Don't do anything I wouldn't do."

He pointed to his forehead with his index finger, chopped the air with a tiny salute, then left the house. The Bronco soon roared to life outside and he backed away without turning on his headlights. The rumble of the engine faded into the distance down the gravel driveway. The hinges of the metal gate squealed as he opened and closed it. Then he was gone, the rumble of the Bronco dissipating into thin air.

I turned to my friends and we must have all had the same look, one of weariness and sleepiness. The moon's pale light shown through the windows of the lake house, casting its night spell. We couldn't help but stretch our arms and yawn, victims to exhaustion.

"Maybe we should try to get some sleep," Randy suggested.

It seemed like a reasonable thing to do, so we all made ourselves as comfortable as we could on the hard wood floor—Brian and Randy with their sleeping bags, and me and Miguel with our rolled-up towels as makeshift pillows.

"We should do some exploring around the property tomorrow," Miguel suggested, which also seemed like a reasonable thing to do. We all agreed.

"And map where to bury our treasure!" Brian added.

We all laughed, then talked a little longer about girls and comic books and movies and arcade games. Eventually everyone was asleep except for me and as I laid there on the hard wood floor, I listened to the owl sing his night song some more.

Hoo huh hoo. Hoo huh hoo.

The next thing I knew, I was swimming in the darkness of my sleep.

12.

I awoke to the sound of Pop Tart wrappers rustling and tearing. I wiped the sleep from my eyes and sat up, the shafts of morning light blasting the room through the bay windows. All three of my friends were sitting up and eating Pop Tarts, already wide awake and ready for adventure.

"How long have you been up?" I said wearily. I wasn't a morning person, per se. My three friends shrugged as they chewed their breakfast. "Got one for me?"

Randy picked up a package on the floor and tossed it to me, my breakfast tumbling into my lap. Then he pulled the second Pop Tart from his own packaging and inserted it halfway into his slit of a mouth, pushing it slowly the rest of the way with his index finger, like a letter being inserted into a mail slot. A look of contentment bloomed on his face, his jaw gnashing his breakfast.

Miguel jumped to his feet, one of his hands over his groin area. He was distressed to say the least.

"Where's the bathroom?" he said, dancing a urination two-step. "I gotta pee!"

"You always gotta pee," Brian replied. "And there's no bathroom in our Cabin of Seclusion. No electricity either."

"Then where do I *go*?"

"Out of doors, I guess," Brian said, shrugging his shoulders. "In nature. Where else?"

"Nature?"

"Outside, you dufus!"

Miguel sprinted for the back door, flung it open, and ran outside. The three of us just had to see where he was going to whiz, so we hopped up and positioned ourselves by the back door, peering out the door window, and eating our Pop Tarts while witnessing Miguel's desperation for bladder relief. He ran like a madman to the nearest tree—his arms and legs flailing like a crazed windmill—and whipped out his whizzer. The sight of him gleefully relieving himself on the cedar tree initiated my own bladder's natural response.

"I think I gotta go, too," I said, patting Randy and Brian on their shoulders, then joining Miguel by the whizzing tree.

Miguel continued to urinate for what seemed like an eternity, even long after I was done with my own liquid elimination.

"I really had to go," he said, then sighing, the spot at the base of the tree where he peed a muddy swamp.

"I see that," I said, pulling up my shorts and walking away.

A little way in the distance, just off the north face of the peninsula where the Meyer lake house occupied, stretched a different pier than the one Tony tied the motor boat to during our lake tour. And out in the calm waters of Canyon Lake, Tony sat in his motor boat, slowly navigating toward the pier, his sunglasses reflecting sunlight and his cool, teenaged irreverence. He had several groceries bags in the boat and what appeared to be an ice cooler, most likely filled with sodas for us. As the boat got closer and closer, the gurgling outboard motor belched louder and louder, until he cut it. He floated the last few feet, then secured the boat to the pier with a length of nylon rope. Miguel and I ran down to meet him.

"Top of the morning to you!" he said, lifting a brown, paper grocery bag to Miguel, then one to me. "What are you ass bandits up to?"

"We had to take a whiz," I said, extending an arm for another grocery bag.

"That's natural," Tony said, sliding the ice cooler on the pier, then climbing out of the boat.

"Thanks for bringing us supplies," I said.

Tony lifted the cooler. "No problemo. I can buy a lot with a hundred bucks."

The three of us trudged back to the lake house. Inside, Tony set the cooler on the kitchen counter. Miguel and I set the grocery bags on the floor where we slept, and where Randy and Brian patiently waited.

"You gonna hang with us?" Randy said to Tony, rubbing his hands over his close-cropped hair, as if that would make it look better. It didn't seem to move at all.

"I can't right now. I gotta work. But I'll be back tonight with Victoria. How's that?"

"Vic-tor-ee-uh," Randy cooed. That made Tony laugh.

"Settle down, Romeo. She's my girl."

"I know."

"Good. Just a clarification."

"What time will you be back?" I said.

"Oh, right after nine o'clock. Cool?"

"Coooool," I replied. "But what do we do until then?"

"I don't know. Go explore. It's beautiful out here," Tony said, then he flashed us a peace sign with his right hand. "Later dudes."

He quickly left, the back door slamming. We stepped over by the door and watched him through the window walk down to the pier, jump in the boat, and cruise away quickly after pulling the starter cord. The boat skipped across the wake of another motor boat with a trailing water skier, then disappeared around the peninsula. We looked at each other.

"Time to explore!" Brian exclaimed. "Let's go!"

"What about our stuff?" Miguel said, looking back at our supplies and backpacks on the floor.

"No one is coming around here. Nothing to worry about," I told him, which eased his apprehension.

Outside, it was an unusually cool morning for summer with a gentle breeze coming in from the Hill Country and across the top of the now placid lake water. We walked down to the pier and examined its sturdiness compared to the rickety one on the other side of the peninsula. But since it appeared to be a dead end for fun—mostly because Brian couldn't swim—we decided to not cross it. We walked down a grassy slope to the pebbly shore. The vast amount of smooth rocks next to the water invited us to play a game of skipping rocks, so we each hunted and pecked for the perfect, flat, smooth rocks to throw. A feisty game ensued but quickly subsided after a few rounds. And as we tossed the remaining rocks back on the ground, I spotted something very unusual. I knelt on one knee and carefully picked it up. What I found astonished me: a large snail shell.

I stood up and examined the peculiarly large shell, the exterior pearlized in swirls of pink and white, its size close to that of a small peach. With my friends around me, I turned it over, then brought it closer to look inside the opening.

"It's like the shell in that stupid book *Lord of the Flies*," I said, pretending to put it to my lips so I could blow it like a trumpet.

"Ewww!" Miguel protested, which made me laugh of course. Unlike the rest of us, Miguel was rather squeamish, almost comically so, even with an abandoned snail shell. The slimy slug was nowhere in sight and yet he still recoiled in terror.

"You mean, like the conch?" Brian said. "I wanna see it."

I handed him the large snail shell, so he could examine it himself. He looked it over, then handed it back to me, pleased to have witnessed such an anomaly.

"I never finished that book," Randy said. "Too depressing."

"That's the truth," I confirmed. "It's a bummer."

"You gonna toss the shell in the lake?" Randy said, a mischievous look on his face.

"Nah," I said, putting it in my pocket. "Gonna keep it as a souvenir."

I noticed Randy looking at something behind me, so I turned to see what he was looking at. And there it was out in the water: Sometimes Island. With water lapping at one side, its jagged contours lifted out of the lake like the back of a prehistoric creature, like a dinosaur with a plated spine wading in the water. Cedar trees dotted the top ridge and swayed in the Hill Country breeze. Its presence out in the lake was eerie and mysterious.

"I really want to explore that island," Randy said. "Do you think people go on it?"

"I'm sure somebody's been on it," Miguel said. "Somebody's been on Sometimes Island at somewhere, someplace... sometime."

We all laughed.

"Nice poem," I said, patting Miguel on the back.

"Wait a minute!" Brian blurted. "I have something. Wait right here!"

Brian tore off, running toward the Cabin of Seclusion at full speed, and we weren't quite sure what he was up to. The three of us looked at each other and shrugged. Seemed strange he would run off so quickly, but we continued to daydream about the possibility of Sometimes Island being occupied at some time in history, maybe by cognizant apes, or long-extinct creatures we didn't even know about.

"I bet somebody's been out there. People like to claim places. Be rulers and stuff. Right, Miguel?"

"Totally," Miguel agreed. "History tells us that."

"Do you want to go out there?" I said, scratching my head. "Tony said it was dangerous to get too close. Rocks and stuff under the water."

"Yeah, I know," Randy said. "I'm still curious."

Just then, Brian came tearing back, one of his arms flapping as he ran, the other arm tucked close as if he was clutching a football. Once he got to us, I saw what he was clutching: a pair of binoculars.

"Check it out!" Brian said, holding them with outstretched arms. "We can spy on the island!"

"Coooool!" I said, reaching out for the binoculars, but Randy snatched them away. "Hey!"

"I wanna see first!" Randy said, raising the binoculars to his face, but he didn't know how to focus or adjust them. He just randomly turned knobs and flexed the middle hinge. "They don't work. I can't see shit!"

Brian grabbed them back, huffing impatience, then adjusted the hinge before placing them in front of his eyes. "You gotta adjust them to your face, then focus. Like this."

Brian looked out at the island and the three of us without binoculars shaded our brows with flat hands, trying to see the best we could. Brian narrated what he was observing.

"I see rocks. Some tall grasses. Some cedar trees—"

"Anything good?!" Randy demanded.

Brian slowly lowered the binoculars and stared at Randy.

"Like what? An arcade?"

"Nah! Something valuable," Randy said, smirking.

Brian rolled his eyes again, then raised the binoculars back up to his face.

"I see some birds perched up in the trees."

"Birds?!" Randy said. "Lame!"

"I guess what Randy is getting at," I began. "Does it look like Sometimes Island has ever been occupied by humans?"

Brian appeared to scan the length of the island and back. "That's a negative."

He dropped the arm with the binoculars to his side. Randy snatched them out of his hand, raising them to his face, and struggled to look through them.

"How do these things work?" he said.

We all laughed at Randy's frustration. I looked back behind us to see what was around, peering at a line of trees up the incline.

"We should go up there and explore," I said. Brian and Miguel nodded while Randy continued to fumble with the binoculars. The three of us walked up the incline toward the wooded area, leaving Randy behind. He called out to us.

"Wait for me!"

When he caught up to us, we were already deep into the woods. Dried leaves crunched under our feet as we walked farther from the lake house and deeper into the platoon of tall trees. The Hill Country breeze rustled the canopies of the trees, birds occasionally flapping and squawking above us. As we trudged through the leaves and moist soil underneath, the omniscient presence of nature enveloped us, insulating us from the sounds of civilization near the marina and campground. The muffled din of animals and insects unconcerned with our existence greeted us: squirrels cracking nuts, birds leaping from branch to branch, and beetles scurrying along rotting tree trunks.

"It's so cool," Brian said. "I could live out here." He gazed up at the trees and their interlaced canopies.

"Kinda creepy," Randy said, looking around. "What if there was a murderer out here?"

"A murderer?" I said, chuckling. "Like Jason from *Friday the 13th*?!"

"Or worse—Michael Meyers," Randy added. "Nobody would know we were even out here. Dead. My mom would have a hissy fit."

"Mine, too," Miguel said, and we could hear his teeth chattering. "My mom would put a curse on you, dude. *Una maldición.*"

"What does *that* mean?" Brian said, stopping in his tracks and turning to Miguel. He cocked his head, waiting for an answer.

"I just told you. A *curse,*" Miguel replied, putting his hands on his hips. "Are you not listening to me?"

"I don't understand Spanish. That's a *foreign* language, *compadre.*"

"*Compadre* is Spanish too, numb nuts," Miguel said.

We all laughed. Miguel could be pretty funny when he wanted to be, but he abruptly quit laughing and jumped back what seemed like three feet.

He yelled. "What is that?!" Then he pointed to the ground.

I looked to where he was pointing, a small mound of dried leaves and twigs with something off-white underneath. Brian—being the outdoorsy type and less inclined to be afraid of things in nature—swept the dried leaves away from the mound with his right foot, revealing the skull of an animal with a line of ants exiting an eye socket. Randy and I squealed, then hopped back to where Miguel was standing. Brian placed his hands on his knees, then bent over at the waist to get a closer look. An inquisitive harrumph escaped his mouth, then he swept more leaves away from the skull.

"It's a deer," he called out. He squatted down to get an even better look. "It's been dead for a while."

"Gross," Randy said, wrapping himself in his arms. It always surprised me when Randy seemed scared of something, being that he was so big for his age. Never judge a book by its cover, they say. "I'm staying over here."

At this point, Brian had a long, straight twig and he was poking the skull's eye socket, and jabbing at the line of ants.

"We should head back to the Cabin of Seclusion soon," I suggested. "Maybe eat a snack. Maybe snoop around the house. We might find something good there. You never know."

"Yeah!" Brian cried out, jumping up, and tossing the twig. "Treasure!" He sprinted full speed past us and back in the direction we came. As he ran, he yelled. "I want some candy!"

I looked at Miguel and Randy. "Who else wants some candy?"

"We do!" my two friends said, and we ran back the way we came. We hoofed it out of the woods and back to the pier, then ran up the grassy incline to the Cabin of Seclusion: our temporary home away from home.

13.

The afternoon meal we ate once we got back to the Cabin of Seclusion can be described in only one way: a junk food massacre. We plopped on that dusty hard, wooden floor with only one plan of action, and that was to eat everything in our cache of snacks. The ravenous hunger pangs we all experienced at that age were extraordinary to the point of ridiculous. All our parents complained about our bottomless pits for stomachs at one time or another; I'd heard it myself at various sleepovers at each other's houses. My own mother complained every single Saturday morning about my unusual propensity to scarf down twenty or more pancakes in one sitting, even though she continued to satisfy my requests for more griddle cakes with aplomb. Why didn't she just say no? Randy, of course, could usually out-eat the rest of us simply because he was much larger in stature. His ability to shove copious amounts of junk food into his gash of a mouth was legendary. Even my parents hid our snacks whenever they heard he was coming over. But don't underestimate Brian and Miguel, either. I've seen these two tag-team on several boxes of Little Debbie cakes like a ruthless wrestling duo, laying waste to dozens of cakes in a single sitting. This time at the lake house was no different. Unmoored by our parents' watchful eyes, we stormed the grocery bags and ate everything: fried fruit pies, cookies, snack cakes, chips, and jerkies, then guzzled two to three sodas a piece. It was a horrifyingly glorious display of gluttony that I'm certain would've given all our parents big, fat heart attacks. I think we assumed that Tony would just bring us more snacks later that evening. And besides, we were really hungry. Eating everything wasn't just a challenge; it was inevitable.

I remember feeling so full that my t-shirt and the loose elastic waistband of my shorts felt unbearably restrictive, so I peeled off my shirt, slid my shorts down an inch or two to give my gut some room to expand, and laid back on the wood floor, Bloody Billy's backpack underneath my head as a pillow.

"That was bad to the bone," I said. I patted my stomach, then belched. My friends laughed.

The others followed my lead and peeled off their shirts, then laid on the wood floor with whatever they could find under their heads for support. The afternoon was much warmer than the morning time and the cool Hill Country breeze subsided to leave behind an oppressive humidity that settled on the peninsula like a dense fog. Being in the shade and solitude of the lake house was nice, although not air conditioned. We didn't care, though. We were free.

"Bodacious!" Randy added.

"Tubular!" Miguel yelled.

"I got nothing," Brian said, then snickered. "I'm just happy."

"Me too," I agreed.

"I could live out here," Brian said, gazing up to the rafters of the lake house, contemplating something. "It wouldn't be hard for me. I know how to rough it. Or we could just make this place more livable."

"Maybe we could buy this place," Miguel said, which elicited excitement from everybody including me.

"That would be rad!" Randy said, sitting up, then pointing to me. "Dude, how much we got in the backpack?" He snapped his fingers at me, as if to say *Chop chop*, which was annoying. I was chilling out.

Upon further consideration, I didn't know for sure how much cash we had, having randomly plucked small wads of bills here and there to pay for snacks and rides. I sat up and unzipped the backpack, then spilled its contents onto the wood floor: money, papers, snack wrappers, and the 25-caliber American Derringer pistol.

Brian and Miguel sat up, too. And when all my friends saw the gun clunk on the floor, they all said the same thing: *Whoa!*

"Dude," Randy said, leaning forward to pick up the gun. "I didn't know you were packin' heat." He examined it, then his face flushed. He looked at me surprised. "Is this *the* gun from—you know?"

"Yeah," I said sheepishly.

"I thought your step-dad got rid of it?"

"My mom asked him to, but he just put it in the garage."

"I wanna see it!" Brian said, extending his hand to Randy, who willingly gave it to him. Brian jumped to his feet and dashed toward a window, pointing the gun at an imaginary target in the distance. "We could definitely live out here with this for self-defense."

"Give it back," I said. Brian reluctantly complied. "Sorry I didn't tell you about it. Just thought we might need it. I don't know why."

I slipped the gun back into Bloody Billy's backpack. Brian and I sat back down.

"So, how much cash we got to buy this place? Let's count it!" Miguel said. He gathered the bills together and tapped the growing stack as he retrieved the money from the floor, mostly twenties and fifties with an occasional hundred or ten-dollar bill. Once he gathered them all, he began to count—licking his thumb to help with separating them—organizing the bills on the floor by denomination. "Twenty, forty, sixty..." And so on.

We watched him. Even—I dare say—cheered him on.

"Seems like a *lot*!" Randy gloated.

When Miguel was done, he announced, "$1,780."

Again, we collectively declared: *Whoa!* It certainly seemed like a huge amount of money, and to four middle-schoolers in 1986, it was. Just not enough to actually buy our beloved Cabin of Seclusion. Even if it was enough to buy it, the property's ownership was in family-estate limbo.

"We should ask Tony about buying it when he comes back," Brian said, laying his arms across his gut, then farting. "I sure am sleepy."

Brian laid down on the wood floor and so did Randy, obvious victims of a debilitating sugar crash. I opened the backpack so Miguel could put the money back in it. I zipped it shut, laid it on the floor, and used it as my pillow again, laying down with the rest of my friends.

"It sure would be cool if we could buy it. Make it our... What do you call a perfect place to live?"

"A utopia," Miguel answered.

"Yeah, our utopia. And, if we can't buy the Cabin of Seclusion, then we can decide how to split the money later," I said, daydreaming a scene projected up in the rafters, a mental movie of me buying piles of comic books with wads of cash.

"Or bury it!" Brian said. "I wanna bury it! *Please!*"

We chuckled, then soon drifted off into an afternoon nap brought on by the sugar crashes, and the lull of daydreams.

***

I awoke to the cacophony of someone banging on the back door, and yelling.

"Get your hands up!" the intruder yelled, then banged on the door some more, the racket rattling the rickety bones of the lake house.

My body involuntarily jerked up at the waist as I rubbed the crust from my eyes. I discovered my friends writhing on the floor around me, startled with the disturbance. The intruder banged harder on the door and yelled louder.

"You're under arrest, you ass bandits!" he called out, then laughed.

"Oh, stop it!" a young woman's voice said, followed by the sound of skin being smacked.

"Hey!" the intruder said, and that's when I knew it was Tony.

The phosphorescent sunset was fading into twilight and I realized that we had napped for a long time, comatose from the junk food massacre earlier. The back door opened and the sound of feet stomped across the wood floor. The next thing I knew, I was looking up at Tony and his girlfriend Victoria. I forgot how pretty she was, and I was instantly embarrassed for sitting shirtless on the floor.

"Sorry, we fell asleep," I said, finding my shirt, then pulling it over my disheveled head and onto my scrawny body.

"I can see that," he replied, lifting a sixer of beer in one of his hands. "Brewsky?"

I shook my head. Victoria slugged Tony's arm.

"They don't like beer. They're good boys. Remember?" she said, then knelt in the middle of our sleeping circle and turned on the camping lantern. It glowed softly, casting dim shadows on the walls. She looked around at the mess of candy wrappers and soda cans we'd strewn about on the floor along with our backpacks and towels. She winked at me.

"Yeah, I forgot," he said, walking into the kitchen and setting the sixer on the counter. He opened the drawer where he stashed the weed and set it next to the beer. He pulled a small glass pipe from the front pocket of his worn jeans and began packing the bowl, pressing the weed into it with his thumb. "Maybe they'll like *ganja* better." He set the pipe ablaze with a Bic lighter and inhaled deeply, then a blast of white smoke erupted from what seemed like every orifice in his head. He hacked a staccato cough: phlegmy, hoarse, and euphoric.

Victoria laughed. “Doubt it.” She turned to me and smiled, but her cheerfulness quickly withered. For the first time, she got a good look at my face and the bruised halo still orbiting my eye. I had forgotten all about it, but Victoria hadn’t seen us since the camping trip.

“Oh my God!” she cried out. “What happened to your eye?”

“Got into a fight,” I replied, then thumbed to Miguel. “He got it bad, too.”

“Jesus!” Victoria covered her mouth with both hands. “I hope you got in a good punch or two.”

“Me, too,” I cracked. “I don’t remember.”

“Well then,” she began, patting me and Miguel on our hands. “What do you boys want to do?”

I was stricken with embarrassment, not being used to a pretty girl talking to me, especially after just waking up from a deep sleep. I looked over at Randy who was sitting up by now and pulling his t-shirt over his head. He winked slyly, and tilted his head as if to say, *You go, stud!* Seeing that I was also stricken with an immediate case of girl-induced laryngitis, he offered a suggestion for me.

“We could put on a show for you guys. I love to tell jokes. I wanna be a comedian one day.”

“A show?” Tony said, then coughed some more. His face turned bright red and he forced a smile through the coughing.

“Yeah!” Brian chimed in, also standing now and pulling his shirt back on. “He tells jokes. And I have *survival* stories.” He thumbed his chest as a proud smile appeared.

“Like a talent show?” Victoria said. Tony handed her the glass pipe, then sat down next to her. She took a small drag and softly exhaled wispy strands of smoke. “That sounds like fun.”

Miguel added, “And I can give a presentation about benevolent and malevolent rulers of history. I know all about ‘em!”

"A presentation?!" Tony said, then snickered longer than you would expect someone to snicker at such a comment. He was high as can be. "*That's* funny."

"What will I do?" I said. I didn't think I had a particular talent or knowledge to present to everybody, so I was a bit miffed about how I would fit into our little talent show.

"Dude," Randy began, then stood next to me and firmly placed his hand on my shoulder. "You're a great artist and storyteller. I'm sure you'll come up with something."

I smiled at his revelation. I mean, I knew I liked to draw and tell stories, but I didn't think of myself as a *great artist.* That moniker was beyond my comprehension at the time, but I certainly appreciated his adulation.

"Thanks, dude," I said.

"All right, all right. We don't need to circle jerk," Tony said, then snickered again. Victoria slugged his arm. "Hey! Quit hitting me."

"You're such a jerk!" she scolded him.

"Sheesh," he said, standing up. "Let me go get the snacks from the Bronco. You guys get ready. I got the munchies. Be right back."

Tony stomped out of the lake house. Victoria looked up to us from the floor, obviously feeling the effects from the marijuana. She had a content look, one of tranquility. She pulled her knees to her chest, then wrapped her arms around her bent legs to steady herself.

"So, how does your show work? Who goes first?"

"I will," Randy said. "I have a comedy routine."

"Ooo," Victoria said. "How exciting!" She clapped lightly.

Since the camping lantern was on the floor, its glow clung beneath it, casting eerie shadows above it. I could see Victoria looking strangely at us and up at the ceiling, as if maybe she was hallucinating. She cocked her head to the left, then tilted it to the right, as if trying to make out the spirits of the lake house's previous owners, their souls occupying the space around our heads and in the rafters. She leaned forward and picked up the lantern by its top handle.

"Here," she said, handing it to Randy. "Whoever's turn it is, hold this. The speaker gets the lantern. That's how we'll know it's their turn."

"Good idea!" Randy chimed in, holding the lantern up to illuminate his face. "So, I'll go first. Then I think Brian should go next. He's got some great survival stories to tell. Right, dude?"

Brian nodded an agreement, punctuated by a thumbs up. Randy continued.

"Then I think William should go next. Maybe tell a Spider-Man story or something like that. Cool, dude?"

I also nodded. Then added, "You're like our MC."

"Yeah!" he said. "I'm the MC!"

"And a dufus," Brian cracked, which prompted spontaneous snickering.

"Whatever," Randy demurred. "Then Miguel should go last and talk about marvelous rulers and beneficial kings. Cool?"

"Malevolent and benevolent," Miguel retorted, which bothered Randy. He didn't like to be corrected in front of the rest of us.

"You know what I'm talking about!"

Miguel nodded reluctantly. He didn't seem too excited about the talent show or his place in the roster.

"I'll do my best," he said, then sighed. "I don't like to speak in front of people."

"People?!" Randy said. "We're not people. We're your *friends*."

A smirk slid across Miguel's face. "I know. I'll do it."

"Attaboy!"

Tony came back in, stomping over to where we were gathered, a couple of brown, paper grocery bags cradled in his arms. He gawked, noticing we were not in the same places we once were when he went outside.

"What the fuck is going on?" he said. "Why are you holding the lantern?"

"Whoever holds the lantern," Randy said. "Gets to be the presenter. Victoria came up with that."

Tony looked down at his girlfriend sitting on the floor, then smiled.

"That's a great idea. Couldn't have thought of a better one myself," he said, sitting on the floor next to her. He fished a bag of chips out from one of the grocery bags and handed it to her. The surprise gift pleased her. "When does the show start?"

"Now!" Randy said. "Lady and gentleman. And boys. I am your MC for the evening. My name is Randy—"

"We know your name!" Brian heckled.

Randy blasted lasers of contempt from his eyes at Brian, who shrugged. Randy continued.

"Welcome to our first show at the Cabin of Seclusion!"

"The what?!" Tony said, looking at Victoria.

"That's our name for the lake house," Randy said, extending his arm like a TV game show host and presenting the inside of the lake house as if it was a grand prize. He continued. "I am your first entertainer for this evening. I have always wanted to be a stand-up comedian. So, here's my first attempt in front of a real audience."

The five of us scooted closer to Randy, sitting in various poses on the floor. He cleared his throat, then took a deep breath. What happened next was a comedic revelation.

"What's the deal with bathroom passes at school being on a wood block? We take them in the stall whenever we take a crap, and hand it back to the teacher when we're done. Then the teacher gives that poop-covered block to the next kid. That's disgusting!"

We all burst into laughter, particularly Tony, who was stoned to the bone. Our raucous reaction encouraged Randy, who continued assuredly.

"And what's the deal with the Salisbury Steak in the cafeteria? It looks like the lunch lady pooped out a real stinker, hammered it flat, then covered it in gravy. That's sooooo disgusting!"

This joke elicited even louder laughter, so Randy continued for the next couple of minutes, spewing gross joke after gross joke about the various things we all hated about school, the chores our parents made us do, and the minutiae of pre-teen life as a middle-schooler. I guess you could say he was playing to the crowd. Even Tony and Victoria were rolling on the floor. Although they were in high school, in actuality, they weren't too much older. Randy just ate up our enthusiastic reactions to his gross-out jokes. He quickly concluded his set.

"Tip your waitress and bartender, folks! I'll be here all week!" he said, taking a bow and absorbing the adulation from the rest of us. He beamed proudly. "Our next entertainer is someone we all know well. Our friend William!"

Randy offered me the lantern and I stood up after taking it. I looked around the room then down at all my friends, sitting in the quivering, soft glow of the lantern. I felt a paralyzing fear in the pit of my stomach—the fear that comes from being judged or chastised—and Randy could see my hesitation and reluctance. He threw out a life line.

"Tell everyone the story you told me the other day. The one about Spider-Man and Doctor Doom."

I appreciated his assist, then nodded knowingly. I cleared my throat and began.

"So, I have this pocket book copy of the first six issues of *The Amazing Spider-Man*..."

I took a deep breath and imagined the illustrated pages of my book, then the story just poured out. I told them with loving detail about the sinister plot Doctor Doom hatched and the ways Spider-Man thwarted his plans. I described the thrilling action of Steve Ditko's fluid art with the purple prose and zippy dialog of Stan Lee's script. I even played out some of the fight scenes with faux body slams and haymaker punches. I felt like I had them in the palms of my hands and stuck the landing when I finished my routine.

"And that's what inspired me to call Tony about picking us up and bringing us here."

I took a bow. Everyone applauded politely, although not raucously like after Randy was done. But that was OK. I didn't feel like dying anymore; I felt exhilarated and a little relieved it was over. I handed the lantern to Randy the MC, who then introduced our next entertainer: Brian. After a quick bit of applause, Brian procured the lantern and began his part of the show.

"Rather than attempt to entertain you, I would like to answer any questions you may have about survival. I will soon be an Eagle Scout and I know a lot about—"

"What do you do if you get bit by a snake?" Tony blurted. "I've always wondered about that."

Victoria gave him the stink eye and he mouthed *What?* in return.

"Well," Brian began, his eyes rolling up to sort through the various survival techniques in his mind, looking for the correct answer about treating a snake bite. "That all depends on the type of—"

"What if a water moccasin bites you? Will you die? Cause I see them all around and in the lake. I mean—"

Victoria slugged his arm.

"Hey!" he complained. Victoria smirked.

Brian continued, and eventually fielded all types of questions from us, like how to make a composting toilet, what bugs are OK to eat, and where are good places to look for clean drinking water. It was an enthralling presentation actually. I was surprised to learn just how much Brian knew about survival in the outdoors. I had no doubt that one day, he would be a fantastic Eagle Scout. When he was done, we all clapped as he gave the lantern back to Randy.

"That was amazing!" Randy said. "Our last entertainer needs no introduction... Miguel!"

He handed the lantern to Miguel after he stood up and he reluctantly took his place in the middle of the room. He closed his eye and inhaled deeply, a look of tranquility washing over his face. The corners of his mouth perked up, then he began to recite something that seemed like he spent weeks preparing. He spoke with the studious confidence of a college professor.

"I have always been fascinated with rulers from history, particularly the benevolent and malevolent ones. Benevolent ones were kind to their kingdoms. Malevolent ones were cruel dictators. An example of a benevolent ruler would be someone like King James I of England, who allocated funds to support the arts and made reforms for the welfare of women and children. An example of a malevolent ruler would be someone like Adolf Hitler, a leader who abused an extraordinary amount of personal power."

We marveled at the confidence Miguel exuded while he talked about this topic that consumed his passion. It seemed like we were witnessing the beginnings of a prolific career as a professor or some such professional. Little did I know back then just how prophetic that was. He spoke in measured tones, and placed emphasis on certain words with the wave or chop of a hand, like an orchestra's conductor performing a séance on his unwitting musicians.

"I think it's fascinating how a ruler chooses to lead. I've always felt that if I was to rule a kingdom, or if we ruled this place around the Cabin of Seclusion—our kingdom—then we would be benevolent rulers or lords or kings."

"Can a lady be a lord?" Victoria said, interrupting his speech. Tony glared at her.

"Of course, she can," Miguel said. "I'm a feminist, you know. Ladies can be lords, too."

"Radical!" Victoria said, raising her palm to Miguel for a high-five.

"Thank you! That is all," Miguel said, taking a bow.

We clapped as he sat down, congratulating ourselves on a show well done.

"What do we do now?" I said.

"Finish this beer, that's what," Tony said, offering a beer to me. I shook my head. "Man, you mean I have to drink all this beer myself?"

"I'll help you finish," Victoria said, taking it from his hand. She pulled the tab from the top, a foamy blast erupting from it.

"Cool, baby."

"What if we wanted to buy this lake house?" I said to Tony, who was giving Victoria goo goo eyes.

He turned to look at me and scratched his stubbly chin. "Yeah, I don't think you can. It's in estate limbo like I told you before. Besides, even if it was for sale, I don't think you could afford it."

"We have money," I said. "Lots."

"Oh yeah? How much you got in that backpack of yours?"

"$1,780."

"Wow!" he said, sitting up then scratching his scalp. He took a swig of beer before continuing. "That's a good amount of dough, but it wouldn't be enough to buy this place. You probably need a hundred thousand, at least."

"Oh," I said, dejected. "That's too bad."

"Yeah, I'm sure you guys would make awesome lakers. Maybe one day you'll own a place out here. It just probably won't be this place," he said, then he cast an amorous gaze at Victoria. The two nodded, as if knowing an unspoken language that only the two of them were fluent in. Tony stood up and offered his two hands to Victoria, helping her up to her feet. "We gotta get some *sleep*, then get up before sunrise."

"Before our parents wake up," Victoria added.

"So, hand over those sleeping bags."

Brian and Randy groaned, knowing they would be sleeping on the hard wood floor with me and Miguel, then reluctantly gave them the two sleeping bags.

"We'll see you in the *mañana*."

"Good night," Victoria said.

"Good night," we all said to them.

They walked to the other side of the house, entered a room, and closed the creaky door behind them. A series of muffled sounds could be heard, at first a dull thud like the sleeping bags hitting the floor, then a clumsy combination of footsteps as if the two of them tripped over each other's feet. Followed by dead silence. We looked at each other, our eyebrows raised like fighting caterpillars, then we burst out laughing. Randy turned off the lantern, and laid down with his head on his rolled-up towel.

"Might as well try to sleep," he said. "We should get up early and explore our kingdom some more since we're the lords of the manor."

"Yeah!" Brian said. "And finally bury our treasure!"

We all snickered, then made ourselves as comfortable as we could. After saying our good nights, everyone quickly fell asleep, except for me. I stared up into the rafters for what seemed like hours, listening to the owl sing his night song. *Hoo huh hoo, hoo huh hoo.* I heard a rustling outside and my curiosity got the best of me, so I got up and crept over to a window facing the direction of the sound outside.

I pressed my nose to the grimy glass of the window, peering out into the inky darkness, swathes of moonlight illuminating some of the lake house property. Out along the perimeter where the trees lined the edge, a lone wolf stared back at me with glowing yellow eyes, standing still as a statue, not even blinking. It peered straight at me, looking into and through my own eyes, staring into my soul and the secrets kept down there. Secrets so mortifying that I wouldn't dare tell anyone. There was an eerie calmness to its presence, and it seemed the night breeze stopped as it stood there staring. The owl stopped hooting, too. And the longer I looked at the wolf, the more I felt a hypnotizing hold take over me, as if it was seducing me. Scared, I closed my eyes to protect myself, then rubbed them for a second or two, to see if maybe my eyes were betraying me. When I finally opened them again, the wolf was gone. It vanished.

That's when the owl started up again. *Hoo huh hoo, hoo huh hoo.* I scanned all the visible property for the wolf, but he was gone. Finally, I tip-toed back over to where my friends were lying on the wood floor. I laid down, too, and tried to sleep, but I was consumed with the fear that the wolf might come in and eat us all. I pulled my towel over my head in an attempt to hide.

Please go away wolf, I thought. *Please don't hurt me and my friends.*

14.

From what I've been told, sometime early the next morning before there was sunlight, Tony told us he was leaving to take Victoria back to her parents' house and that he would be back to get us in the motor boat, so he could take us back home to Converse. His parents expected him to perform his work rounds for the marina—dropping off supply orders (food, toiletries) to the various families living in anchored sailboats out in the bay—and only then would he be able to give us a ride back home. I say I was told this because I don't actually remember Tony telling us anything; all my friends told me much later. But strangely, what I do remember was a lucid dream so vivid that it has stuck with me to this day, and not the reality of the early morning's events. Has that ever happened to you? I've had dreams that appeared so real that sometimes I question my own memories.

Here's what I dreamt. I believe now that I was so gobsmacked from the wolf sighting that night that I willingly fell into a lucid dream, one where I was conversing with the wolf through the window. The wolf spoke perfect English and was more than happy to answer any questions I had for it. I asked it through the window things like, *What is your favorite thing to eat?* (Turns out it's fawns) *What do wolves do for fun?* (They like to perform practical jokes on the members of their wolf pack) And the most important question of all: *What do you think of humans?* (They're more ambivalent about humans than I assumed) But the strangest part of the dream was not the conversation I had with the wolf. It was that Tony was interrupting me *in the dream.* He was telling me that he'd be back for us in the motor boat, but I kept telling him to stop interrupting the conversation I was having with the wolf. (The wolf's name was Jasper, by the way) I was so annoyed with Tony in my dream because the wolf threatened to leave if he continued to interrupt us. The last thing I remember was yelling at Tony, *Go away! Just go away!*

I awoke to my friends laughing at me while they ate Pop Tarts and drank soda for breakfast. It was a sad realization that the conversation with the wolf was only a dream. I rubbed the crust from my eyes, then stretched my arms.

"Who-thh are you telling-thh to go away?" Randy said, his mouth full of Pop Tart. He slurped from a can of Big Red, then belched.

"Tony," I said, rubbing my stiff neck.

"Tony?" Brian said, chuckling. "He left a while ago with Victoria. Said he had to get her home, then go to work." He shoved the rest of a Pop Tart into his mouth, almost too large of a piece to fit, then crumpled the wrapper into a tiny ball. He cocked his arm up as if to shoot a three-pointer in the final seconds of a tense NBA basketball game, then launched the wadded wrapper over all our heads and into a trash bag hanging on the side of the kitchen counter. The unexpected completion excited him. "Three points!"

Randy slapped him on the back and Miguel clapped.

"Nice one!" Randy said, then turned to me. "Tony asked us to clean up after ourselves. He left the trash bag for us."

"All right," I said, then sighed. "It's been cool here in the Cabin of Seclusion. I wish we could stay longer."

I picked up my package of Pop Tarts and tore open the wrapper. A can of Pepsi was there for me, too. My friends were already finished with their breakfasts and were picking up after themselves, putting their garbage in the trash bag while I ate.

Miguel hummed a work song that I believe was *Relax* by Frankie Goes to Hollywood.

"Maybe when we get back, we can figure out how to buy this place," I said, my mouth full of food. The Pepsi popped when I pulled the can's tab, then hissed, a mass of carbonated soda plopping down to the hardwood floors.

"How are we going to do that?" Randy said, standing by a window and looking out at the bay at the sail boats bobbing in the water. "Tony said we wouldn't be able to buy it."

"What does he know? He's just a teenager like us," I scoffed.

"That's true," Randy said, returning to where I was sitting on the floor.

Brian and Miguel played a tense game of one-on-one basketball, using whatever trash they could find as the ball: crushed cans, wads of paper, or whatever. Randy scooched closer to me to give them playing room.

"Maybe we could convince one of our parents to buy this place," he said, scratching his scalp. "Brian's maybe?"

"Yeah, that's a great idea!" I said, raising my voice so Brian could hear. "What do you think, Brian?"

He stopped in his tracks, allowing Miguel to run around him and slam-dunk a soda can unimpeded.

"In your face!" Miguel cried out, dancing a victory jig.

Brian placed his hands on his hips. "If I talk to my parents about buying this place, then they will be suspicious."

"Why's that?" I said, wadding up the wrapper after the last bite, then tossing it at the trash bag. It didn't go in.

Brian sat down with me and Randy.

"You don't think they'd be suspicious if I asked them *out of the blue* to buy an abandoned lake house? Sounds weird just saying it out loud."

"Well, you don't have to say it like that," I said, rubbing my chin and thinking of a better sales pitch. "You could say... Dad, mom. I have an excellent *investment* opportunity."

My three friends laughed, particularly Brian, who slapped his knee then threw his head back, his laughter billowing up to the rafters.

"That's funny," he said, then sighed. "Too funny."

Miguel returned to the window and looked out at the bay.

"When do you think Tony will be back?" he said. He pressed his nose against the window, shading his eyes with one hand. The morning sunlight was bright and intrusive. "I think I see him!"

"Is he coming in this direction?" I said.

"No. He's driving around the boats out there in the middle of the lake. Or at least I think that's him," he replied, then stammered. I could tell he was mulling something over in his mind, something important. "Do you *drive* a motor boat? Or do you *boat* a motor boat?"

"What are you talking about?" Brian said, then laughed. "You always ask the weirdest questions."

"The boat," Miguel said. "When you operate it. Do you drive it or boat it?"

"Who cares!" Randy blurted.

"I do," Miguel said. "I like to know these things."

"Nerd stuff," Randy scoffed.

"Maybe," Miguel said, returning to where the rest of us were sitting. "What do we do until he comes back?"

"I guess just make sure this place is cleaned up and pack our stuff," I said. "Then back to reality."

"Sucks," Randy said. "The Thousand Oaks Gang is gonna hound us all summer."

"We should bury the backpack before we leave," Brian suggested. "Like in the trees behind the house."

"That's not a bad idea," I said. "Let's do it after we clean up."

"Radical!" Brian said, standing up. "Let's clean up then."

The rest of us stood up, then scoured the lake house for food wrappers and soda cans and cigarette butts and whatever else we could find. As we picked up after ourselves, I decided to tell my friends about what I saw the night before while they were all sleeping.

"I saw a wolf last night," I said, which of course stopped all my friends.

"What?" Brian said.

"A wolf. While you guys were out cold last night. I heard something out back, so I decided to look out the window. It stared back at me."

"Was it by itself?" Brian said.

"Yep."

"That's crazy. They usually travel in—"

"Packs?" I said, then we both laughed.

"You read my mind!"

"That's what friends do," I said, then picked up a flattened soda can and tossed it at the trash bag. The can bounced off the counter edge, then clunked on the floor.

Brian pshawed. "You really need to practice your jump shot."

I rolled my eyes, then picked up the errant can, putting it safely in the trash bag. Outside, the sound of a motor boat grew louder, and I assumed it was Tony coming back for us. I raised myself on my toes and glanced out a window, seeing a motor boat approaching the pier.

"Tony's coming," I said to my friends. "We better finish up, so we can go home."

"What about the backpack? I thought we were going to bury it," Brian said.

"We can bury it quickly before we get in the boat."

"All right."

We picked up the last of the trash as the sound of the motor boat grew louder and louder, then abruptly stopped. I remember thinking that Tony had returned faster than I expected, and I wondered how we were going to bury the backpack out amongst the trees without a shovel or any tools. As I daydreamed about the four of us attempting to dig a hole with sticks and branches, Tony banged loudly on the back door.

"Come in!" I shouted.

But he didn't open the door. I looked at my three friends.

"Should I open it?" I said to them.

They shrugged. Then Tony banged on the door again, louder this time.

"It's not locked!" I called out. "Just come in!"

The banging continued, louder and louder. I thought maybe the door was locked and decided to just let him in. The door rattled as he banged on it. I trotted to the door. When I turned the door knob, I realized it wasn't locked.

"See!" I said, as I swung the door wide open. "It's not locked."

Tony was there all right, but he wasn't the one banging on the door. Tony was kneeling on the ground with a stream of blood draining from his battered nose. A guy that looked strikingly like Miguel's older brother Rogelio was standing over him, holding the nape of his shirt in a clinched fist. And another guy who looked remarkably like Bloody Billy was closest to the door, both his hands clinched into angry fists. He raised them, then slowly cracked his knuckles, which elicited a smirk.

"Good morning, sunshine," Bloody Billy said to me, but I was in shock and didn't reply.

All I could think was, *Am I still dreaming? What is going on?*

"You look surprised," he said, then lunged at the door, shoving it open. The force of the door knocked me back and I toppled to the floor on top of Bloody Billy's backpack. "I'll just let myself in."

I snatched the backpack and scurried to the opposite side of the lake house, standing in front of an array of windows overlooking the placid bay. My three friends were there, too, and we huddled tightly. Bloody Billy stomped a few steps then stopped, looking around the lake house, taking it all in.

"Nice hideout you got here," he said, then sneered at us. "Too bad I'm gonna have to burn it down."

15.

Now, it may seem coincidental to you, dear reader, that Bloody Billy and Miguel's brother—that jerk Rogelio—just happened to appear at the back door of the lake house, but there really was a very simple and practical explanation that was working itself out long before they showed up unannounced, although it wasn't clear to me while that bastard was goading us at the time. You see, I found out much later that while we did our best to conceal our little adventure from our parents, our juvenile parlor tricks didn't fool everyone. Rogelio was the one that caught on to our mischief when he noticed four BMX bikes lying in the grass outside his house. It didn't register with him at first, but when his parents mentioned at the dinner table that Miguel was spending the night at Brian's house, the presence of our bikes gave him pause. He snuck into Miguel's room soon after dinner and snooped for additional incriminating clues. He swept everything off Miguel's desk onto the floor with an angry arm. He yanked open all the drawers of his dresser, then tossed the clothes on the floor along with the drawers. But when he noticed Miguel's phone on his bed, that's what gave us up.

That stupid, baby blue, slimline telephone.

According to Miguel—who later found out the whole story from his parents—Rogelio picked up the phone and pressed the one button that would give our shenanigans all away: the redial button. I was the one to make the last phone call to Canyon Lake Marina—wanting to tell Tony to park down the street instead of in front of the house, so he wouldn't give us away—and that fateful mistake was what brought Rogelio and his cruel leader out to within close range of our Cabin of Seclusion that morning. They pulled up to the marina in that wicked Camaro and stormed the marina store where Tony unfortunately was sitting behind the counter, collecting the supplies he needed for the boaters waiting patiently in the bay for their morning delivery. They roughed him up real good and in a matter of minutes, he was explaining in exquisite detail where we were and what we were doing. I don't blame Tony, really. I'm sure it was hard keeping a secret when a jerk like Bloody Billy was pulverizing his face. So, once Tony told them he had planned to pick us up in the motor boat after his morning deliveries to bring us back to the marina, so he could drive us home, Bloody Billy had new plans. And this was when the real danger for us finally materialized. It was all fun and games until Bloody Billy and Rogelio showed up.

That stupid, stupid telephone. Why didn't I put it back where I found it?

Back inside the lake house—our Cabin of Seclusion no more—I clutched Bloody Billy's backpack tightly to my chest as my three friends clutched onto me, huddled against the bay of windows like scared fawns cowering from a hungry mountain lion. I think they knew—just as I knew—that I was the source of Billy's ire. He tapped the floor with his scuffed, steel-toed boot, as if knocking on the hatch to hell, then pulled a Zippo lighter from his pocket. He flipped the lighter open and lit it in one fluid flick of his wrist and snap of his fingers, like a magician revealing a trick from his shirt sleeve. He raised the lighter in front of his face.

"I bet this shack will burn like a... like a..." He turned to Rogelio who was still standing outside the door with Tony's shirt in his clinched fist. He called out, "What does that Doors guy say in the song?"

"Huh?" Rogelio replied, oblivious. "What song?"

"You know?" Billy continued, then attempted to sing. "*And our love will be a funeral...* What does he say?"

"Fire?"

"No, you idiot!" Billy said, then stammered, humming the melody of the tune that perplexed him. He turned back to face us, humming some more. "Hmm hmm hmm, *come on baby light my fire.*"

As Bloody Billy struggled to think of the words to The Doors infamous song, *Light My Fire*, I slowly unzipped the backpack and carefully slid my hand inside. I reached down to the bottom and squeezed the grip of the 25-caliber American Derringer pistol, waiting for the opportune time to pull it out.

"I don't know the words to that song," Rogelio said, Tony's shirt still in his grasp. Tony slowly shook his head at his predicament, or maybe it was the asinine conversation he was being subjected to listen to when he'd rather be back at the marina, flirting with Victoria.

Thinking about it now, I don't blame Miguel's brother. That song was an earworm with a weird rhyming scheme. Most people couldn't recall the correct lyrics.

"Nevermind. I'll think of it in a bit," Billy said, pulling an unfiltered cigarette that was dutifully perched above his ear and slid it in his pursed lips. He lit the cigarette with his Zippo, then swept the lighter against his thigh, snapping the lid shut. He slipped the lighter back into his pocket. "I believe you have something of mine."

At this point, the backpack felt as if I was clutching a boulder, its bulky presence weighty and unruly from the guilt of all the events that led me and my friends here. I thought of throwing it or dropping it, maybe possibly launching it at Billy's face to distract him enough so we could run, but none of these scenarios seemed reliable as an escape plan. How would we then get out of the house? Break a window? Tackle Billy? I clutched the backpack tighter and attempted to retreat further away, but my friends and I were already pressed against the windows. We were trapped. I gripped the pistol tighter, waiting for the opportune time to pull it out. But the tighter I gripped it, the more I kept thinking, *What are you waiting for, dummy? You're just gonna get pounded again!*

So, I unsheathed the pistol from the backpack. With a stiff yet shaky arm, I pointed it directly at Bloody Billy. He chuckled when he saw it, like I was an inexperienced magician pulling a floppy, fake rose from a limp top hat.

"Now, what are you going to do with that 'cept make me mad?" he said. He took one stepper closer to us, sucking on his cigarette. He exhaled toxic smoke from his tar-stained nostrils.

I slid my finger across the trigger, debating if I really had the guts to pull it. The cold sweat pooling under my arms and dripping from my forehead told me otherwise. I was really nervous. I steadied my gangly arm the best I could. Bloody Billy's face blurred in my line of sight.

He took another step and another drag from his smoke. "Just give me the goddamn backpack and maybe I'll let you go. Maybe."

"Don't come any closer or I'll shoot!" I cried out. My arm shook.

Even though the pistol was small, it was getting heavier by the minute. That's what happens when you hold your arm straight out for more than ten seconds. My arm transformed into a block of wood, then a row of bricks, then into a hunk of iron. The pain was excruciating. I figured the longer I waited, the more of an advantage Bloody Billy would gain. He took another step closer, his body engulfed in cigarette smoke. Time slowed down. His body motion sludgy and deliberate, like he was walking through the waist-high water of an angry river. Every thought that flashed through my mind, every plea for a defensible motive, led me to this: shoot the bastard. I could claim self-defense. I had three reliable witnesses and Bloody Billy was a notorious bully.

"This is my last warning!" I screamed, but he didn't heed it.

He continued to call my bluff.

But I wasn't bluffing.

I closed my eyes. I braced myself. I grit my teeth.

I pulled the trigger.

Then, nothing happened.

For a brief moment, I opened my eyes and I could see on Billy's face a sign of regret, a slight tinge of *Oh shit!* But once he saw my surprise, he lunged at me.

"I'm gonna kill you, ass wipe!" he bellowed.

But Randy had other ideas. He lunged, too, blocking Billy like a football tackler, their heads and shoulders hitting with a dense thud. They grappled in front of Miguel, Brian, and I—their arms flailing, their feet shuffling for better footing, fists pounding flesh. It was a terrifying sight, the two of them fighting, drops of sweat and spittle flying everywhere, the stench of testosterone. Remarkably, Randy shifted his weight and slid an arm through Billy's legs, then lifted his body off the ground under his crotch with the crook of his arm. Billy was shocked to find out just how strong Randy was; I could see it on his smug face while dangling above us. Randy rotated his torso, then body-slammed Billy with all his strength. The lake house shook after the boom of Billy hitting the floor, but that didn't stop him. Billy continued to swing his arms and kick his legs while on his back, like an angry crab.

Outside, Rogelio unclenched his fist and let go of Tony, so he could come inside to assist his gang leader. Tony seized his opportunity to jump off the back porch and run for the woods, not offering to assist us or anything. He quickly vanished amongst the stately trees. I don't blame him. It was an unfortunate turn of events for all of us. Back in the lake house, Rogelio grabbed Randy by his neck and arm, trying to push him away from Bloody Billy, but Randy was a belligerent mass of resistance. He held down Billy with one arm and swung at Rogelio with the other. The three of us were petrified, which I'm sure irritated Randy.

"Run, you idiots!" he yelled at us, and we didn't wait for a second command.

We ran around the mound of bodies and out the back door. As I ran, I dropped the useless pistol on the ground while clutching the backpack under my arm. Miguel, Brian, and I jumped off the back porch and retreated toward the line of trees. But, for some reason still unknown to me, Brian stopped and held out his arms to keep Miguel and I from running in the woods.

"Something tells me it's a bad idea to run in the woods!" he said, panting.

"Then what do we do?!" I said, also panting.

The three of us quickly scanned the area, looking for an escape route. Miguel pointed toward the pier. "The boat!"

"Yeah!" Brian agreed, strangely. "The boat!"

"But what about Randy?" I said, looking back at the lake house. The sound of fighting could be heard through the cracks of the weathered, wood siding.

"We'll wait for him in the boat. When he comes out, we'll call for him."

"Good idea!" I said, then we ran to the pier, the backpack under my arm and me limping behind my two friends.

We got to the pier in a matter of seconds and I knelt to hold the gently rocking boat close while my two friends got in. There was no sign of Tony to ask how to start the boat, but I remembered watching him pull the starter cord a couple of times, so figured I could do it myself. Once my friends were in the boat, we all turned to the lake house and waited. The boat rocked side to side. The yelling coming from inside was indecipherable, but it sounded angry and terse. Then, there was silence. I looked at Brian and Miguel, who both shrugged. Brian gripped the side of the boat, remembering he couldn't swim, as the water craft bobbed. Then Miguel pointed to the lake house.

"There he is!"

Randy burst from the back door and was booking it to the pier, his arms swinging wildly, his feet kicking up grass and dirt.

"Start the boat!" he yelled as he ran toward us.

A few moments later, Bloody Billy and Rogelio ran out the back door, too, chasing after Randy, their faces maroon with anger. I pulled the starter cord on the motor as hard as I could, but nothing happened. The motor wheezed, then died.

"Pull harder!" Brian commanded. "Really yank it!"

"I did!" I replied, then pulled again as hard as I could.

Still nothing.

"Start it!" Randy yelled again, running as fast as he could with the two bullies on his heels.

I pulled on the starter cord again, but no luck.

"Dang it!"

"Let me try!" Miguel said, then pushed me aside.

He grabbed the starter cord handle and yanked it so hard, I thought he was going to rip it off the motor. He fell back on his butt and the engine roared to life, grey smoke and orange sparks erupting from the back.

"You help Randy in the boat! I'll drive!" Miguel said, sitting on the rear bench and gripping the motor tiller, ready to steer it.

"OK," I said, getting in front of the boat.

By this time, Randy reached the pier and was stomping across it.

"I'm gonna jump!" he said, then leapt on top of me, almost sending the two of us off the side of the boat, the vessel wobbling wildly.

But we didn't fall out. Miguel accelerated the motor boat and we pulled away from the pier. I looked back and could see Bloody Billy and Rogelio stomping across it, their faces so red they looked like they'd burst. About halfway down, Rogelio stopped in his tracks, but Bloody Billy kept running. As we pulled farther away, I expected Billy to stop running too, but he didn't. He ran to the edge of the pier, then without hesitating, jumped into the water.

"Billy jumped in!" I yelled, pointing back.

Randy and I watched as Bloody Billy appeared to be swimming with large breaststrokes—his head and arms bobbing high above the water, then back under and up again—and I thought it strange that he thought he could catch us by swimming in the lake. The boat was flying across the water at full speed by this point, the engine screeching loudly and our hair flapping in the wind. I felt a sigh of relief slip out my mouth, but the motor was so loud that I couldn't hear it. I turned to see where Miguel was steering the boat, Sometimes Island looming ahead in some light fog out in the middle of the bay not too far away. I remember thinking to myself that as long as Miguel could get us around and past Sometimes Island, then we'd be safe. I turned back to see if I could see Bloody Billy swimming in the water, but I didn't see him anymore. Maybe we were too far away to see him. Maybe he was resting in the water, deciding if he should keep swimming, or if he should swim back to the pier because his pursuit was futile. Either way, I didn't care. We escaped from the two bastards and we were on our way to freedom. Or so I thought.

Randy cheered, jutting both arms in the air.

"Fuck yooooou!" he screamed, then bellowed. "You assholes!"

The rest of us began to cheer, too. It was hard not to, this stupendous moment feeling something like a victory, watching our main tormentor ill-advisedly jump into the lake. We attempted to give each other high fives and the like, but as Miguel steered the motor boat toward Sometimes Island, I had an icky feeling in my gut. Call it intuition or fear or whatever, but whatever the feeling was, it snapped me out of my celebratory mood. All I could think about was what Tony told us before on our first boat tour: *That's Sometimes Island. Can't go on it, though. Your boat would get ripped apart from the jagged rocks that surround it under the water, if you tried to land near it.*

"Miguel!" I cried, but it was too late.

There was a loud bang, then the feeling of catching air that you get in the pit of your stomach like the moment before a roller coaster barrels down the first, tall incline, as my head lunged forward then down into my knees. It felt like I punched myself in the face. Then the next thing I knew, I was underwater. I immediately flapped my arms to swim and I felt the backpack under one of my arms, impeding my strokes. I pushed on it, soon feeling it beneath my feet as I kicked my legs, then it disappeared as I tried to swim back to the surface. That was the last time I saw or felt the presence of Bloody Billy's backpack. The power I felt from possessing it was released with every stroke of my arms, with every frantic kick of my legs, as I struggled to get to the air. It probably sank immediately to the bottom of Canyon Lake, where it belonged.

I burst to the water's surface, then swam toward Sometimes Island, eventually climbing on top of a large rock. I was able to sit on the slimy rock, the cold water at my waist, my legs submerged beneath lapping water. The motor boat was upside down and floating away from Sometimes Island, but I didn't see any of my friends. I tried to stand on the rock, but it was too slippery. I cried out for my friends.

"Randy! Miguel!" I yelled. "Brian!"

But all I heard was the motor, still running and upside down with the propeller up in the air, spinning wildly. The submerged motor abruptly stopped. The boat sank amongst rings of gurgling water, morphing into placid ripples, then a shimmer of refracted sunlight. The boat was gone. I scanned for any sign of my friends. I choked on some tears, worried that they were all dead, and I was all alone. But the next thing I knew, I heard coughing and gasping, and my three friends were clinging to another rock behind me and closer to the island. I was relieved that they were alive, safe, and sound close by.

But for how long?

PART III.
Boat Wreck on Sometimes Island

16.

When Randy, Miguel, Brian, and I were in the sixth grade, we used to ride our bikes outside of the neighborhood to find buildings with access to their roofs. It didn't matter what kind of buildings: schools, convenience stores, car dealerships, whatever. We had this thing for getting up high and surveying the area. Being on top of buildings made us feel powerful, free, and even a little naughty. The business owners hated it—some of them even called the cops—but we couldn't get enough of it.

One time, we noticed a strip mall with an unsecured ladder on the back of an auto insurance business. It was a building we hadn't been on top of before. We decided to ditch our bikes in an overgrown grassy field behind the strip mall and climb up. Randy, Brian, and Miguel went up first and I stayed on the ground, on the lookout for angry business owners or malicious security guards. Randy was the last one up and, once he was on the top, he leaned over and told me to come up the rear. As I scaled the squeaky, rusty ladder, Randy spotted a curious security guard walking around the side of the building. He probably saw us on a security monitor or something like that and decided to investigate, or at least smoke a cigarette. I scurried up, but my feet slipped. I fell one rung and my quick descent stopped cold when my crotch hit the rung. The pain launched fireworks into my eyes and I felt like I was going to pass out, but I was able to cling to the ladder and not fall to the ground and crack my head open. The security guard noticed my predicament and ran over. Randy watched the entire episode from the roof, and felt helpless. He cried out for me to come up the ladder to escape. He leaned over the roof edge, extending his hand. But I was only halfway up. I didn't see the security guard coming, but I knew he was there because of Randy's pleading. I wanted to climb, but I was petrified from pain and shock. I vividly remember looking up at Randy and seeing the fear in his eyes. He was extending his hand as far as he could to me, almost as if he was about to fall down the ladder, too. He kept pleading, over and over.

"Reach my hand! I'll help you up! Come on!"

I thought about this time when I clung to the strip mall roof access ladder while I swam from my rock to the rock my friends were on, just after the motor boat sank in the angry waters of Canyon Lake. The water was considerably choppier around the island and the wind howled ruthlessly. Randy reached down to help me up on their rock, which was just as slippery as the other one. I wouldn't have been able to climb on it without his help. With Miguel and Brian bracing him, he grabbed my hand and effortlessly pulled me out, and plopped me on the rock. I was always amazed at just how strong Randy was. I'm sure he pounded Bloody Billy and Rogelio pretty good before running out to the motor boat.

"Dude, you all right?" he said, panting.

"I think so," I replied, squeezing out the front of my drenched t-shirt.

"Why am I always helping you up places?"

"Beats me," I said, then shrugged.

"I pulled him out, too," Randy said, thumbing back to Brian who was right behind him, shivering with his backpack still strapped around his shoulders and standing next to Miguel, who was also shivering. "You know he can't swim."

"Yeah," I said, dejected.

"What happened to the backpack?" Brian said. His teeth clattered from the effect of the wind on his wet skin.

"Fell off and sank," I said. "How did you keep yours on?"

"Don't know," he said. "Just did."

The four of us stared at each other. We were dumbfounded. Thirty minutes before, we were getting ready to go back home. Our parents wouldn't have been the wiser about what we had done that weekend, I was certain of that. We would've seen other kids around the neighborhood enjoying their summer (riding their bikes, swimming at the pool) and we would've bragged about our weekend to whoever would listen, but no one would've believed us. It would've been our secret trip—a couple of blissful days at our Cabin of Seclusion—the place no one in middle school knew existed, nor would our parents have fathomed we had the gumption to go to. I mean, Brian's parents knew of the abandoned lake house, but I don't think they ever would've imagined us paying a high-schooler to come pick us up and take us to it. It was pretty unbelievable. It was even more unbelievable that we were standing on Sometimes Island and staring at each other like a bunch of idiots.

I turned around and peered at the lake house. It was farther away than I thought it would be from the vantage point of the island. It appeared to be a small, brown dot, and I couldn't see if Rogelio or Tony were still around. I then turned to see how far the marina was and it wasn't even a dot (I couldn't see it at all actually), although I could make out a few sails here and there of the boats anchored in the bay, but they appeared to be more like crumpled, white triangles bobbing on the water than boat sails.

I turned back. Fear loomed large. "What are we gonna do?"

"And what are we gonna eat?" Miguel said. "I'm already hungry."

"I bet you have to pee, too," Brian said, then rolled his eyes.

"Yeah, that too," Miguel said, his head bobbing in agreement.

Randy craned his neck over the rest of us, surveying the island. Something caught his attention. Then he looked down at the rock we were standing on and how far it was from the island.

"We should try to get to those rocks that look like a staircase, then climb up higher away from the water," he said, looking to all of us. "Can you guys do it?"

I looked down to see just exactly how far we were from the rock staircase and, it seemed to me, that the distance between the rock we were standing on and the bottom of the staircase on the island was about three or four feet. Not too far, but one of us couldn't swim. I pointed this out to Randy.

"Yeah, I'll help him. Can you two get across yourselves?"

Miguel and I looked at each other, then nodded.

"Great. You two go first. Then I'll go and help Brian."

Miguel and I didn't even hesitate. We climbed down the rock into the water, which turned out to be about as deep as up to our necks, but easy enough to cross without any problems. Once we got to the rock staircase, we began our ascent. Randy jumped in and out of the water in one swift motion. He turned to Brian and insisted he follow.

"Jump in, dude! I'll help you!"

Miguel and I watched from the top of the rock staircase. Brian shook his head.

"Come on! You won't drown. Just jump and I'll grab your hand."

With such a profound fear of water, it was a miracle that Brian was as close as he was to becoming an Eagle Scout. Seemed like being able to swim would be a requirement for a Boy Scout. Don't you think? Brian hesitated, shaking his head and wrapping his arms around his torso, as if holding himself in such a way would transport him somewhere else far away like to his living room in the safe confines of his house, watching reruns of *Gilligan's Island* or *The Beverly Hillbillies* like he'd done so many times before, without fear of drowning.

"All right then," Randy said, taking one step up the rock staircase. "See you later!"

This was enough motivation for Brian. I'm sure he didn't want to be left stranded on that slippery rock away from the rest of us. He leapt as far as he could. Randy knelt close to the water and extended his hand. Brian pulled himself up Randy's arm onto the island, his feet frantically kicking at the water, his fingers penetrating Randy's skin like cat's claws in a tree trunk. He was relieved to be out of the lake.

"Thanks, dude," he said to Randy, who patted him on his sopping shoulder.

"No problem."

They both climbed the rock staircase up to where we were standing, where we would later learn was the tallest point on the island. From this vantage point, we could see everything around us, just like standing on one of the roofs of the businesses we would scale after school. Except for a few birds flying above, there didn't seem to be any other living things close by. And we were completely surrounded by water with green and brown scribbles of land and trees way out toward the horizon.

Brian was standing closest to me, both of his arms wrapped around his torso as if he was hugging himself. He loosened his self-hug, then patted the outside of his upper arms, a gentle act of self-motivation.

"Let's survey this island," he said, and began trudging across a ridge that started where we were standing and seemed to stretch across the entire length of the island. He walked with both arms stretched out like he was traipsing across a high wire. We followed him in the same fashion.

We quickly discovered that there wasn't much on the island, mostly an abundance of rocks with sparse vegetation. There were scattered patches of wild grasses jutting up from cracks in the rocks, mostly covered in grass burrs—or as we called them: sticker burrs. There were a few rather tall cedar trees, and they swayed carelessly in the wind. The tallest of them all was a bur oak tree. (Brian pointed out this fact and explained that bur oaks had no relation to sticker burrs, in case you were wondering) The bur oak was the only tree on the island with some sort of canopy, casting an oblong shadow on part of the island; the cedar trees were like giant twigs with little for leaves. Once we got to the other end of the island, we looked out to the mainland, which seemed like miles away, the tops of the tree-covered hills mere squiggles of oaky green dashed across powder blue sky. A loud sigh escaped from my mouth as a profound realization materialized after gazing across that dark, cold water.

We were stranded.

"Well, guys," I said, raising my hand to my brow, then shading my eyes with it. "I think we're screwed."

"You got that right," Randy agreed. "Screwed City."

"Screwed Central," Brian added.

"Just *plain* screwed," Miguel said.

I couldn't have agreed with my friends more.

17.

We sat on the jagged ground within the oblong shade of the bur oak tree, gazing in the direction of the lake house. No boats sailed or motored by, and the only sound we could hear—besides occasional sighs from each other's mouths or the grumbling of our stomachs—was the rustling of the Hill Country wind in our ears. I was starting to get hungry, but telling my friends that fact seemed too obvious, and maybe a little cruel. I was certain they were getting hungry, too, and we didn't have anything to eat as far as I knew. But maybe the backpack sitting between Brian's legs would yield something for the group.

"Hey, Brian?" I said, then waved a curious hand to get his attention. He was staring off in the distance as if looking through the window of a pet store at a puppy he knew he could never have. "Wha cha got in the bag?"

"I don't know," he replied, then unzipped the backpack and rummaged through it. "Let me look."

He jabbed his hand around inside, then pulled out his pair of binoculars, still wet from his quick plunge in the lake, but nothing else.

"I got this," he said, then raised them to his face and adjusted the focus with the center knob as he looked through them. "We can keep an eye on shit."

"Oh yeah? What do you see?"

He pulled the lens covers off and held the binoculars steady to his face, examining something off in the distance that I imagined was the lake house. Sometimes he would squint, then adjust the knob that sat in the middle again for better focus.

"I don't see Rogelio," he said, then squinted some more. "I don't see Tony. I don't see Bloody Billy, either."

"I hope that bastard drowned," Randy said defiantly, tossing a pebble into the lake. "He deserved to drown."

"Yeah," Miguel agreed. "*Él es un pendejo grande.*"

"I don't know what that means, but I agree," I cracked. All my friends chuckled.

Brian turned his head and set his sights on what I imagined was the marina.

"Maybe someone will sail by soon," he said. "Maybe..."

"Yeah," we all said.

Maybe someone would sail by. Maybe a rescue crew would fly over. *Maybe.* And more maybes. The longer we sat on the rocky terrain with the tree's unsympathetic shadow slithering closer to the trunk of the tree, the more it seemed less likely that someone would just happen to notice us sitting on this sad excuse for an island. As far as we knew, we were the only ones in the entire world that knew we were sitting on Sometimes Island.

"I know!" Brian said, jumping up and smacking his forehead. "Remember what they did in that dumb book *Lord of the Flies*?!"

"I told you I didn't finish it. Too depressing," Randy muttered, then picked up a flat, glossy rock the size of a half dollar and threw it side-arm across the water, attempting to skip it, but it plunked in the water instead and sank.

"They used Piggy's glasses to light a fire, so a ship would see them. Let's try to start a fire," Brian suggested.

"None of us wear glasses, dufus," Miguel said, then scoffed. "Got any matches in that backpack of yours?"

"No, just the binoculars," Brian replied.

"Figures," Miguel said.

We sat in silence, staring off in various directions. I noticed Brian fidgeting with the knob on the binoculars, and it seemed to me at that moment—observing the lenses refract light at the end of the black and white shafts—that they were the closest thing we had to glasses.

"I know!" I blurted. "Let's use the binoculars to start a fire!"

"The binoculars?" Brian said, looking quizzically at them. "How would that work?"

"I don't know. They have lenses like glasses, though. Right?"

Brian examined the binoculars, turning them around to see the glass on both ends, and quickly deduced he couldn't argue with that rationale.

"Seems legit," he said, then stood back up. "Let's try it. You guys gather kindling and leaves and stuff, and I'll see if I can light it on fire."

Brian knelt back down and gathered rocks, forming a circle to create a makeshift pit to start a fire in. The three of us split up and explored, looking for dried twigs and grass and leaves that we could bring back as kindling. Sometimes Island was pretty barren, almost like the surface of the moon. We were able to gather a few things for kindling, but not much. When we all returned to where Brian crouched, we dropped what we foraged into the fire pit.

"That's it?" Brian complained. "You barely found anything."

"Yup," I confirmed, punctuated with a wilting whistle. "That's it."

"Well, I'll see what I can do."

Brian suspended the binoculars above the sad pile of twigs, then glanced up to see where the sun hung in the sky. He strategically turned the binoculars, then adjusted some more. Once he was able to train a pinhole-sized bit of refracted light onto our lame excuse for kindling, he steadied his hands.

"It may take a bit," he said confidently. "But I think I can do it."

"Great!" I said, patting Randy and Miguel on their backs. "We'll have smoke signals in no time!"

"Maybe," Randy grumbled. His apprehension was palpable.

We watched Brian for maybe five or six minutes, but it seemed like an eternity. The pinhole-sized bit of refracted light rested in place like a white freckle on a dry, brown leaf. But there was no fire, or even smoke. Brian remained undaunted.

"May take a bit," Brian repeated. "Just a bit."

Randy sighed. "I'm gonna sit in the shade."

He began to walk in the direction where we sat earlier, but the tree's shadow slid further away in the other direction.

"If we don't find shade, then we're gonna roast in the sun," Randy said.

He scratched his scalp and I could tell he was irritated, maybe because he was hungry, or with his frustration of being stuck on this island. I certainly was feeling frustrated and I was definitely hungry, but I didn't know what to do. The hunger pangs in my gut distracted my mind, leaving little room for rational thought.

"Maybe you guys should try to build a shelter while I try to start this fire," Brian suggested.

Seemed like a good way to occupy our time. The three of us looked at each other, dumbfounded. None of us had any idea of how to build a shelter, let alone what to look for to build one. In fact, if the building materials we found weren't Legos or Lincoln Logs, then the possibility of the three of us building a shelter was close to zero. Randy rolled his eyes at our predicament.

"Come on and follow me," he said, then sighed. "I'm sure we'll find something to build a shelter with."

We followed Randy along the top ridge of the island, first looking down the side where our boat crashed. I stopped and gazed at the water. The lake gently lapped at the bottom of the island and the rocks just underneath the surface. Time seemed to stop as a vivid daydream played in my eyes of the boat sinking, its rear end up in the air with the motor still spinning, as it slowly disappeared into the depths, eventually hitting bottom next to Bloody Billy's bloated corpse. I shook my head, ending the daydream.

"Nothing but rocks down there," I said, then caught up with them.

"Yeah," Miguel agreed. "Nuttin' from nuttin' leaves nuttin'."

As we approached the other end of the island, Randy stepped down a foot or two on the opposite side from where we crashed, then noticed something in the water, which was as still as glass.

"I think I see something!" he said, then slowly climbed down the jagged backside of Sometimes Island. Where the water kissed the rocky skirt of the island, Randy pulled a piece of wood too large to be a branch and too small to be a log, but seemed promising enough as a piece of building material for a shelter. It was a start, at least. "A piece of wood!"

I stepped down a foot or two with the thought that I could help Randy pull the piece of wood to the top of the island by handing an end to Miguel to help us the rest of the way. I watched Randy wrestle with it, grabbing the gnarled end, then lifting it out of the water. It was a pretty good-sized branch, maybe six or seven inches in diameter and five or six feet in length. It was a rather straight piece of wood, too, as luck would have it.

"I bet we can use this," he called out as he struggled to pull the branch up the steep backside of the island. But when he got about halfway between the water and where I stood, the water-logged piece of wood fell apart, the rebellious half dropping behind him, then tumbling back in the water. He examined the other piece still in his hands as it, too, fell apart.

"Oh man," he moaned.

But he didn't lament too long about it as Miguel yelled from up top, pointing in the opposite direction like a crazed sailor, happy to see land after months stranded out at sea. "Over there! Look!"

Randy looked down to where Miguel was pointing, then descended, carefully stepping or sliding over rocks, some the size of boulders.

"Be careful!" I pleaded.

"See it?!" Miguel called out.

"Yeah!" Randy replied.

When he reached the bottom, he pushed a rock aside, then pulled a rusty metal *For Sale* sign out of the water. He lifted it above his head for me and Miguel to see. It said on the front:

FOR SALE
BY OWNER
CALL 210-493-2707 FOR INFO

"I got it!" Randy yelled.

"Can you bring it up?" I said, worried.

"Yeah!"

We watched Randy climb back up, refusing any help.

"I think this'll work."

We followed Randy back to where Brian knelt on the ground, hunched over his makeshift fire pit, his arms stiffly extended with the binoculars in his hands. The kindling looked just as it did when we left him: not on fire. He looked up at us. "I hope you had better luck than I'm having. This stuff won't light!"

"We found something to use for shelter," Randy said, showing him the metal sign.

"Wicked!"

"I just don't know where—" Randy said, looking around. "Oh, I know."

A few feet away were two, wispy cedar trees, just far enough apart to act as beams for a makeshift roof. He wedged the metal sign horizontally between them, not much higher than where his head rested on his shoulders, creating a simple shed.

"Tah dah!" he cheered. "Shelter."

Miguel and I examined the structure and the amount of shade it provided. It didn't provide much, maybe a square of shade that was three by three feet, but it was better than no shade at all.

"We'll be awfully crowded under there," I said.

Miguel shook his head. Brian jumped up, frustrated.

"Damn it!" he cried out. "Damn! It!"

He hung the binoculars around his neck, then came over to examine the shed, too.

"Good thing I like you guys. We'll have to snuggle under there to get shade."

"Yep," I said, then snickered. "Snuggle time!"

Randy and Miguel groaned as Brian and I fought for the best spot in the shade. Not even being stranded on an island kept our competitive natures at bay.

"You're a couple of dingleberries," Randy said.

"Yep," Miguel agreed. "Stinkin' dingleberries."

18.

Later that day, the island and the wind sang us a duet called Boat Wreck Blues. The hunger pangs tweaked our dispositions even more, but Brian was the only one of us skilled enough to do something about it in our unfortunate situation. He promised us he would catch a fish, but only if the rest of us continued to try to ignite a fire in our makeshift fire pit using the binoculars. We quickly agreed to his proposal. But after ten minutes of roasting in the sun without any progress on a lit camp fire, the three of us decided to hunker under our *For Sale* sign shelter and watched Brian fish for dinner from our shady vantage point. He was using a long, grass stalk as a fishing rod with a piece of cotton thread he pulled from the bottom seam of his t-shirt tied to the end of the stalk as the fishing line. For bait, he tied a sticker burr to the thread's end, thinking it would act as a hook when a fish tried to bite it. The only problem was, the sticker burr simply floated on the water instead of sinking, and no fish seemed interested in his bait, or maybe there weren't any fish in our vicinity. Either way, Brian's lack of fishing success curdled his ego.

"Why aren't they biting?!" he said, stomping on the slimy rock he precariously stood on. Not having much experience around water (remember, he couldn't swim), his angry feet slid on the slippery platform of rock, and he fell on his back. The shallow bit of water splashed on top of him—on his face and chest—sending him into a panic. Maybe he thought he was about to sink in the lake, or maybe he thought he was done for. Either way, he booked it from the rock to the top of the island faster than what seemed humanly possible. The three of us almost died from laughing, which irked Brian.

He peeled the wet t-shirt from his back, wrung the lake water from it, and huffed.

"Screw you guys!"

We laughed some more until Brian finally smiled. He knew we weren't making fun of him. It was just too humorous not to laugh at.

"Ha ha. Very funny," he said, flinging his sopping wet t-shirt over his shoulder. There wasn't enough room in the shade for Brian. But since he was wet, he seemed happy to sit in the warm sun.

"You would think at least one boat would've come around by now," Brian said, then wrung out his t-shirt again.

"You would think," I agreed. "Not one dang boat."

"Not one!" Miguel said. It almost seemed like he was going to cry, but he simply sniffled and turned his head.

We all looked out across the lake in the direction we believed the marina floated by the shore. I couldn't see it at all and it seemed like the sailboats scattered across the bay bobbed lifelessly in the water. Or maybe those buoyant objects were dragonflies dancing on the surface of the lake. I couldn't tell anymore. When hunger eats you from the inside and the heat bakes you on the outside, reality can retreat into the parts in the mind where dreams and nightmares come from.

"One will come by eventually," Randy said. He cracked his knuckles with the certainty and confidence of a seasoned gambler. "I'm sure of it."

"Yeah," I agreed, although skeptical. It seemed like the population of lakers and campers and fisherman were extinct.

"I mean, Tony knows we're out here. Right?" Randy said, looking at me. He scanned my eyes for an affirmation.

"I don't know if he saw us crash out here. He ran into the woods when Rogelio jumped on you and Billy," I said, looking at the ground between my legs. There was a line of ants marching within a crack and my curiosity was piqued. "He probably has no idea we're out here. Hey, how do you think these ants got out here?"

Randy pulled a stalk of grass from the rocky ground and snapped it in half, then in half again. "How would I know. This sucks."

We sat under the *For Sale* sign in the summer heat for what seemed like an hour, watching birds fly above us and the occasional disturbance down at the water line that could've been a discombobulated fish or cranky turtle. I jabbed at the line of ants with a brittle twig, contemplating different, plausible scenarios that brought the ants from the mainland to the island. Our stomachs sang a baritone folk tune about destitution and regret when something caught our attention: a speed boat.

Brian jumped to his feet and jabbed at the air with his index finger. "A boat! A boat!"

We all jumped up and flapped our thin arms like excited birds attempting flight for the first time and squawking for the mother bird's attention. The speed boat skirted along the horizon—water spraying out from the inboard motor onto the turbulent wake that snaked from the back like billowing smoke—then made its way into the middle of the bay. As it headed in our direction, its motor roared louder and louder, and soon we could see that the speed boat was pulling a slalom skier who knifed back and forth across the boat's wake, occasionally catching air when hitting the wake's frothy outer seams.

"Hey! Over here!" we pleaded in unison.

The sight of the boat was very exciting, but the idea of being rescued was even more exciting. I knew we didn't want to be on that island much longer than we had to. We jumped and yelled and flapped our arms as much as we could.

"OVER HERE! HEY!"

As the boat approached the island, it became apparent that the skier was exceptional in skill. As he skimmed back and forth across the wake, he performed a variety of flips and acrobatic moves that mesmerized us. Our pleading turned to gandering. We watched what appeared to be a double backflip that the skier performed as effortlessly as me scratching my butt.

"Did you see that?" Randy said, a tinge of astonishment in his question.

"Yeah," the three of us replied enviously.

But soon, the boat skirted close enough that we could see the driver's grizzled face with dark sunglasses perched on his sunblocked nose, his sunbleached hair flapping at the back of his head, and his shoulders also slathered with white sunblock. The driver swiveled at his waist, looking out in front of the boat then looking back at the skier, and back again, repeating at short intervals. There wasn't anyone else on the boat to watch the skier. And the driver definitely didn't see us, that was for sure. We restarted our pleading in earnest as the boat approached closer.

"OVER HERE! HEY!" we called out together.

We flapped our arms as wildly as possible. The motor boat roared as it skimmed across the lake, drowning out our cries for help. The driver didn't look in our direction and neither did the skier, who was too occupied with his skiing performance to look at the typically abandoned island. We cried out louder and louder, but eventually the boat turned at the orange buoys to avoid the jagged rocks that surrounded Sometimes Island just under the surface of the water, and made its way out into the safer, open water of the lake. The skier followed, flipping and jumping to his heart's content. The boat and the skier soon vanished around the back of the peninsula, the one with the Cabin of Seclusion: our previous residence.

"They didn't see us," Miguel said, then sighed.

He walked back over to the *For Sale* sign shelter and plunked down in the shade. Brian and Randy joined him soon after. I was the only one left flapping my arms and jumping for attention. I heard the sound of my voice and realized my friends were not with me. I turned back to see them—dejected and tired—but I tried to remain hopeful.

"They'll come back this way," I said, joining them under the sign. "I'm sure of it."

No one said anything.

We sat in the shade without saying a word to each other for what seemed like a few hours. The speed boat never came back our way. The blazing sun slowly descended behind some poofy clouds—edging its way closer to the hilltops in the distance—and with its descent came the armada of hungry mosquitoes. They swooped in with the humid evening breeze and attacked us relentlessly, our unprotected skin a feast for the bloodsuckers. Miguel noticed them first and swatted his arms and legs with his hands, occasionally leaving a bloody stain on his skin where an insect used to be.

"Blech!" he protested. "So gross!"

The rest of us swatted our unprotected appendages. But we couldn't keep up with the insect barrage. There seemed to be millions of the bloodsuckers and nowhere on the island for us to hide from their mindless attack. So, as the evening turned to night, we surrendered.

"You know," Brian started, then swatted a mosquito on his forearm. A bloody splat appeared on his skin. "If you rub mud on the mosquito bites, it helps them stop itching."

Randy examined Brian. "Where do we get mud? There's nothing but rock on this island."

"We can make our own," Brian said. With his fingers, he swept a tiny pile of dust in the middle of his crossed legs, then hocked a loogie in his palm. He held his palm above the small dust pile, and with his index finger he pushed the loogie onto the pile. He mixed his own mud and dabbed a small amount on one of his mosquito bites. "Like that."

"We'll be spitting all night to make enough mud to cover these damn mosquito bites!" Randy complained.

We all laughed, then got to work spitting and dabbing. And I hate to admit it, but Brian was right. The mud did help with the itching, even though we all smelled like spit and dust and bad breath. Once the sun dipped behind the distant hills, the soft glow of twilight entertained us, which eventually turned to a black curtain speckled with stars, and the mosquitos retreated across the water with full bellies. The lights from the marina and the campgrounds illuminated the edge of the lake, some dancing like fireflies. And the bright moon bathed us in a corn yellow glow. The Milky Way spread across the chasm of sky, our galaxy's brilliance aglow with speckles of light and gamma rays from stars far, far away. We managed to all lay down under the *For Sale* sign shelter like four sardines wedged between the two cedar trees. Normally, the touch of each other's skin would be repellent. But that night, it was comforting. No one complained.

I remember being mesmerized by the sight of the Milky Way. It wasn't something we saw at night in our home town, being that the sky there was filtered through the glow of city lights. But on Sometimes Island, the Milky Way was as clear and brilliant as the Christmas tree my parents setup in our living room every winter.

"It looks amazing," I said.

"It sure does," Brian agreed. "Seeing it is one of the coolest parts about camping."

As we took in the brilliance of the night sky, a familiar sound interrupted us. It was a sound I had heard before, recently in fact. It sounded like this: *Hoo huh hoo. Hoo huh hoo.* I sat up, looking for where the bird call was coming.

"Did you hear that?" I said, looking around us, then up.

It called again: *Hoo huh hoo. Hoo huh hoo.*

About twelve or fifteen feet above us sat an owl in the bur oak tree. It's yellow eyes glowed—reflecting the pale moonlight—as it looked back down at me. Occasionally, it would blink. The contours of its body blended in with the crooked lines of the tree branches, an effective nocturnal camouflage. I was surprised that, not only could I see it, but that it sat there staring back at us.

I pointed in its direction. "Guys! There!"

My three friends sat up to see the owl, which startled it. It spread its wings wide, then leapt into the air, flapping its wings with long, swooping beats. As it ascended in the sky, something fell in front of us, dropped from a clinched claw. The object hit the rocky ground with a thud.

"It dropped something," I said, then got on all fours and slowly made my way to it. But once I realized what it was, I gagged. "Yuck!"

"What is it?" Randy said. He crawled over to where I was to get a look. He gagged, too, when he saw it. "Ugh! A dead mouse!"

The poor creature was disemboweled, its entrails flopped out of its slit-opened belly onto the dusty ground.

"Ewww!" we all cried out. Randy and I crawled back under the shelter with Brian and Miguel, holding our folded legs up to our chests as if shielding ourselves from the natural violence that ended that poor rodent's life.

"Maybe—" I started, gagging again. "Maybe, it thought we were hungry and dropped us a snack."

"That's gross!"

We didn't see or hear the owl again that night, but its presence left a pallor of dread. Would it harm us? Or worse, drop more dead animals on us? We didn't know, but eventually decided unanimously that we would try to get some sleep instead of worrying about it.

"We should look for something *else* to eat in the morning," Brian suggested.

And with that, everyone laid back down to sleep, supine as we were on the rocky ground under the *For Sale* sign shelter. Quickly, everyone drifted into sleep, except for me. I laid awake for another hour or so, listening to my friends snore a new duet with the Hill Country breeze. I thought I saw the owl flying across the sky, or maybe I was only dreaming.

19.

When I woke up the next morning, the first thing I saw was Randy peeing into the lake. I rubbed my eyes thinking I was dreaming because it was a strange sight to see. When I sat up, I also saw Brian peeing into the lake, his shorts crumpled down around his bony ankles and his tan butt bare in the breeze for all to see. And a few feet from him, Miguel was squatting on a rock taking a dump. The turd shot out from his behind, then quickly flopped in the water like a runaway train you'd see in an old-timey movie dropping off the end of a broken suspension bridge, then tumbling down to certain destruction into a ravine. The sight of my friends relieving themselves made me laugh out loud, but also made me realize that I had to pee, too. I couldn't remember the last time I peed, but it didn't matter. I joined my friends for an emergency piss into the lake.

I yanked my shorts down. "Ahhhhh!" The relief to my bladder was exquisite.

"You got that right," Randy said, putting his shriveled carrot back into his shorts. He slapped me on the back, altering my urine stream to splatter my shoes. "Don't miss!"

"Dang it!" I said, adjusting my stream back to the intended target. I peed as fast as I could to avoid another disturbance from my friends.

Randy, Brian, and I sat back under the *For Sale* sign shelter while Miguel remained on his rock, still squatting. He looked perplexed.

"Guys?!" he cried out. "You got any T. P.?"

The three of us laughed.

"Nope!" Brian said, then laughed again uncontrollably.

Miguel grimaced.

"Well, what do I do about... you know?"

"Wash your butt in the lake?" Brian suggested.

"I'm not doing *that!*" Miguel whined, then sighed. "Can you bring me something to wipe with?"

"Like what?" I said. I had no idea where we'd find any toilet paper or something even approximating toilet paper.

"Here," Brian said, then he grabbed a bur oak tree branch on the ground near us, about the diameter of a pencil and a foot long with five dried leaves at the end in the configuration of a star. He plucked the leaves off the branch, then folded them carefully and neatly into a square as if creating origami. "Give him this."

I took the small square from Brian and rubbed it between my fingers. It was dry, brittle, and course, not worthy of rubbing against your butt, emergency situation or otherwise.

"OK."

I stood up and wiped dust from the seat of my shorts with my free hand, then stepped down to where Miguel was squatting on the rock.

"Here," I said, handing him the dry, brittle square. "Brian said use this."

Miguel examined the rough "toilet paper" and grimaced again. I joined my friends back in the shade. We watched Miguel swing his hand around to his backside—the brown square clinched in his fingertips—but the minute he dabbed the square against his butt, it disintegrated into bits and left his fingers unprotected from the residue of his defecation.

Miguel cried out in horror. "I got poop on my hand!"

He screamed, then without warning, jumped into the water. Once his head bobbed above the surface, he used his left arm to keep him above water and his right hand rubbed his backside underwater to clean himself. He was quite dismayed about it. The three of us on land cackled at his dilemma. For a brief moment, it seemed we forgot that we were stranded on the rocky island and were having fun like we were on vacation or something.

Miguel swam a few feet away from where he cleaned himself, as if to avoid any of the dirty water around his butt from washing back over him. Once he was far enough away, he flipped on his backside and casually swam, exhibiting a leisurely backstroke for a dozen strokes or so. He then turned over and approached the island with a sturdy breast stroke, his mouth clinched shut to avoid letting in the foul water that he left behind. But something caught his eye and his swimming strokes became more determined.

"Hey guys! I found something!"

This got our attention. We stopped laughing.

"What is it?" I called back.

"You won't believe it!" he said, climbing out of the water.

He trudged back up to where we were—drenched to the bone and his sopping curly hair clinging to his head—with a very familiar object in his hand: a soda can.

"Look!" he said, excited. "A can of Pepsi Light!"

"Whoa!" we all said.

"And it's not opened!"

The coloring on the can as well as the Pepsi logo were sunbleached and it appeared to be at least a few years old. One end bulged as if it might have been shaken and ready to burst at some point, but didn't, the carbonated explosion in suspended animation. The other end had traces of green algae clinging to it. Pepsi Light wasn't our soda of choice—although all our mothers drank plenty of it along with Tab and Diet

Rite—but who were we to complain? It was like a gift from Mother Nature, an offering of something she knew her creatures of the woods wouldn't want, but her creatures from the city certainly would.

"You think it's still good?" Randy said, curious. He licked his lips.

"There's only one way to find out," Brian said, then snatched the can out of Miguel's hand.

"Hey!"

Brian yanked the aluminum tab off the top of the can, tossed it over his shoulder, and took a swig.

"It's flat but yummy!" he said, pleased. He licked his lips, then wiped his mouth with his forearm.

"Let me try," I said.

I took a swig, then passed the can to Randy who did the same, then finally to Miguel. And like that, the Pepsi Light can was empty. Miguel turned the can upside down above his mouth to show us how much remained inside. One amber drop fell out.

"That was fast!" Miguel said, then crumpled the can and tossed it on the ground.

"Maybe there's more," Randy said, peeling his t-shirt off and tossing it in the shade of the *For Sale* sign. He trudged down the incline and jumped in the water. Miguel quickly followed him.

"Wait for me!"

I wanted to follow them, but once I saw the look of fear on Brian's face, I decided to stay behind with him. I pointed to a jutting rock to our left and suggested we watch Randy and Miguel from that vantage point. Brian smiled and nodded. He followed me to the rock and we sat on the end—our feet dangling—and we watched Randy and Miguel splash around, looking for more cans of soda or anything else worth consuming. A cool breeze came in and tickled our backs.

"How long do you think we'll be stuck here?" I said to him.

He shrugged. "I have no idea. Seems no one knows we're here."

He plucked a bit of scraggy grass from a crack in the rock, then dropped it in the lake. The blades floated like miniature rafts.

"I know. I was hoping Tony would come looking for us, but he probably doesn't know we're here either."

"He probably thinks we ran home or called our parents or something."

"Yeah," I said.

We sat in silence for a couple of minutes while we watched Randy and Miguel down in the water—splashing each other instead of looking for more sodas—until I had a realization.

"Do you think we should create some rules while we're here?"

"Rules?" Brian said. His face scrunched as if I suggested something preposterous. "You mean like laws or something?"

"Yeah. It's probably what adults would expect from us. Right?"

Brian was collecting an assortment of pebbles in one hand and, once the pile had gained some substance, tossed them one by one into the lake with the other hand.

"We don't need any rules since there aren't any adults here. What would rules do for us anyway?"

I didn't have an answer. I guess I hadn't pondered before that day the reasons why rules existed. I just followed whoever seemed to be in charge. I was just that type of kid: a stickler for the rules.

"Maybe they would help keep us busy?"

"Keep us busy?"

"Yeah."

"The reason adults have rules is to keep kids in line and to keep other adults occupied while they do whatever they want behind their backs."

"No, they don't," I answered, but then immediately regretted my answer.

"Yes, they do. Adults hate rules. They tell kids to follow them, but secretly they hate them, too. It's true."

He tossed a few pebbles onesie-twosie into the lake, then hurled the rest of the pile all at once. The shrapnel dotted the surface of the water.

"We should just be kids and not have any rules. It'll be better that way."

"OK," I agreed, but I was also confused. "But isn't being in the Boy Scouts about following rules?"

Brian nodded. "I don't know if I want to be in the Boy Scouts anymore."

This was a startling revelation, to say the least. I mean, Brian admitting that he didn't want to be a Boy Scout anymore? He was as close as can be to becoming an Eagle Scout, the tippy top of the scouting hierarchy of ranks. I wasn't sure at the time what caused his change of heart, and I wasn't ready to find out either.

At this point, Randy and Miguel were thrashing water at each other and laughing, their offensive hacks becoming more forceful with every swipe. As we watched them, I noticed some movement on the lake toward the horizon. I jabbed Brian in the ribs with my elbow. "Look!"

Out in the bay in the direction of the marina, a couple of small, white triangles skirted along the horizon, then turned toward Sometimes Island and grew larger as they approached. The triangles raised slightly and billowed, revealing their sailboats underneath.

"Look!" I cried out, then jumped to my feet, flapping my arms above my head. "Hey!"

Brian jumped up and we both cried out as loud as we could, both of us waving our arms to catch the attention of whoever was on those sailboats. Randy and Miguel turned to look in the direction we were shouting and saw the sailboats.

They quickly swam back to the island and climbed up to where we were. The four of us called out desperately.

"HELP! HELP!"

Just like the speed boat the day before, the sailboats turned to our left once they got close to the orange buoys, the signs for danger lurking below the water. But the two sailboats moved much slower than the speed boat, and without the noise of the engine drowning out our pleas, so it seemed the potential for them to hear us was much higher this time. We jumped and screamed and flapped our arms.

"HELP US! OVER HERE!"

The two sailboats—each maybe the length of a school bus—slowly made their way past the island. The first boat had two people on board: one man at the back holding the tiller to steer and a woman near him cranking the ropes of the sails. The second boat also had a man and woman steering and controlling the boat, but had an additional passenger—a little boy sitting on the bow at the front. The little boy saw us calling out to them from the island, and he stood up, holding a suspension rope with one hand, and waving to us with his other hand. He called back to who I assumed were his parents, pointing at us and demanding they look, but they didn't. They were too busy navigating.

"HELP US! HELP!"

As both sailboats passed the island and made their way out to the open waters of the lake, we jumped and screamed as much as we could. The little boy on the sailboat eventually stopped waving and sat back down on the bow. And just as he did that, the foot on my gimp leg landed on a rock and twisted my ankle. I toppled to the ground, almost knocking my friends off the jutting rock.

"Ah shit!" I cried, as my body crumpled into a useless pile.

Randy quickly scooped me up in his arms and carried me over to the shade of the *For Sale* sign shelter. He gently laid me on the ground.

"You all right, dude?" he said, worried.

"Yeah, but I hurt my leg."

The pain was excruciating—muscle memory conjuring the moment the bullet from the 25-caliber American Derringer pistol tore through my leg in elementary school—and I gripped my hip to try to relieve it.

"Sit still," he said.

"But what about the sailboats?"

He looked up, sighed, then looked back at me.

"They're gone."

Brian and Miguel sat with me, too.

"I'm sure another boat will come," Miguel said. "I hope."

He and Brian looked in the direction of the marina, then shook their heads.

20.

Later, Brian and Miguel continued to sit with me in the shade as I nursed my sore hip while Randy searched down by the waterline for something else for us to eat or drink. After Miguel found the can of Pepsi Light, Randy was certain there was more for us to consume down in the cold, murky water. He just had to look hard enough to find it.

"If Miguel found a diet soda, then I can find something too," he demanded, stomping down to the water. The rest of us were skeptical, but we also didn't want to tell him to not look.

The sun slowly set for our second evening on Sometimes Island, inviting the armada of mosquitos back for another feast of our blood. This time, we had grown more accustomed to them and didn't swat at them as much as the night before. There wasn't anything we could do about them anyway. We could dab the bites with spit-mud all night long, but the more we dabbed, the more the mosquitos were determined to keep stabbing our skin in fresh spots. It was useless to even fend them off. Brian was more worried about my hip than the bloodsuckers anyway. He was an attentive medical aide.

"Let's try to lift your leg."

"OK," I said. I attempted to lift my gimp leg, but the pain in my hip was excruciating. A yelp escaped my lips. "It hurts too bad."

"Then don't move it," Miguel insisted, placing a hand on my shoulder.

A lethal amount of toxic guilt consumed me. Our fathers and step-fathers—the ones we all missed the most at that moment because they would've known exactly what to do to survive or even get off that island—taught us that crying or showing any emotions was a sign of weakness, so I tried my best not to cry. But I couldn't help it. The pain in my hip was too much to bear. At first, one of my weary eyes eked out a single tear. Then, without warning, both my eyes sprung a leak. I sobbed uncontrollably. The abject display of emotion startled my two friends. I knew they, too, suffered under the oppressive regimes of their fathers' toxic masculinity. But soon enough, their gentle pats turned into comforting embraces—the only thing that calmed me down.

I held both my friends in my arms. "Thank you."

Randy must have heard my crying from down by the water.

"Is everything all right?" he called out.

"Yeah, no problem," Brian replied.

"OK. Just checking."

Randy continued to search. Once the sun hid behind the distant hills, twilight swirled across the sky in strokes of pink, orange, and yellow, like an unseen giant from the ancient past had painted his impression in wide swathes in the sky. It was a mesmerizing atmospheric display. Miguel was in a contemplative mood.

"How long do you think we'll be out here?" he said.

"You got me," Brian replied. "I'm not a bettin' man so..."

"You're not even a *man*," Miguel said, then pshawed. A shower of spittle rained on me from Miguel's tempestuous lips.

"Ewww! You spit on me!"

The three of us laughed, which was encouraging. Even in the worst of times, humor was a salve for what ailed us. It seemed no matter what, if we were all together, then we could get through whatever was troubling us. Encouraged by our laughter, Miguel continued.

"What if this island had secrets like on *Gilligan's Island*?"

"What do you mean?" Brian said.

He and I trained our eyes on Miguel, who continued enthusiastically.

"You know how they're always finding stuff on *Gilligan's Island*? Or they seem to make themselves at home by making whatever they want out of stuff on the island?"

"Yeah," Brian and I both said.

"Sometimes, they seem so comfortable that they don't even act like they want to leave the island at all."

"So, you're saying there might be something like a hidden room underground filled with stuff for us, like food?"

"Maybe," Miguel said, smirking. "Would be nice, wouldn't it?"

"Yeah," I said.

"Who do you think is hotter: Ginger or Mary Ann?" Brian quizzed us. He rubbed his chin while pondering his own answer.

"Ginger!" I squealed. Both my friends giggled.

"What about you, Miguel?"

He scratched his scalp, then inspected his fingernails. He always seemed to have a habit of doing that: inspecting his nails after a scalp scratch. He never seemed to find what he was looking for whether it was lice or dandruff or whatever scalp condition worried him.

"I like Mary Ann. She seems more like girlfriend material. Ginger is kinda slutty."

Brian laughed. "I like slutty." A smirk slid across his face.

"Perv," I said.

"Yup."

"How about this?" I continued. "Who's hotter: Mary Ann from *Gilligan's Island* or Mary Jane from *Spider-Man*?"

"Wait a minute?" Miguel said. "One's on a TV show and the other is in comic books. You can't compare them in real life?"

"*Real life?!*" I cackled. "Neither one of them are real life."

Miguel began to argue his point when a gust of wind screeched from behind us, shoving our backs adamantly, reminding us that we were in the midst of Nature and not merely on summer vacation. The wind probed our ears and billowed our shirts, and even pushed our hair into our eyes—except for Brian's Afro, which did its best to maintain its suave symmetry. It was as if Nature was doing its damnedest to get our attention, even though Nature wasn't aware just how stubborn a group of teenaged boys could be with their attentiveness. There was a reason the fathers from our generation claimed we were obstinate or hardheaded, declaring the best way to grab our attention was a heavy hand or a commanding bark. Nature hadn't been as brusque up to that point, preferring a subtler, more passive aggressive approach. But that was about to change. All of a sudden, we heard Randy screaming.

"Owwwww!" he cried out, down by the water.

Without even thinking, Brian jumped up and trounced down to help him. Miguel stayed with me. Soon enough, the two of them appeared under the *For Sale* shelter with us, Randy's arm bent around Brian's shoulders for support, both drenched with lake water from the waist down. Randy clutched his left wrist, his limp hand swollen and red with two maroon dots oozing blood. A look of grotesque fear hung on his face like one of those ancient wooden, tribal masks you'd see mounted on a city museum wall.

"A snake bit him," Brian said. "Probably a water moccasin."

"What do I do?!" Randy said, worried. He panted and looked around like he wasn't sure if he was in a dream or not.

"Hold on. I know," Brian said, then peeled his t-shirt off his back. He twisted the t-shirt around Randy's wrist, then pulled Randy's hand towards him. "I'm gonna have to suck it out."

"Suck what out?!" Randy protested, retracting his swollen hand. The look on his face turned from fear to disgust.

"The poison," Brian said, then sighed. "Do you trust me or what?"

Randy also sighed then acquiesced. He gave his hand back to Brian, who gently examined it. He turned it over looking at the palm, then back.

"I'm going to ask you to look away," Brian commanded. Randy reluctantly did, and Brian got to work. He sucked on the two bloody spots on Randy's hand then spit—his face twisting into a look of disapproval so pronounced that it was almost comical—then sucked and spit some more. After a few more fervent rounds of this, he released Randy's hand. "I hope that helps."

Brian stood up, then trudged back down to the water. We could hear him slurping handfuls of dirty lake water, then spitting it out. The twilight dissipated, and the curtain of night hung high in the sky. Randy and I laid next to each other on the cold ground, me clutching my hip and Randy clutching his hand to his chest.

"I hope we make it off this island *alive*," Miguel said.

"Yeah," I said.

"This isn't like *Gilligan's Island* at all."

I was thinking the exact same thing.

21.

The funny thing about hunger: you don't know what true hunger is until you experience it. Those rumblings in your gut around your typical breakfast, lunch, and dinner times aren't true hunger. That's your brain tricking you, making you think you're hungry, when you're really not. If you simply ignored the gastric rumbles, then they would stop after ten or fifteen minutes, but no one ignores them. After two or three days without food, true hunger sets in and *those* hunger pangs are excruciating, the true definition of gut-wrenching. And that's what started happening to us after two full days on Sometimes Island. Our bodies sent warnings to our brains that they would eat themselves from the inside if some food wasn't dropped down into our stomachs pronto, and our brains panicked. We wrapped our arms around our midsections to quell the rumblings, but that didn't do anything to ease our hunger. Earlier that day, we did drink some lake water—the four of us kneeling and lifting cupped hands filled with silty liquid to our parched lips—but the hint of spilt gasoline from motor boats and urine squirted from drunk boaters was a rancid reminder that we were not drinking clean water. It was difficult to swallow more than a gulp or two.

Once the night sky hung above us—the stars twinkling within the inverted crevice of the Milky Way—Brian suggested we hunt for constellations as a way to keep our minds preoccupied. It was a fun idea until we realized none of us knew enough about where to actually find the constellations. Brian thought he could locate some, but it didn't seem like he knew what he was looking for. Still, it soothed us looking up into space at the twinkling dots, so much so that Brian and Miguel quickly fell asleep. Both snored like fog horns.

Randy and I couldn't sleep, probably from the additional pain we each experienced: my hip and his snake bite. And Randy was sweating profusely, probably from the poison circulating through his body. I could feel the humid heat coming off his pasty skin as we laid next to each other, looking up into the obsidian black night sky. Randy cleared his throat as quietly as possible and wiped his brow with his forearm.

"Do you think we'll die out here?"

The dreadful thought had crossed my mind, but I didn't want to say it out loud, as if verbalizing my fear before now would make it come true.

"Nah. Someone will come for us."

"Oh yeah? *When?*"

I didn't know, so I shrugged. "Soon, I hope."

Randy wheezed through pursed lips, then something caught his attention.

"Look!" he said, thrusting up his chin, signaling for me to look up.

The *For Sale* sign obscured some of our view of the treetop, but I could see a large bird clinging to a branch up there, with the black ceiling of space hanging above it and white speckles of stars and satellites casting distant light, soon followed by a familiar sound: *Hoo huh hoo, hoo huh hoo.*

"Maybe it'll drop us another dead mouse for a snack?" I said. "I'm so hungry I could eat a dead mouse."

"No way, man!" Randy said. "I wouldn't. I'm no animal."

He shook his head defiantly and lightly clucked his tongue.

"You'd rather *starve* to death?" I said.

"Probably."

"That's silly!"

Randy nudged my ribs with his elbow, then shushed me.

"You'll wake up those two honking dipshits," he said.

"Sorry," I said, struggling to keep the giggles inside.

"And don't be sorry, but do have some dignity. You know?"

"OK," I said. "I'll just starve to death with you, then. Very dignified like."

He nudged my ribs again. I guess he wasn't a fan of my sarcasm.

"I never, ever thought about dying before, until I was down in the water looking for something to eat," he said, then stammered. "I guess I always took my mom and our full fridge for granted."

"Yeah," I said. I was feeling guilty about the same thing. "We're just dumb kids."

"Real dumb."

"I sure would love to be going through my folks' fridge right now."

"Me, too! What would you get?" he said, excited. He propped himself up on one elbow, but the shift in his body weight brought him discomfort. "Ow!"

"You OK?" I said, propping myself up, too.

"Yeah, my hand hurts. That's all."

"Oh."

"So," he began, then took a deep breath. "What would you get?"

I looked up and inventoried the refrigerator and freezer in my mind, or at least how I last remembered it to be. It was hard to decide.

"A vanilla Drumstick!" I said. For those of you who don't know, that's not a chicken leg or a stick to smack a drum with; it's a chocolate-coated, vanilla ice cream cone with chopped peanuts in the chocolate coating. It's delicious. Trust me.

"Ooooo!" he said. "I'd destroy one of those right now."

"What about you?"

"Shoot, I don't know." He fell silent and, I assumed, inventoried his mom's refrigerator in his mind. "My mom baked some chocolate chip cookies last weekend and stashed some in the back of the fridge. She thinks I don't know they're there, but I do. I'd gank some of those cookies and eat them slowly."

"With a glass of milk?"

"Duh!"

We both laughed out loud, which almost woke up Brian and Miguel. They twitched and moaned, but didn't wake up. They were deeply entranced by their slumber. Randy and I covered our mouths with our hands to keep from laughing louder. Right then, we heard the owl leap from its brittle branch and flap its broad wings a few times—batting humid air and buzzing insects down with great force—then watched it glide through the air, illuminated by the moonlight across the great expanse of water that separated Sometimes Island from where the marina and campgrounds were on the other side, until we couldn't see it anymore. I envied the ease in which it could escape from the island whenever it felt like it, something we didn't have the fortune of being able to do.

A pshaw flopped from Randy's parched lips. "I guess no dead mouse this time."

"Guess not. Stingy old owl."

"So rude!"

"Selfish!"

My stomach interjected, groaning loudly, clinching my insides. I laid my arm across my stomach to soothe it.

"All this talk about food isn't helping, is it?" Randy said. He picked a booger, then unceremoniously flicked it. He probed his other nostril, but found nothing.

"Not really," I said.

"Maybe tomorrow, we can ask Brian and Miguel to go down to the water to look for some food or something."

"OK."

"I'm sure another boat will come by tomorrow."

"I hope so," I said, then sighed. I laid back down on the ground and looked up at the stars. If I kept still long enough, I could see a shooting star or an airplane with its flashing red light. I couldn't locate any constellations, but I was OK with that. A chill was in the air and we both shivered.

Randy laid back down, too, with a groan.

"This sucks," he said.

"Does your hand still hurt?"

"Yeah, a lot. But I'm not sweating as much right now."

"That's nice."

"Maybe we should try to get some sleep."

"OK."

Randy closed his eyes and soon snored softly. He must have been more tired than he thought. Me, I wasn't tired at all. And I couldn't lay still long because the rough ground with its pebbles, sticker burrs, and dried twigs stabbed my ribs and spine through my t-shirt. Every few minutes, I would have to fidget and find a new position for my body to lay, before repeating the process again in hopes for at least a little comfort. It was useless, though. And nothing made it more apparent that I wasn't home than lying on the hard, rough ground without a roof over my head or a blanket to keep me warm.

This was the first time in my conscious memory that I ruminated about my life and the real danger I found myself in. Before the boat wreck on Sometimes Island, I don't think I contemplated my existence and the possibility that my life could end. It was a sobering experience for a middle-schooler. I thought about my parents and wondered how much my mom missed me. Surely at that point, she knew me and my friends were missing. *How much pain am I causing her?* I thought. *Would she be mad at me for running away?* I even missed my step-dad, Steve, and would've preferred his solemn presence to the predicament I was in on that unforgiving island with the wind laughing at us and the owl dropping dead mice. I thought about my friends' parents and wondered how they felt, too.

Then mental images of all the things I would miss if I perished on that island marched through my mind—a strange parade of unfortunate missed opportunities—like my first kiss, which hadn't happened yet since I hadn't met a girl I wanted to kiss by that point. Or getting my driver license and first car at sixteen years of age, which I later learned would be a 1978 Honda Civic with a 60 hp engine, the perfect car for me. Or going to the senior prom with Carly Simpson, who would then go down in history as the first girl I kissed and the first one to break my heart in two. She crushed me after the prom. But if I were to die on Sometimes Island, then none of these things would come to be. I would rot on the island, my bones collecting dust and housing spiders, along with the skeletons of Randy, Brian, and Miguel. My eyes watered. My heart ached.

Knowing that coming out to the lake was my idea, I felt an oppressive amount of guilt, even if the Thousand Oaks Gang had something to do with it. I even felt bad for Bloody Billy, if you can believe that. I was sure his mom missed him, too. But on second thought, decided that even his own mother probably didn't like him. He was just too much of a degenerate to be loved. My immature mind put the blame for our predicament squarely on Billy, the one who put us on the path to escape to the Cabin of Seclusion and our eventual wreck on Sometimes Island.

"It's all that jerk's fault," I whispered to myself. "Yup, his fault."

I imagined Bloody Billy at the bottom of the lake, his face and neck bloated, bottom feeders sucking on his blanched arms, his shirt billowing in the water while moonbeams danced around him, and his backpack lying in the silty lake bed not too far from him just out of reach, a school of minnows pecking at it. I had no idea how deep the lake was at the point where he vanished or if moonbeams could reach the bottom of the lake or even if there were bottom feeders down there, but just the idea of this soothed me. I joyfully thought about Billy's watery grave while looking up at the stars.

"That son of a biscuit," I whispered to myself, then immediately thought of my mother making breakfast back at home, popping open a can of Pillsbury Biscuits and laying the circles of dimpled dough on a baking sheet. "Mmm, *biscuits*."

I soon fell asleep—a deep, deep black hole of sleep, without dreams of scrumptious breakfasts or sunken bullies.

22.

I woke up to witness Miguel peeing in the lake and Brian—standing on the jutting rock—peering through his binoculars across the lake. Miguel's urine stream was more like a splatter as he mercilessly blasted the lake water in fits and starts. His urination was a fluorescent yellow spurt of water out the end of a withered straw, the spurts shooting in random directions. It looked painful, although he didn't audibly reveal if it was or not. Once he was done, he pulled up his shorts, snapped the elastic band at his waist, and returned over to where Randy and I were lying on the ground. Randy was still asleep, his swollen hand and arm on his chest like a swaddled baby.

Miguel plopped down next to me, quite chipper for the early morning hour. "Good day, sunshine!"

"Hey," I said, rubbing the crust from my eyes. "What's he doing?"

I set my gaze on Brian. Miguel turned to look.

"Oh, he's just watching. Hoping to see Tony or someone."

"And?"

"*Nada*," Miguel replied, then picked up a stray pebble and tossed it in Brian's direction. It skidded on the ground, missing Brian's legs, and plunked in the water. "But he's on a mission."

I shifted my body position and noticed that the pain in my hip wasn't as bad as the day before. I slowly lifted my leg without much pain—raising it, then lowering it, then rotating it in small, circular motions—which pleased Miguel.

"Look at you!"

He jumped up and ran to where Brian stood on the jutting rock, jabbing him in the ribs with a pointy index finger.

"Hey! William's getting better!" Miguel exclaimed.

The jab caused Brian to reflexively bend at his waist, turning his entire body into a greater-than symbol.

"Why'd you do that?!" Brian said.

"Do what?"

"Poke me!"

"I barely touched you," Miguel said, rolling his eyes at Brian's frustration.

I looked over at Randy and he turned on his side, a quick herky-jerky type of turn like he levitated, then commanded to turn against his will by a wizard. He snorted, then snored some more. Brian and Miguel came over and squatted next to me.

"You doing OK?" Brian said. One corner of his mouth turned upward in a hopeful gesture. "You look better."

"Thanks, dude. I feel a little better. Did you see anybody out there?"

"Not yet."

"Keep lookin'."

"How's he doing?" Brian said, then thumbed in Randy's direction. Some blades of grass were stuck in his Afro like needles in a pin cushion. He noticed me looking at his hair, so he patted it, and a couple of blades fell out.

"Sawing logs," I said.

Brian winked, then returned to his post on the jutting rock—his binoculars pinned to his face. Miguel dusted off a spot next to me and sat down. It seemed strange that he would dust off the ground considering we were both filthy as pigs. Maybe it was a habit from our more civilized life back home and the constant scolding from our mothers to not get things in the house dirty. Miguel was noticeably gaunt, a withered facsimile of my friend—his eyes a little sunken, his lips a little ashen. His tangled hair, dotted with grass and sticker burrs, flickered in the breeze. But his withered state didn't seem to hamper his good disposition.

"I had a dream last night," he started, then cleared his throat.

"Oh yeah? What about?"

"I had a dream that my brother was being nice to me and rescued us. Weird, huh?"

He looked at me for an affirmation, knowing full-well how I felt about his dastardly brother.

"That would never happen in a million years."

"So true," he said, picking up another pebble, and launching it at Brian. The pebble skidded on the rocks, ricocheted up, then pegged Brian behind his right knee. He yelped, swinging the binoculars down while he rubbed his leg. "Bullseye!"

"Screw you!" Brian said. He glared at Miguel, then lifted the binoculars back to his face, returning to his lookout position. "Can't you see I'm doing something important here."

"Looks like you're just standing there," Miguel teased.

Brian's pshaw morphed into a loogie, which he spat into the lake. But his protestations quickly turned to a celebratory dance. He jumped up and down, waving his arms in the air.

"Hey!" he yelled, waving his arms furiously and yelling out into the giant, watery chasm.

Miguel and I were perplexed, to say the least.

"What's up?" Miguel called out.

Brian continued his pleas, not looking back at us.

"There's a boat! Look out there!"

I sat up while Miguel stood up. And sure enough out on the horizon was an object skirting across the water that certainly could've been a boat, if not a mirage from our collective imaginations. Our commotion awoke Randy, who sat up and rubbed his crusty eyes with his good hand. He seemed to be a little lost, as if awaking from a 100-year slumber and he didn't quite know where or who he was. Then he carefully shook out the tingly sleep from his swollen hand. He winced as he cradled it gently back against his chest.

"What's all the racket?"

"Brian sees a boat!" Miguel called out.

The look of surprise on Randy's face was priceless. His eyes bulged wide while his jaw dropped open, revealing his skeptical tongue.

"Really?"

"Yup," I said. "Look!"

Randy miraculously stood up—pressing his lame hand against his chest and shading his brow with his good hand—as he peered out across the water, squinting. Hope is a miraculous thing. Even the faintest bit of hope elicits will power from the deepest recesses of downtrodden souls. As if yanked to life by a puppet master, Randy and Miguel both joined Brian, all three jumping and screaming their brains out, trying their best to get the driver of the boat's attention to where we were stranded on damned Sometimes Island. I sat in the cool shade of the *For Sale* sign and watched my crazed friends as they pleaded to be seen. I could finally see the faint stirring of water way off in the distance, and I could hear the muffled buzz of the boat's motor. It skimmed across the water, but not in our direction. It seemed to be heading toward the Cabin of Seclusion.

"I think it's Tony!" Brian cried out. "But where's he going?!"

Brian stopped jumping so he could examine the boat's course through the binoculars. He kept them trained on the boat while Randy and Miguel continued to yell and wave their arms.

"Keep it up!" he said, turning his head to stay with the boat. "It is Tony. He's going to the lake house. Maybe when he cuts the motor, he'll hear us."

Randy—now seemingly unaffected by the poison from the snake, and full of life—stopped yelling and reached for the binoculars.

"I wanna see!" he said, then snatched the binoculars out of Brian's hands.

"Hey!"

"Just let me look a sec," he said, peering through the lenses and adjusting the focus knob. He squinted his eyes, then dropped his arms, a look of astonishment washing down his face. "It is Tony."

It's funny what the adrenaline created by this type of excitement will do to the infirmed. Just like Randy, I quickly joined my friends on the jutting rock without any concern for my once hurting hip. The only sign remaining from Randy's ill reaction to the snake bite was that he was still sweating profusely, even on that cooler than usual morning; the jaundice color of his skin had returned to normal. Brian snatched his binoculars back from Randy and narrated Tony's every move, since the rest of us couldn't see that far. It was obvious Tony couldn't hear us anyway, just as Brian's narration revealed.

"What's he doing now?" I quizzed Brian.

"He's tying the boat to the pier. And now he's getting out of the boat... and walking toward the lake house."

"Is anybody with him?" Miguel said. He scratched his scalp, then examined his fingernails, finding nothing of concern.

"Nope. He's all alone. Now, he's walking up the steps to the back door and... he went inside."

"Do you think he thinks we're still there?" Randy said.

Brian lowered the binoculars. "What are you asking me for?"

"I'm not asking *you*. I'm just talking out loud."

"Then be quiet. You're making it hard for me to tell everybody what he's doing."

Brian raised the binoculars back up to his face. Randy defiantly stuck his tongue out at him, which cracked me and Miguel up. Unconcerned, Brian squinted his eyes as he looked through the binoculars.

"He's coming back outside. Now, he's... just walking around. Looking on the ground or something."

"He must be looking for clues," I said. Randy and Miguel agreed.

Brian continued. "He's walking around the lake house. He's out of sight, probably walking around the other side."

"I wonder what happened to Rogelio," Miguel said.

"Probably went back home," I said.

Miguel shrugged.

"I see him again!" Brian continued. "He's walking back to the pier. And now he's..."

Brian stopped, then lowered the binoculars and rubbed his eyes with his free hand, digging out any blurriness with a swiveling fist. Then he raised the binoculars.

"He's looking this way. He's just standing there with his hands on his sides. Just looking."

"Do you think he can see us?" Randy said.

"I don't know. But he keeps looking this way. Now he has his hands over his eyes. He keeps looking at me!"

"Do you—" I began, but Brian cut me off.

"He's getting back in the boat. Now, he's... he got the motor running. And now he's coming this way!"

Brian dropped his arms and a big smile slid across his face, beaming like a thrilled child on a hopeful Christmas morning. The four of us knew the promise of what was transpiring.

"We're gonna be rescued!" we all cried out.

We couldn't contain ourselves. The excitement of the possibility of being rescued was too much to keep inside. We hooted and cheered.

Little did we know what would happen next.

23.

Our nightmare was over. We were rescued. The sight of Tony navigating his motor boat towards Sometimes Island was as exciting as the time Brian's parents revealed the entertainment for his seventh birthday party was Mister Mystical the magician. We about crapped our pants back then just with the mention of the magician's moniker, and we about crapped our pants again at the sight of Tony: our rescuer. Brian kept his binoculars trained on Tony's boat as he continued to narrate his progress, even though we could see Tony perfectly fine at this point for ourselves. The distance between his motor boat and our place on the island had drastically reduced, and we continued to jump and scream to keep his attention. But the lake grew angry—the surface boiled and stabbed at the hull of Tony's boat, rocking it side to side as he approached us. The lake wasn't ready for us to be free kids quite yet.

"He's getting closer," Brian said. "Almost to that orange floaty thing."

"We can see him perfectly fine. He's not that far away," I told him.

He dropped his binoculars and scanned the lake with his bare eyes. "Oh, you're right."

"Maybe we should go over there so we can be closer to him," I said, then pointed to a spot down the island where another jutting rock plateaued, the top of it sticking out from the island like a granite diving board.

"Good idea!" Brian replied.

We made our way to the flat rock—large enough for all of us to stand on—then continued to watch his progress. Once he was close enough to the orange buoy, he throttled the motor in what I imagined was reverse, then cut it. He steadied the boat with an oar.

"Hey! Are you all right?!" Tony called out.

We were so excited to be rescued that all we could do was cheer and flap our arms like baby birds elated with the return of their absent mother, but Brian had better ideas.

"Hey guys, calm down. He can't hear us," he said. The three of us stopped cheering. Brian cupped his hands around his mouth and cried out. "Come closer!"

Tony stared blankly at us. "Are you all right?! I can't hear you!"

"Come closer!" Brian repeated.

Tony watched us as if he was waiting for us to respond, the oar in one hand propping him up in the boat and his other hand on his hip. Maybe it was the wind out on the water past the buoys or various noises from the marina and the campground that kept Tony from hearing Brian's pleas. We didn't know. The frustration we felt was palpable. We wanted desperately to get off that island and the fact that Tony was so close yet so far was disheartening.

"I can't come any closer!" he called out. "Hey! Can you hear me?!"

"YES!" we all said. "Help us! Help!"

Tony shook his head, then set the oar down in the boat. He climbed to the back, pulled the starter cord which awoke the idle motor, then turned the boat toward the marina and headed that way. We pleaded for him to come back, but he didn't.

"Where's he going?" I said.

"I don't know," Brian said. "Maybe to get more help. At least he knows we're here, though. That's great news!"

"Yeah," Miguel said, dejected. "Hopefully."

"I guess all we can do is wait," Randy said, gently supporting his wounded hand. "I'm sitting in the shade."

Randy trudged back to the *For Sale* sign shelter, then sat in its oblong shade. The rest of us soon joined him—our knees to our chests and our sullen eyes leering in the direction of the marina—happy to get a respite from the blazing morning sun. The wind picked up and hissed, occasionally screeching. *How long do we have to wait?* I remember thinking. I'm certain my friends were wondering the same thing. My stomach growled like a wounded beast and I laid my forearms across my belly to quell it.

"I could eat a horse," I lamented.

"I second that," Brian added.

"Me too!" Miguel said. "And ladies and gentlemen, we have a quorum!"

The three of us laughed, something I hoped would ease our desperation. I turned to Randy and slapped him on the back, hoping he'd join in, but instead he wilted and laid on his side.

"Randy, are you all right?"

"I think I'm gonna die," he said.

His skin turned a color I can only describe as spoilt milk and beads of sweat oozed from his furrowed brow. He clutched his wounded arm at the wrist as he writhed on the rocky ground.

I turned to Brian and Miguel. "I hope Tony comes back soon."

They both nodded. I gently rubbed Randy's back.

We sat under the *For Sale* sign shelter for what seemed like an eternity, only shuffling our sad configuration when the sun's movement pushed the cool shadow of our shelter a few inches here and there. The dryness of my mouth was excruciating and felt akin to wool cloth lining my tongue and the roof of my mouth. I gave up on licking my lips as it just made them feel worse. To keep my mind occupied, I asked

Brian to hand me the binoculars and I secretly hoped that observing the water would conjure a rescue boat of some sort. I scanned the horizon in hopes of seeing something promising, but saw nothing.

As I sat there, I experienced a feeling that I can only describe as stupefying lethargy. The combination of exhaustion, hunger, and dehydration infiltrated my body and left me with the feeling that I was sinking in quicksand. Thoughts entered my mind of the comfortable numbness of sleep and nothing sounded better than falling fast asleep and never waking up. It's a horrible thing to admit—the idea that death was enticing. But for a brief moment, it was, until Brian slugged my arm.

"What's that?" he said, pointing to the lake.

I blinked my eyes a few times before lifting the binoculars. In the distance was a blurry mass approaching us, something that looked like a tortoise floating on the water, and as it slowly approached, I soon realized it was a pontoon boat, or what I would later learn Tony called a party barge. The shiny aluminum railings and pontoons glimmered in the sun and from the reflections off the water. Its maroon canopy perched above it like a sad beret, and underneath were two people I was grateful to see: Tony driving and Victoria standing at the front.

"They're coming for us!" I said.

Brian grabbed the binoculars from my hands and peered through them. "It's Victoria."

We looked at each other. "We're saved!"

Brian, Miguel, and I couldn't contain our excitement, giving each other high-fives and such. I even patted Randy on the back to let him know of our fortune. He simply groaned.

"Stay here with Randy," Brian told me. "Miguel and I will go wait on the rock for them."

I agreed, and my two friends sprinted over to the jutting rock, jumping up and down and waving their arms. Soon enough, the party barge puttered as close as Tony would allow it. He cut the engine and joined Victoria at the front. This time he had a megaphone in his hand.

"Can you hear me?" he called out.

"Yeah!" both Brian and Miguel replied.

"Just so you know, I can't get any closer than this. Do you think you can swim to us?"

"Yeah!" Victoria added, but realized she needed the megaphone. She grabbed it from Tony. "Do you think you can swim to us?"

Brian and Miguel stopped jumping, then turned to me and Randy sitting under the *For Sale* sign. It was apparent to them that Randy and I weren't in the position to swim out to the party barge in the angry lake water. Besides, Brian couldn't even swim at all on a good day. Swimming was just not an option.

Brian turned back to Tony and Victoria, his hand cupped next to his mouth. "Randy and William are hurt, and I can't swim!"

Tony and Victoria looked at each other, obviously perplexed about what to do, when Victoria began furiously pointing at the water. Tony ran to start the engine, then slowly reversed the boat's position from a nearby buoy and the jagged rocks lurking just underneath the water's surface. Once he was ten feet back or so, he cut off the engine again, returning next to Victoria.

He raised the megaphone to his mouth. "If I throw a rope to you, can I pull you to our boat one at a time?"

Brian looked to me once more, but I could see he already knew the answer.

"No, we can't!"

Tony and Victoria turned to each other, both shrugged then argued about what to do next. They seemed irritated and frustrated with equal measure when Victoria began furiously pointing at the water again. Tony quickly ran to the back of the boat, but didn't make it fast enough this time to crank the motor. The party barge lunged toward the buoy as if an angry, underwater creature maliciously pulled it. One of the pontoons jutted up from the water followed by the sound of its aluminum underside ripping open, like the death knell of a radioactive dinosaur in a Japanese monster movie from the 1950s. Tony fell to the platform while Victoria clung to the side rails of the party barge.

"Oh no!" Victoria cried out. "Now you've done it!"

"Oh shit!" Tony yelled.

He grabbed a safety pole from the side rails—the kind someone would use to pull in a drunken passenger who inadvertently tumbled in the water while partying—and pushed the party barge back from the wicked rock just underneath the water's surface.

"We'll be back!" he yelled, then quickly started the motor and maneuvered the party barge back in the direction of the marina.

Victoria appeared at the back of the boat, holding the side rail with one hand and the megaphone with the other.

"We'll be back!" she called out. "We promise!"

The party barge slowly made its way to the horizon, then slipped underneath it, disappearing as quickly as they came. Brian and Miguel sulked back to where we were under the *For Sale* sign shelter and joined us in the shade.

"Well," Brian began, then sighed. "That sucked."

"Sucked balls," Miguel added.

"Yup," I said. "Another quorum."

24.

Growing up in the 1980s afforded me and my friends a certain amount of freedom. We were not watched or monitored the way kids are nowadays. But this also came with a certain level of disconnectedness that many now also have a hard time comprehending. When Tony and Victoria floated away, my friends and I had no idea when they would be back. There was no way for us to communicate with them or the marina or anyone else in the surrounding area. We were far away from our mothers and fathers, and they had no idea where we were; for all they knew, we were still at Brian's house. The fact that Tony even found us was a miracle in itself. If he hadn't noticed the flickering reflections from Brian's binoculars, then he never would've driven his motor boat out to Sometimes Island. Remember, he told us that no one ever went out to the island. It was just too dangerous—for many reasons. So, yes, the fact that he spotted us out there on that desolate place in the middle of the lake was miraculous. He told me a number of times later that before we were stranded out there, he rarely even looked at the island while he was working at the marina, almost like it was invisible, or it simply blended into the horizon while he puttered around doing menial tasks. I think about this all the time. We were sitting at death's door, and didn't even know it.

We stared in the direction of the marina for hours, waiting for Tony and Victoria to come back, maybe with a bigger boat, and hopefully with more help. Not even the sight of other boats and skiers excited us anymore. They just ignored us anyway like we were pests. We just wanted our friends to rescue us, so we didn't jump and holler at the sight of these unwanted boaters. But we couldn't ignore the hunger pangs in our twisted stomachs. Miguel and I implored Brian to dig deep in the recesses of his mind for any information from his Boy Scout training that would maybe help us identify something on the island to eat.

"There has to be some leaf or plant we could eat. Right?" I insisted.

"Yeah, something," Miguel added.

Brian was stumped. He told us he clearly remembered lessons about which wild berries were safe to eat and which to avoid like the plague, but there weren't any berries at all to discern on the island. He shrugged no matter how much we protested.

"Sorry, dudes. I already feel helpless as it is," Brian said, then tossed an innocent pebble into the water.

"And *you* want to be an Eagle Scout?" I said sarcastically. "I thought you guys knew everything about survival?"

"I said I was sorry!" Brian snapped, then quickly jumped up and stormed off, leaving Miguel and I perplexed.

He stomped to the other end of the island and plopped down at the furthest possible spot where he could sit without falling into the water. Miguel indicated with a tilt of his head that we should go over to where he sat, imploring me with those sad brown eyes of his. I felt bad for teasing Brian. It wasn't his fault that the Boy Scouts didn't teach him how to survive while on a deserted island with three of his useless friends. So, I patted Randy on the back—whispering in his ear that we'd return shortly—then Miguel and I made our way over to where Brian sulked. On the way, we gathered a variety of leaves, twigs, and stalks of grass that had potential to be eaten. Then we both sat down with him. I extended one of the green leaves I found on the ground in front of his face, twirling it between my index finger and thumb, exhibiting its potential deliciousness.

"Do you think I can eat this?" I said. "Looks yummy."

Brian glanced at it, then turned his attention back to the lake. "I don't know. Why don't you eat it and see?"

"Maybe I will."

"Then do it."

"Yeah," Miguel agreed. "Just eat it."

"OK, I will."

I slowly raised the leaf to my unsuspecting mouth. I opened it wide—comically agape. Miguel watched with anticipation. Brian continued to ignore me.

"Here I go," I said.

Brian then watched my progress from the corner of his eye and as the leaf got closer to my mouth, the more he turned his head to watch. Then without warning, I shoved the leaf in my mouth and chomped on it.

"He actually ate it!" Miguel called out, then burst out laughing, rolling onto his back, kicking with excitement.

Brian's eyes bulged with astonishment like he knew something I didn't, but that I would soon find out. As I chomped on the leaf, the bitterest of acrid liquids covered my tongue and elicited my gag reflex immediately. I spit out of the half-chewed leaf and coughed.

Both Brian and Miguel were on their backs laughing hysterically, kicking their legs up and punching at the sky with celebratory fists. I even had to go down to the water (in spite of my sore leg and the excruciating pain it caused going down there) and rinse out my mouth, scraping the last of the bitter leaf from my tongue with my finger nails. Dirty lake water was better than the horrific taste of that insidious leaf.

"It's disgusting," I said.

They continued to laugh at me, their arms now draped across their bellies. I didn't like being the source of their amusement, but it was better than discontent between us.

Brian sighed. "That was hilarious."

"So funny," Miguel agreed.

I returned to where they were sitting and sat down.

"Glad that I amuse you. Still friends?" I said, extending my hand to Brian for a reconciliatory shake.

"Of course," he said, shaking my hand with an extra firm grip, then he twisted his arm so he could pin me to the ground. We wrestled for a bit, but not in a competitive way. We were just horsing around when Miguel cried out that he saw something down in the water.

"Look! Money!"

Brian and I quit wrestling and we watched Miguel go down to the waterline and pull a soggy $100 bill from the cold, dark water. He stepped over mossy rocks to get back to where we were standing and held the limp bill up for us to see, pinched between his thumb and index finger.

"Do you think that's from—" I said, then looked out to the lake at the spot where I remembered seeing Bloody Billy's head bobbing in the water for the last time.

"Maybe. Who knows? Did you know American money is made from a remarkable material that's like cloth?"

Brian and I looked at each other, then both shook our heads.

"It'll air dry in fifteen or twenty minutes. You'll see."

Brian and I shrugged at this new information about American paper money.

"Let's go back with Randy," Miguel suggested. "It'll dry just as fast over there. Too bad we can't eat it."

We made our way back to where Randy was laying under the *For Sale* sign. It was nicer sitting in the shade while we waited for the $100 bill to dry. And to be rescued. Fifteen minutes quickly went by and Miguel's theory about how fast the money would dry was proven correct.

"See?" he said to Brian and me, then handed us the $100 bill to examine. Sure enough, it was dry as can be and felt remarkably like any old bill. "I want to make something for you."

He extended his hand and I gave the bill to him. First, he folded it in half. Then he flattened it and used the line down the middle as a guide for his impromptu origami project. He held the paper close to his face and folded it a number of times while his tongue jabbed in and out of his mouth, revealing his intense concentration. After performing a dozen or so origami folds, his project was complete. He placed it in his palm and showed us.

"A paper airplane!"

"Whoa!" we said in unison.

He handed the paper airplane to me.

"Maybe a plane like this will rescue us soon," he said.

I pinched the paper airplane between my index finger and thumb, then examined its aerodynamic lines. I swung it through the air as if to throw it, but didn't.

"Throw it to me!" Brian commanded.

So, I did, but it crashed quickly on the rocky ground instead of landing in Brian's outstretched hands.

"Piece of crap," Brian said, which made us all laugh.

Randy moaned, then turned on his other side. His skin was grey and damp. He pulled his knees to his chest and laid on his side in the fetal position. We didn't dare touch him.

After a few minutes, our excitement about the paper airplane dissipated with the realization that maybe—just maybe—Tony and Victoria wouldn't be back as soon as we'd hoped. There was no sign of them at all and Randy seemed to be getting worse as time trudged on. He moaned and groaned in a state of listless irritation and we didn't know what to do except to comfort him by whispering well-wishes. Our presence seemed to calm him sometimes, but his worsening condition worried the three of us. *Is he going to die?* I thought to myself. How could I face his mother if that happened while we were stuck on Sometimes Island?

As night fell, we did as little as possible to expend energy, lying together on the ground like cadavers. All my friends slept as I gazed up at the Milky Way—I held the paper airplane in my hands, every once and a while zipping it through the air above my head—and I wondered if the owl would hoot or, at least, pay me a visit by sitting on a branch up in the bur oak tree. If he dropped a dead mouse this time, then I would most likely eat it, particularly since Randy was asleep and couldn't chide me about not having dignity or something like that. I was so hungry that dignity was something I just wasn't worried about.

So, rather than think about dead mice or dignity or food, I decided to put the paper airplane in my pocket and count as many stars as I could in an effort to go to sleep. The last thing I remember was that I counted ninety seven stars before I, too, fell asleep. I must have fallen into a very deep slumber because the next thing I remember happening was like something out of a dream. It was like a UFO was coming down from the sky and—little did I know—it was coming for us.

PART IV.
Rescue of the Benevolent Lords

25.

During elementary school, not only was I obsessed with *Spider-Man* comics, I was also addicted to movies about extraterrestrials and spaceships. That time from the mid-1970s through the mid-1980s was the pinnacle of alien movies in my opinion. There were these stone-cold classics: *E. T. the Extraterrestrial*, *Star Wars*, *Cocoon*, *Alien*, just to name a few. But the greatest of them all—the *coup de grace* to all arguments about alien movies of the period—was *Close Encounters of the Third Kind.* It had amazing special effects, but it was also very realistic in its portrayal of government conspiracy as well as the alien abductions. A viewing with my parents during a dollar matinee was revelatory to my young, impressionable mind. As I watched—transfixed, mesmerized, and stuffing my face with buttered popcorn—I remember my parents telling me afterwards, "This is exactly what would happen."

"How what would happen?" I said, worried.

"An alien *invasion.*"

I agreed with them, not only because they were my parents, but because the depiction of the aliens was so realistic and plausible that I had no doubt it would be true. Scenes like the alien scout ships flying through the toll booths or the abduction of the little boy outside his rural home or the final landing of the gargantuan mothership on the top of Devils Tower burned indelibly into my adolescent imagination. I was certain—as certain as any little kid could be—that *Close Encounters of the Third Kind* was an accurate depiction of what would happen if aliens came to Earth. It was a documentary of what was to come for humanity.

So, when I was awakened by an ominous sound from up above and those all too familiar searching, incandescent lights beamed down from the inky black, night sky, my first thought was, *I knew it was true!*

I sat up and watched the strange object approach the island from up above—two shafts of light radiating the water and a glow from its bulbous fuselage—and it emitted a rumble similar to the sound of someone boxing your ears repeatedly. *Thwump thwump thwump.* I was flabbergasted, to say the least. And as it got closer, a gust of forced air pushed up to the island from the water and launched shrapnel of dust, pebbles, twigs, and sticker burrs into my bare chest and face. My friends awoke from the attack of island debris, immediately covering their eyes with their hands. The *thwumping* became audibly clearer as it got closer, as well as the realization that this unidentified flying object was actually very identifiable. Brian was the first to verbalize this fact.

"Tony sent a helicopter to rescue us!"

The reflection of the search lights off the murky water illuminated the helicopter from below, and it was clear to us that we would probably be getting off that godforsaken island soon, as long as we didn't get impaled by shrapnel first. The force of the air and the debris pummeling us was almost too much to take, so we crawled behind some cedar trees and the bur oak tree and held onto the trunks tightly, using the base of the trees as a shield from the dangerous debris. The *For Sale* sign wriggled in between the two trees it was pried between, broadcasting an irritating sound similar to a clown blubbering his index finger between two slobbery lips through an amplifier. The closer the helicopter descended, the stronger it blew. Inevitably, the *For Sale* sign just couldn't stay put. It launched from between the two cedar trees out into the dark water behind us like a crazed Frisbee, floating a moment after it splashed, then quickly sinking to its doom. I turned back to find my friends gripping the trees for their dear lives. I knew we were being rescued, but it was a terrifying way to rescue us.

Hovering above the island, I could see there were two men in the helicopter. The pilot spoke to us through a speaker mounted below, but his voice was indecipherable. He sounded like every adult character in every *Charlie Brown* cartoon I ever watched: muffled, squawky, and incomprehensible.

"I think they're trying to tell us something!" I yelled out to my friends.

Brian nodded. Miguel and Randy hugged their trees and didn't make a move.

"I wonder what they're saying!"

After a couple of stanzas of unintelligible squawking, the helicopter hovered in place like a gigantic wasp, occasionally adjusting its search lights to different locations on and around the island. Maybe they were surveying the scene. Maybe they were contemplating an ill-advised landing. Maybe they just didn't know what they were doing. I never found out, to tell you the truth. Believe me, later in life, I asked everybody just what the hell this helicopter pilot was thinking, but nobody could tell me. It remains a mystery to this day. But at the time, as I gripped my tree and looked up to the helicopter the best I could, it seemed like the only hope we had to be rescued.

It hovered long enough to sweep all the loose debris off the island, the shrapnel attack finally relenting. I noticed something descending from the bottom of the helicopter, but I couldn't tell what it was at first. It lowered through flashes of light, a line of some sort dangling from below the fuselage, at one point illuminated enough to reveal to me a rope with a triangular handle at the end of it. Then I realized what the helicopter pilot was attempting to accomplish: rescue via flying trapeze.

"They dropped a rope!" I cried out.

Brian returned a puzzled look, which morphed into a grimace. As young as we were, we both realized what a dumb idea this was and wondered which adult came up with this ridiculous rescue plan.

"I'm not hanging on to that!" Brian yelled. "I can't swim! Doesn't *everybody* get that by now?!"

As the trapeze descended closer to us, the pilot squawked another stanza of garbled instructions. This was the misguided attempting to rescue the inexperienced. This was—in so few words—a disaster. The helicopter maneuvered closer to the island, the dangling trapeze twirling under the forced air of the helicopter's spinning blades. The farther it descended, the faster it spun.

"This is crazy!" I cried out.

"I'm not doing it!" Brian screamed. "Not doing it!"

Soon, the dangling trapeze swayed in the air as it spun, swinging an invisible circus performer back and forth. The invisible performer grew more and more daring, swinging wider, the trapeze wobbling. Before long, the trapeze unilaterally changed its purpose from a rescue device to a dangerous flying object. Its swinging radius grew wildly and more erratic. Once the helicopter pilot noticed what was happening below to his rescue line, he adjusted the helicopter's position. But the tilted blades forced more air toward the island, sending the trapeze on a hurtling course toward an unsuspecting cedar tree. The branches ensnared the trapeze and the rope slithered around its catch like a snake hungry for a quick kill. Losing its freedom, the helicopter's engine revved loudly, performing a panicked shimmy as its motion was restricted.

"It's gonna crash!" I screamed.

All the cinematic logic in all the 80s action movies told me this. It was supposed to crash. *Rambo* movies told me this. *Indiana Jones* movies told me this. *James Bond* movies, too. The helicopter's engine revved even louder as it tilted in an effort to escape the cedar tree's grasp of the rescue line. Like a rowdy dog pulling on its owner's leash, the rescue line grew taut to the point of almost snapping, and the tension created seemed to pull the helicopter closer to the water. And right when I thought it was going to crash—plugging both my ears with stiff index fingers as I prepared to brace myself for an explosion—the rescue line snapped with a whip-crack screech. And the next thing I knew, I was on the ground, under a dog pile of friends.

"Stay down!" Randy commanded. He must have tackled the three of us to the ground to protect us. He was so big and heavy, we had no choice but to stay down.

The rescue line screeched and hissed like a prehistoric creature as it whipped above us, then splashed into the water behind us. The cedar tree dropped all its needles in a shower of panic. And the helicopter ascended into that deep, dark sky, its *thwumping*, rhythmic din pulsating toward the clouds, its fluorescent lights beaming at the hills. It hung in the air for a moment or two like a ruminating wasp, then it was gone with a quick tilt to the right, the beating of its blades still reverberating in my ears after it vanished.

Brian, Miguel, and I elbowed our way out from under Randy, or what appeared to be the ghost of Randy. His skin was pallid, almost translucent, and his sulking face glowed in the dark. He sat down where our *For Sale* sign shelter used to be, the roof now at the bottom of the lake, and he shook cedar needles from his hair.

"That was crazy," he said, then coughed up a loogy.

"Totally," I replied.

We sat with Randy as the night embraced us with the hope for a rescue gone.

26.

The next morning, no one needed to pee, mostly likely the first signs of dehydration. That urgent feeling we usually felt first thing in the morning—whether at home with our loving families or on that godforsaken deserted island—had dissipated along with our hopes of being rescued. The helicopter that visited us in the night seemed more like part of a collective nightmare than an attempt to rescue us. *What normal adult thought* that *was a good idea?* I kept thinking to myself. It just didn't make any sense. Even I, at such a young age, saw the absurdity of a helicopter / flying trapeze rescue mission of four preteens in the middle of the night. It was asinine, really; any middle-schooler would've told you that.

But as the sun slowly ascended and the four of us rubbed our crusty eyes covered with dust and debris from the botched rescue mission, we could smell the evidence of civilization in the air, my friends and I only separated by a cruel body of water that—in the grand scheme of things—wasn't the greatest distance we would have to cross in our lives, as impossible as it seemed at the time. The water churned just enough to let us know that we were not getting across it, no matter how hard we tried. Besides, Brian couldn't swim, as he stoically reminded us. What we smelled floating across the angry water was exhaust from engines, wafts of fragrant cedar and oak trees, and the scent of the most delicious of all Texas traditions. It was so strong that Brian, Miguel, and I sat up, tilting our sniffing noses up in the air like hungry beasts.

"I smell barbeque," Brian said, then licked his dry lips with his sandpaper cat tongue.

"Smells like chicken," Miguel added.

We couldn't figure out exactly where the delicious combination of scents came from, but Brian surmised that the engine exhaust must have been from the marina and the fragrance of a cherished barbeque dinner must have been from the extinguishing grills and campfires of the campgrounds next door. The intoxicating scents drifted to the island on the Hill Country breeze. It was a malicious tease from humanity and a serenade from the sirens of barbeque lore.

"I would destroy some chicken right now," I confessed. Brian and Miguel emphatically agreed. It sounded divine to my malnourished body.

"I could guzzle a 2-liter of Big Red, too!" Miguel said.

"Daaang! That sounds good!" Brian said.

We could've gone on like that until the moment we happily died, reminiscing about family feasts we took for granted and easy snacks we snatched without thinking how hard our parents had to work to provide, anything to appease our dreaded souls from the hopelessness we felt deep in our hearts and empty stomachs. But then a familiar sound returned. It came in with the delicious Hill Country breeze across the churning waters.

The *thwumping* noise.

The *thwump thwump thwump* of helicopter blades.

And the sound of an armada of rescue boats. Like the rumble before an avalanche or the rolling thunder after a heavy rainstorm.

"Look!" Brian cried out, pointing toward the approaching mass.

And just as we hoped—finally—a different, larger helicopter (similar to the ones you'd see in war movies like *Apocalypse Now* or *Rambo*—army green with white, block lettering stenciled on it and a machine gun mounted on its side, although this one didn't have one of those) approached Sometimes Island with dozens of motor boats underneath it: ski boats, fishing boats, patrol boats, even a party barge. It was an exciting vision, which is how it seemed to me because the boats emerging from the smear of hazy horizon across the glittering water appeared to shimmy and sparkle as if ejecting themselves from our mirage of hope. The rumble from the beating helicopter blades and the dozens of outboard motors was the most beautiful sound I had heard since long before our boat wreck on Sometimes Island. I was so excited that I just had to tell Randy, who was still lying on his side in the fetal position. He was a despondent lump of poisoned meat.

"We're rescued!" I told him, shaking his shoulder. But his body was limp, and he simply grunted. "Don't worry. We'll help you."

Brian and Miguel were on the jutting rock by now, jumping up and down, waving their arms frantically, although they didn't have to. We were going to be rescued nonetheless. But they just couldn't contain their excitement. *What will be the first thing we do once we're off this island?* I thought. *Eat hamburgers? Drink sodas? Kiss the mainland under our feet? Hug our parents?* What would you do first? There was nothing more delicious than hope fulfilled.

The motor boats swarmed the island out by the bobbing orange buoys, as if appearing out of nowhere, the way Imperial space cruisers in the movie *Star Wars* exited hyperspace: a screeching halt from light speed. But the helicopter was the prominent savior. It approached the island with a careful descent, its beating blades pushing air on the island like the one the night before did, although every bit of debris on the island had already been swept off. *Thwump thwump thwump* the blades undulated. A commanding voice notified us through a loud speaker—clear as day—that a soldier would be rescuing us, followed by a figure dropping from the fuselage like a spider down its silken thread. I joined Brian and Miguel on the jutting rock and we watched the soldier descend in a fashion that made me think we were witnessing a real-life Spider-Man, his motion almost supernatural in appearance, although wearing bulky, military fatigues instead of a red and blue superhero suit. The helicopter dropped the soldier on its intended target: the jutting rock. Towering over us with sinewy but sturdy arms, short-cropped dark hair, coffee-stained teeth, and mirrored sunglasses, the soldier's confidence was a welcome presence.

And without missing a beat, he commanded us to give him an answer.

"Who's going first?!"

The three of us looked at each other and immediately knew who from our dejected group should go first.

"Randy!" we replied, pointing to where our friend laid on the ground.

With slack in his rescue line, the soldier wrapped a length of it around his right arm and trotted over to Randy, the helicopter hovering patiently in the sky. He knelt next to him, tapped him on the shoulder, said something to Randy through a cupped hand, then placed his right ear close to Randy to hear his response. The soldier nodded a time or two, then unceremoniously hoisted Randy over his shoulder quicker than an Olympic weightlifter, Randy's ragdoll body folding at the waist, his lifeless limbs dangling down. The soldier trotted back to the jutting rock as if Randy weighed only a few ounces, then with his free hand wrapped a safety cord around Randy's waist, which he fastened to a metal loop on his belt. He looked up to the helicopter, communicated something through a headset receiver, then displayed a thumbs up. I could see the pilot nodding, his silvery sunglasses refracting sunlight.

He turned to us. "Decide who's next. I'll be back."

And with that, the slack in the line tightened and the soldier and Randy were lifted about twenty feet in the air. The blades undulated: *Thwump thwump thwump*. The helicopter maneuvered over the waiting rescue boats—nameless do-gooders and boaters all looking up at the helicopter as if witnessing something unbelievable—then delicately dropped the soldier on the party barge. Two people, who appeared to be Tony and Victoria, helped set Randy in the barge, then cheered as the soldier ascended back into the air.

"He's coming back!" Brian shouted.

"Who's going next?" Miguel said. His eyes darted back and forth from me to Brian, then to the helicopter with the dangling soldier fast approaching us.

"I vote for Brian since he can't swim," I said.

Miguel agreed, which caught Brian off guard.

"I don't know, guys," he said, shaking his head. "I'm scared!"

"Scared?" I said. "Did you see how easily he carried Randy? Like he weighed nothing!"

Brian gazed across the water to the party barge where Randy laid waiting for the rest of us, then his head tilted up to the flying Spider-Man, coming back for the next one of us to rescue.

"You think I'll be safe going over all that water?" he said.

The fear displayed on his face was nothing short of dreadful. What could I say to appease my friend? I wasn't quite sure, so I quickly decided to hug him, then said the first thing that came to my mind into his ear.

"Easy street!"

The next thing we knew, the soldier was on the jutting rock with us, the air stirring around us, the water agitated and vibrating.

"Who's next?!" he said.

I could see the three of us huddled together in the reflection of his sunglasses.

I pointed to Brian. "He is!"

The soldier gave a thumbs up, then without asking, hoisted Brian over his shoulder as easily as he did Randy, securing Brian around the waist with the safety cord. He looked up to the helicopter and indicated he was ready. The rescue line tightened, then he levitated into the air. Brian kicked his legs as the soldier ascended above the water, appearing as if he was attempting to swim away from the soldier's grasp, trying to escape from the dilemma that tweaked his anxiety. The motion of his kicking legs wobbled the soldier, who wrapped his arm tighter around Brian in an attempt to get him to stop kicking. The soldier twisted his body, his arm muscles bulging. It seemed as if he was gaining control of Brian's irascibility.

The air became still. The *thwump thwump thwumping* dampened.

Then without warning, Brian mysteriously slid from the soldier's grasp—down his back like famed magician Harry Houdini slithering out of a length of chain—kicking and screaming in a terrified dive head-first down to the lake below. The collective gasp from Miguel and me was as loud as the splash. A white, frothy explosion gave way to bubbly ringlets where Brian disappeared into the dark water, then the enlarging circles of bubbles dissipated into nothingness, the ripples from the splash jabbing at the nearby boats. No signs of Brian: no hands flapping, no hair, no friend visible in the water.

It was Brian's worst nightmare come true. It was his mother's worst-case scenario. It was our collective fear realized. I promised my friend that nothing would happen, but then the worst thing happened. He inexplicably slipped from our superhero's sturdy grasp, plunging in slow motion to the one place he dared not go, the one place he repeatedly told us he couldn't go for fear of drowning. The surrounding sounds of the boats and the helicopter vanished as I looked on in paralyzed fear. Miguel's hands covered the lower half of his face, hiding his terrified O of mouth, muffling his scream of panic, his eyes bulging in disbelief. What could the two of us do? How could we save our friend? We both knew in that still moment that we were useless to help Brian, as much as we wanted to. We were children. We were not equipped to help him. I feared for the worst as I imagined Brian sinking down to the silty lake bed, drifting toward the place where Bloody Billy most likely laid, the bottom feeders dashing away, the backpack filled with money there, too.

Then a commotion from the party barge snapped me from my hypnotized state.

In a split second, Tony dove from the side railing of the party barge into the dark water after our submerged friend. The *thwump thwump thwumping* of the helicopter blades returned along with the cheering of many faceless boaters. We all waited to see if Tony could save our friend. After a few tense moments of staring at the very place where Tony dove in, I saw his head come up from the water. Victoria tossed a rope from the boat, which he used to pull himself closer. A moment later, Brian's head popped above water. He spit and sneezed water from his mouth and nose, then cried for help. Before we knew it, Tony was climbing a ladder on the side of the boat, pulling Brian up by his t-shirt. He eventually turned around and followed Tony up onto the platform of the party barge.

"Thank God!" Miguel said.

We both hugged each other, grateful that our friend was rescued. The soldier appeared again on the jutting rock, appearing as if out of thin air because our attention was focused on Tony and Brian.

"Who's next?" he said. "And can you *not* kick your legs, please?"

"I think Miguel should go!"

"Are you sure?!" Miguel said.

"Yeah!" I said, then placed my hand on his shoulder. "I'll be right behind you."

Before I knew it, I was watching Spider-Man carry Miguel in the air to the party barge, soon joining Randy and Brian as well as Tony, Victoria, and other do-gooders. Then it was my turn. When Spider-Man returned to the jutting rock, he didn't even ask me if I was ready. He flung me over his shoulder, wrapped the safety cord around my waist, secured the cord to his belt, and we were in the air faster than I could comprehend. As we rose above the rocky place that was my home for the last few days—the unforgiving, deserted Sometimes Island—I marveled at just how small it was, and that it didn't seem as far from the mainland as we thought. Flying even higher, the island looked like a toy model, something a young boy would glue together then spray paint, tiny rocks like styrofoam, splintery trees like toothpicks. When you are experiencing trauma, does your brain perceive things to be worse than they really are? Does your perception of time and space change when you are separated from what you know as reality? I wasn't thinking about these things as I flew from the island to my rescue boat. I have thought about these things since then—at night, while sitting up in a sleepless trance—and wondered to myself how we got ourselves into this mess, and how we managed to survive. We had everything against us, but we got through it together. These four kids of Thousand Oaks and Hidden Oaks. These seventh graders from F. D. R. Middle School. The Benevolent Lords of Sometimes Island.

When my feet touched the floor on the party barge, I was embraced by my friends along with Tony and Victoria, both as happy to see us as can be, happy we were alive, happy to have helped save us. We celebrated, our huddle of teenagers jumping like a victorious sports team, except for Randy, who laid crumpled at our feet. When Spider-Man finally asked us if there was anything else for him to do, or any other people to help back on Sometimes Island, it didn't take a genius to figure out what I needed to say.

"Our friend got bit by a snake!" I said, as loud as I could over the cacophony of motor engines and the *thwumping* of the helicopter blades. "He's not doing good!"

Spider-Man looked over to where Randy laid in a helpless mass, then nodded. He barked something into his headset, then scooped Randy up and over his shoulder again, his limp body draping over his burly shoulder. And before we could say goodbye to Randy or offer words of encouragement, Spider-Man was in the air with one of my best friends, up and away, then inside the fuselage of the waiting helicopter. It turned east and flew (I would later learn) to Brook Army Medical Center in San Antonio, Texas, or BAMC (pronounced bam-cee) as the folks around here call it.

Once the *thwumping* sound of the helicopter dissipated after it disappeared over the surrounding hills, the cheering of the boaters in the other boats could be heard. Tony and Victoria beamed as the three of us stood at the edge of the party barge, gripping the metal railing and taking in the congratulatory cheers and well-wishes. It was an amazing spectacle to take in after several days in destitution with no food, water, or adequate shelter. I turned to Brian and Miguel, then flung my arms around them, pulling them close.

"I love you guys," I said to them.

"I love you, too," they both said.

"All right, all right," Tony said, interrupting us. "Let's get you guys back to the marina."

"Yeah," Victoria added. "I bet you're all hungry."

I looked at my two friends, then turned to Victoria. "We're friggin' starving!"

"Then let's go!" Tony said.

He cranked the ignition to the motor of the party barge, then took us all back to the marina, the armada of other boats following behind us.

27.

After Tony secured the party barge to the marina, the five of us—me, Brian, Miguel, Tony, and Victoria—were met with jaunty cheers, toothy smiles, and shoulder pats from a slew of excited people: our parents, police officers, park rangers, Tony and Victoria's parents, fishermen, TV news crew, water skiers, and who knows who else. It was an exhilarating moment. The first faces I recognized in the throng of strangers were my parents—my mother and step-dad Steve—who both embraced me. My mother kissed my forehead while questioning me simultaneously: a loving inquisition.

"So glad you're safe! Why were you out here? I was so worried about you! Are you OK?"

"I'm OK, mom," I said. "Just really hungry."

"Do you want something to eat? Do you want a candy bar?"

I looked up at her. "Yeah, I want a candy bar."

She plumbed the depths of her handbag and pulled a perfectly good Snickers bar from inside. I unceremoniously ripped open the packaging and devoured it. As I chomped the candy bar—as delicious as anything I had ever eaten in my entire life—I spotted both my friends, their sunken eyes glaring at me as I devoured the candy, and I felt soul-crushing guilt. My hunger had gotten the best of me like a smooth-talking transient separating me from a hard-earned dollar.

I turned to my mother. "Can my friends have a Snickers, too?"

My mother wasn't prepared for my request and hastily searched her purse for more candy bars, digging beneath stray cosmetics and rattling keys and multiple pairs of eyeglasses, even though it was apparent she didn't have any more. Instead of admitting her oversight, she commanded Steve to go buy some candy in the marina store. An unexpected sigh escaped from deep within his soul. He sulked away, rummaging in his pant pockets for money to pay for candy.

"Don't you worry. He'll get some for your friends."

To placate my guilty mind, I tore the last of my Snickers bar in two and gave the pieces to Brian and Miguel. They devoured the candy like rabid dogs.

Brian's parents were there, too. Both hugged and kissed him while he licked his fingers of candy residue, telling him about their sorrow when they discovered he was missing.

"I felt like the worst mother in the world," his mother said, sobbing uncontrollably as she pulled his head to her bosom.

"It wasn't your fault, ma," Brian said. He rubbed his sticky hands on the front of his shirt. "And I'm OK."

"I bet your Boy Scout training helped," Mr. Johnson added. Brian sulked and didn't respond.

Miguel's parents were also there—both embracing him and telling him how worried they were when they, too, discovered he was missing—along with Miguel's bastard brother, Rogelio. He stood sheepishly behind his family, not saying a word, both of his hands buried deep in his back pockets, as if he'd washed them of his guilt and concealed them from the relieved throng of do-gooders that witnessed our rescue. I gave him a stare that could burn through steel, and once his eyes caught my intense stare, he looked off in the distance as if watching sail boats, then spun around and walked away, probably to go hide in the car. I was OK with that; I would get my revenge on him later.

Tony and Victoria stood with their parents, both parental sets telling my folks that they were there for them and would help in any way possible, even offering to pay for any medical attention and whatnot. It may well have been a ruse to avoid a lawsuit, especially from Mrs. Johnson, a hard-nosed lawyer that I would later learn was a well-known prosecutor at some point in her career. There were bits and pieces said by Tony and Victoria's parents to mine about how they were just flabbergasted that we were even out there on Sometimes Island, something they'd never heard done before in all the years they owned the marina and the campgrounds, even by their most disreputable customers.

"You might as well have told me they were stranded on the moon," the man standing behind Tony said (his father I presumed and the owner of the marina). "Nobody I know has ever dared go on Sometimes Island. It's just too dangerous. At least that's what I've always been told."

After hearing this, my mother turned me around, then blasted me with a penetrating stare. "Why did you go out there?!"

"It wasn't on purpose," I told her. "We were being chased by—"

Brian and Miguel both grabbed my arms, attempting to stop me from spilling the beans before we could all come to an agreement about what exactly we should tell our parents.

"Dude!" they both said.

I understood this as a demand to stop talking and not incriminate me and my friends.

"Chasing you?" my mother said. "But who..."

"I'll tell you about it later. OK mom?"

She sighed and reluctantly acquiesced. "OK."

The next thing I knew, my friends and I were accosted by the local news reporter and her film crew. She introduced herself as Cokey Ramirez, a reporter with San Antonio TV station KSAT 12—the channel I watched for countless hours of reruns like *The Munsters*, *The Addams Family*, *The Beverly Hillbillies*, and of course, *Gilligan's Island*—and her carefully made-up face with swathes of eye shadow over a thick undercoat of foundation and concealer was very familiar to me and my friends. Her famous mug adorned commercials and news previews, and was flashed in-between all the reruns we consumed after school. She wore a bright, purple business suit and her hair was as straight and glossy black as a freshly tarred highway in west Texas. In person, she was skinnier than imaginably possible, and smelled of gardenias and coffee. The idea that my friends and I would possibly be on TV sent electricity through my body like a jolt of lightning. She pointed a bulbous microphone at me while a bright light mounted on a video camera behind her flooded my retinas.

"How did you survive out there this long?" she said, a hushed silence following her question. She jabbed her microphone at my face.

"I don't know. We just did."

She tilted the microphone back at her. "What did you have to eat on the island?"

The microphone pointed at me again. "Nothing. I tried to eat a leaf, but it was gross!"

A smattering of laughter.

"Nothing to drink either?" she continued. She moved the microphone again closer to my face.

"Well," I said, looking at my friends. Brian nodded for me to continue. "We tried to drink the lake water, but it was—"

"I found a can of Pepsi Light in the lake! We shared that!" Miguel blurted. He folded his arms across his chest in a self-congratulatory kind of way, a toothy grin gleaming. He was really mugging for the camera.

"Pepsi Light?" Cokey Ramirez said, then chuckled. "They may offer you a sponsorship after this!"

"Nah, I like Big Red better. Can I get a sponsorship from them?!"

More smatterings of laughter. The reporter continued, now aiming the microphone at Brian—his face beaming. I could tell both of my friends were enjoying this bit of media attention. It was a stark contrast from the last few days stuck on that unforgiving, rocky island with little hope to survive.

"You know, I'm surprised your time on the island didn't turn into a *Lord of the Flies* situation. That's what they always say about people who get stranded from civilization, that they devolve into savages. Did that ever occur to you while you were out there?"

She pointed the microphone at Brian. "Who do you think we are, lady? A bunch of *jerks*?!"

Cokey Ramirez was caught off guard by Brian's proclamation, but she forced a smile, then chuckled nonetheless. She wrapped up the interview by asking the three of us to stand together so they could film a conclusion for the segment. Camera lights flashed. Salutations were given. People clapped. It was a surreal moment for me and my friends.

But the celebratory moment didn't last as long as I would've liked. While Cokey Ramirez wrapped up the interview, my mother unceremoniously grabbed me by my arm and pulled me close to her, her manicured nails digging into my upper arm. A dour look hung on her face and she gripped my arm even tighter as she knelt in front of me. My step-dad towered behind her, his hands on his hips, his squinty eyes on me like hot glue.

"Billy?" she started, then cleared her throat. That damn nickname again. "There's someone that wants to ask you some questions."

I covered my heart with my hands. "Questions?"

"Yes, he's a lawman," she said.

From the gaggle of people and the thrum of their chatter appeared a burly hand the size of a baseball mitt, extended to me for a shake. As I grabbed the leathery hand, I followed the arm it was attached to up to the face of the man hoping to question me: Sheriff Samuel Hill.

"Or you can simply call me Sam. That's what all my friends call me," he said with a baritone drawl, then chuckled. His grip was firmer than I could bear, reminding me that I was not as mature as I would've preferred. He pumped his shake three times. My hand continued to throb after he released it. "Can I ask you a few questions?"

"Sure," I said.

My mother and step-dad stepped aside, leaving me with Sheriff "Sam" Hill and his deputy, a tall and doughy Hispanic man with a nametag announcing his surname to be "Gonzalez." Sheriff Hill was brusque and monumental like a granite boulder, his furrowed brow dipping in the middle with a penetrating "V," pitch black aviator sunglasses with gold frames disguising the color of his eyes, a government-issued cowboy hat capping his bristly maned head, his grizzled visage punctuated by a mustache that perched above his thin, chapped lips like a corn bristle broom. A toothpick danced across the row of yellow kernels at the bottom of his mouth.

"I understand there were four of you," he began, hocking up a loogy, then swallowing it. "Excuse me. There were four of you to begin with, is that correct?"

"Yes," I said sheepishly.

"Speak up, son. It's loud out here."

"Yes!"

"What happened to him? It's a him, I presume."

"His name is Randy."

Sheriff Hill smirked. "Randy is a fine name. What happened to Randy?"

"He got bit by a snake—"

"A water moccasin!" Brian blurted. He must have been listening to my interrogation and wanted to help.

"And you are?" Sheriff Hill said to Brian.

"I'm one of his best friends," Brian said, a smile as big as a cumulus cloud in the Texas sky.

The smirk on Sheriff Hill's face returned. "Is he dead?"

"No," I told him. "The helicopter took him away when I told the soldier he got bit by a snake."

He rubbed his stubbly chin. "I see."

"Are we in trouble?"

"Why would you think that?" the sheriff said, the toothpick two-stepping from one side of his mouth to the other.

"Because you're talking to me," I said, my vision darting between the old sheriff's face and my worried friend.

"I just need to ask you a few things before you go home with your parents. Is that OK?"

"I guess," I said, looking up to my mother. She returned a stern look along with a slow nod of her head. "It's OK with me."

"Good. So, I overheard you say a little while ago to the fine reporter lady that you were being chased. Is that right?"

"Chased?" I said, looking over to Brian. A look of concern wallpapered his face.

"That is what you—"

And just like a spring shower appearing in the sky out of nowhere, my eyes sprung a leak. I was consumed with so much guilt and anxiety and worry that I couldn't contain the wrestling emotions. The spring shower of tears quickly transformed into a full-on thunderstorm.

Sheriff Hill was caught off guard by my unabashed display of emotion. He patted me on the shoulder—his face turning the color of fresh tomatoes—then handed my mother a business card he pulled from his breast pocket.

"Maybe it's too soon to speak to your son," he said to my mom, clearing a fresh loogy from his throat, then swallowing it. The toothpick danced a jig back to the other side of his mouth. He pulled another card from his pocket as well as a black pen. "If I could have your home number, then I'll call you in a matter of days. My contact information is on my card."

My mother recited our home telephone number to the sheriff, who dutifully scribbled it on the back of the card, then inserted the card in his breast pocket.

"Good day, ma'am," he said, lifting his cowboy hat ever so slightly, tilting his head in a conciliatory fashion. He repeated the friendly tilt to my step-dad. "Sir."

He quickly left the marina, followed close behind by Deputy Gonzalez, which had the effect of pulling a stopper from a full bath; the rest of the boaters milling about slowly filed out, too, as well as Cokey Ramirez and the TV news crew.

My step-dad leaned close to my mother. "Maybe we should take Billy home."

"Good idea," she replied, then patted my shoulder. "Ready to go home, dear?"

I pulled up the front of my shirt to wipe my blubbering face, then noticed my friends receiving similar looks from their parents (time to go!) and the last of the onlookers: Tony and Victoria along with their parents. I wanted to say goodbye to my friends and conceded as much to my mother. She obliged me with a nod. So, I gave quick hugs to Brian and Miguel.

"See you tomorrow?"

"Yeah!" they said. It was wishful thinking on my part. Little did I know we would all be grounded the next day, to varying degrees of punishment and lengths of time. I would get the worst of it.

Then came my goodbyes for Tony and Victoria. I hugged them both.

"Thanks for helping to rescue us."

"Right on, little dude," Tony said. He patted me on the back.

"Maybe we'll see you around again," Victoria said.

"That would be so coooool," I said.

Then my mother put her arm around me and escorted me out to our family car. I got in the backseat of our silver 1984 Honda Accord and watched the marina shrink into the distance as we drove home to Converse, Texas.

28.

Little did I know that my coveted prize for being rescued from a deserted island in the middle of Canyon Lake was a sentence of solitary confinement for the rest of the summer. My parents forbade me from seeing any of my friends, watching TV, talking on the telephone, or riding my bike. I was to stay in my room and think about what I did and the pain I caused my parents as well as the other parents, every day until it was time to go back to school. And I did think about that just a little, but the rest of the time in my room was dedicated to drawing cartoons, writing stories, and reading comic books. In that sense, being sentenced to solitary confinement wasn't half bad. In fact, I rather liked sitting in my room while I drew, wrote, and read to my heart's content. I did miss my friends, but it could've been much worse. I knew I would see them eventually, and I had whatever I wanted to eat and drink whenever I wanted it. It wasn't all bad. Much better than being stuck on that goddamn island, if you'd asked me. But still, I was grounded. My parents were always the strictest during the first week of a grounding, especially the first day or so. But once the week went on and they became distracted by their own bullshit, their watchful eyes wandered and they pretty much left me alone after that.

The following Monday while Steve was at work and my mother was grocery shopping, Brian paid me a quick visit. He rode his bike to my house as fast as he could because he wanted to let me know that Randy was OK and that he was recovering at home. He received antivenom at the hospital soon after the helicopter landed and was sent home after staying one night in the intensive care unit. Being so young and strong also helped his speedy recovery. I was relieved to know he didn't die, which was my worst fear. I didn't see Randy for the rest of the summer because he told Brian his mother was taking him to his grandparents' house in Louisiana, where he would stay until school started again in September. He told me all this while we ate an entire package of Double-stuffed Oreos in my room while my parents were away.

"My parents say Shreveport is a dump and filled with racists," Brian said while patting his auburn Afro with one hand and shoving an Oreo into his mouth with the other. He was always patting his Afro, even though its shape never changed. He wiped his mouth with the back of his free hand after he swallowed his cookie.

"I see. How's Miguel?"

He fished in the package for another cookie, but they were gone. "Good. He told me his parents are making his brother join the army. The jerk deserves worse than that, though."

"Totally," I agreed, but quickly pivoted to more important matters. "Want a vanilla Drumstick?"

"Can't. I gotta go to Sheila's house."

"Sheila?" I said, quite shocked at the unexpected sound of a girl's name. Since when did Brian talk about girls? And why was she more important than eating ice cream with one of his best friends? "Who's that?"

"*Oh, oh, Sheila,*" he sang, then jumped up and attempted a goofy dance move. "*Let me love you till the morning comes.*"

We both laughed as I knew the popular song he was singing by the R & B group Ready for the World, or at least tried to sing. He quickly left on his bike afterwards without saying who Sheila was or where he met her or how attractive she was, although I learned later that summer that he was sneaking out of The Mansion late at night and into Sheila's house, where he loved her till the morning came—just like the song said. To this day, whenever I hear the song *Oh Sheila*, I think of Brian and the mysterious girl who he had clandestine intercourse with, under the roof of her unsuspecting parents' house. This was just the beginning of many bad decisions for Brian concerning girls and women.

Miguel kept in contact with me that summer by mailing letters he typed using *WordPerfect* on his Apple IIe personal computer, then printed on a dot matrix printer. He confirmed what Brian had told me about his brother, Rogelio, and by the end of the summer, that jerk was stationed at Lackland Air Force Base for six weeks of basic training in the blistering Texas sun, although the bit about the army was incorrect. He enlisted in the Air Force instead, as was his father's bidding. I never saw Rogelio again. And I wouldn't see Miguel in person until the first day of school. But I did enjoy his neatly typed, lengthy letters about his specific fascination with history. I got about one a week in the mail. He was busy studying the history of benevolent and malevolent rulers as well as prophets and a variety of religious saviors. He was branching out his knowledge of history and wanted to tell me all about it. Typical Miguel stuff.

He also used the letters to confess secrets like a Catholic used Confession with a priest to shed the guilt from sin. One of the secrets he revealed was his father was the reason the helicopter and soldier saved us from Sometimes Island, being that the helicopter pilot from Randolph Air Force Base owed him a favor. Turns out the pilot was caught drinking and driving one night on the military base by an M. P. (that stands for military police) and when he was taken into the base police station, he begged the commander for leniency, as he didn't want to lose his position as a pilot. Turns out the M. P. commander was Miguel's father. So, when Miguel's father learned where we were stranded and that it was a treacherous place for us to be, he called in his favor to the troubled helicopter pilot who was obliged to help. In the letter, Miguel begged me not to tell anyone about what his father pulled off and I never did, until now. Funny how the world works.

A couple of weeks after my parents brought me home from Canyon Lake, Sheriff Samuel "Sam" Hill paid me a visit. I wasn't told in advance that he was coming. My mother just stuck her head in my room unannounced—as she was prone to do—and blurted it out while I sat on the floor with all my precious belongings spread out around me.

"Someone is here to see you, dear," she said sharply. "Make yourself presentable."

"Who is it?" I said, standing then closing the fly on my jeans.

"Sheriff Hill."

I felt my face scrunch. "Who's Sheriff Hill?"

"From the lake," she said, then opened the door to my room. "Here he is."

"Oh."

I had completely forgotten all about Sheriff Samuel "Sam" Hill, as was standard operating procedure for a boy my age and with such a limited attention span. But once he appeared in my room with his very recognizable features—bristle broom mustache, tanned leather skin, baseball mitt-sized hands, tan and brown uniform, dancing toothpick in his mouth—the memory of who he was, and what he wanted, quickly dislodged from the swamp of my distracted mind. When he entered my room with his cowboy hat in his hand and pressed to his chest, he nodded to my mother, then she closed the door.

"Howdy," he said to me, then scanned my room. He wasn't wearing his sunglasses this time, exposing his penetrating, dirt-colored eyes. Finding a chair at my desk, he extended his large hand to it. "Do you mind if I sit?"

I shook my head. He pulled the chair around and sat down. He motioned for me to sit down on the floor, so I did. His ominous presence in my room made the hairs on the back of my neck stand up. He smelled of cigarettes, coffee, and gun oil. He looked around, first at all the things scattered on the floor, then at the pictures I had taped to the walls. He chuckled.

"This is a boy's paradise," he said, rubbing his stubbly chin. The toothpick in his mouth danced back and forth on his chapped lips. "You like living here with your parents?"

"Yessir," I quickly responded.

"That's good. That's good," he said. "You like comic books?"

"Yessir." As you can see, my answers became stuck in a broken groove, like a scratched LP record under a bouncing needle. Anxiety will do that to a boy.

"I liked comic books, too, when I was a young boy. Superman was my favorite. Where was it he liked to go?" Sheriff Hill swept a hand across his bald crown, smoothing down a few wild strands, then he placed his cowboy hat back on his head where it belonged. "The Fortress of..."

I was shocked at the quick turn of events. A grizzly, old lawman discussing comic books with me in my room? It was unfathomable! My own mother didn't even attempt to discuss comic books with me. How strange.

He continued. "Solitude! That's it. My old brain still works as it should. Sometimes, anyway. The Fortress of Solitude. You like Superman?"

"Yessir," I said, even though Superman wasn't my favorite hero. He was kind of hokey to me and my friends. He was old-fashioned, just like the sheriff.

"Do you have a favorite hero? And don't say *yessir* again, son. I can see you're being polite."

I lowered my head and rubbed my neck. A dozen or more comic books were fanned out on the floor in front of me, in plain view of the sheriff. I felt he already knew my answer to the question.

"Spider-Man. He's my favorite."

"*Spider-Man, Spider-Man. Does whatever a spider can*," he sang with his gravelly voice, then chuckled. "Figures. Do you mind if I ask you a few questions?"

I slowly nodded. What else was I supposed to do?

"Do you know a boy named Billy Callahan?"

I felt a twist in my gut, an awful malicious twist from an evil spirit. I didn't know what to say, so I just stared back at Sheriff Hill. Bloody Billy's ugly face appeared in my mind's eye, staring back at me.

"He went to Robert E. Lee High School. Worked at the sporting goods store last spring. Volunteered at the American Legion on Saturdays helping disabled veterans. Everyone says he was a good kid."

Good kid? I thought. *Since when was Bloody Billy a* good *kid?*

"He's missing. Has been for a while, at least since the time you were out on the godforsaken Sometimes Island with your friends. What are their names?"

I blurted out an answer like an obedient dog. "Randy, Brian, and Miguel."

Sheriff Hill adjusted his hat while I watched the toothpick shuffle back and forth in his gash of a mouth. His bristle broom mustache swept the top of the toothpick.

"That's correct. Randy, Brian, and Miguel. They told me Billy supposedly followed you out to the Meyer lake house. Is that true?"

You talked to Randy, Brian, and Miguel? I thought. *Uh oh.*

"Am I in trouble?" I said, my voice trembling.

"Why would you be in trouble, son?"

I looked down at my comic books, rubbing my neck some more.

"I don't know."

"I'm just trying to find this boy, Billy Callahan. You understand?"

"Yessir."

The sheriff hawked a loogie from deep in his throat, then swallowed it back down. "Why did you go to the Meyer lake house? Did you run away from your parents?"

"No sir," I said. I felt every nerve in my body poke through my skin, exposed to the world.

"You see," I began, sensing the relief that would come if I just told the sheriff the truth. I cleared my throat. "You see, we found Billy's backpack one day after school."

"You *found* it?" he said, more interested now. He sat up and adjusted his cowboy hat. "Did it have anything in it?"

"Well, to be honest, it had money in it and—"

"Money, you say? How much money we talkin' about? Twenty dollars?"

"Well..."

"Fiddy dollars?"

I stammered. "More like a couple thousand."

"A couple thousand?!" he blurted. The toothpick was breakdancing at this point. The sheriff's raised eyelids revealed the yellow of his eyes, stained from years of arduous public service. "And do you think Billy knew you had his backpack?"

I didn't respond.

"Sounds like you didn't find it. In some parts of this great state of ours, they would say you *stole* Billy's backpack."

"Stole it?" I said. This was a shocking development to me.

"That's right. Why didn't you give it back to him?"

"Well, you see," I continued, swallowing a gob of spit first. "He bullied me and my friends. He threatened to—"

"Bullied, huh?" The sheriff pulled the toothpick from his mouth and flipped it around. He slowly inserted the unchewed end back into the chapped slit under his mustache. "I see."

I turned my gaze down to my comic books. On the cover of one, Spider-Man was being choked by none other than The Lizard. I felt the muscles in my neck constrict my esophagus.

"Billy got spotless references. You see, I asked around. Do you understand?"

I nodded.

"Okay, so you *found* Billy's backpack and didn't give it back to him. So, then what did you do with it?" He leered at me, his dirty eyes illuminated. "Tell me the truth."

I racked my brain for the next course of events. I became light-headed.

"Well, you see. I called that boy Tony who works at the marina up at the lake."

"Canyon Lake Marina?"

"Yessir."

"The boy who works for his parents?"

"Yessir."

"Why'd you call him?"

"To come pick up me and my friends and take us to the old lake house."

"And you took the backpack with you?"

"Yessir."

The sheriff inhaled deeply. "I see. And did you pay Tony any money from this backpack you may have stole?"

I didn't answer right away. I searched his dirt-colored eyes for any sign of hostility or judgment, but I didn't find any. He just looked at me the way you look at an instruction manual for an appliance.

"Maybe. I can't remember."

"And you realize that the Meyer lake house is private property. In some places, they would say you were trespassing."

"But it's abandoned!"

The sheriff's eyebrows slowly raised.

"Son, don't you raise your voice at me," he said, wagging an indignant finger. "That's not polite."

I looked at the floor. "Yessir."

"So, let me get this straight," the sheriff began, then rubbed his chin, the toothpick jabbing at the heavens. "You and your friends took a stolen backpack to private property, then broke in?"

"The back door was open..."

"No matter. That's still illegal entry. How did Billy find you?"

"I don't know. He just showed up and threatened to beat us up."

"Because you had his backpack?"

"Yessir."

"So, then what'd you do?" He leaned back in the chair, splayed his legs, then adjusted his pant waist.

"We ran away from him and got in a boat."

"A boat? Where'd you find a boat?"

"At the end of the pier. Tony brought it."

The sheriff leaned forward. "So, you and your friends got in a boat. Then what?"

"We started it and tried to get away."

"Did Billy get in the boat with you?"

"No, he jumped in the water as we pulled away."

"And that's when you went out to Sometimes Island?"

"Well..." I began, then stopped. The events of that day riffled through my mind in no discernible order. "We didn't want to go to the island. It was an accident. We crashed into a rock."

"And Billy? Did he swim out to the island?"

"He tried to. I saw him in the water. Then he disappeared."

The sheriff sat up, stiffening his back. "He disappeared in the water? You're saying he drowned?"

"I don't know."

At this point, without warning, my eyes sprung a leak. Again, just like at the marina. Then with the initial appearance of tears, a wellspring of emotions burst out. I sobbed profusely. The sheriff sighed, then roughly cleared his throat. He unbuttoned his left shirt pocket and pulled out a handkerchief, then handed it to me.

"Calm down, son. I'm not here to make you cry. Just asking questions."

"Am I in trouble, mister?" I said, words wedged between sobs and gasps for air.

"No, no, you're not in trouble. I'm just trying to find that boy, Billy Callahan." He unbuttoned his right shirt pocket, the one under his shiny badge, and pulled out a Dum Dum lollipop, then handed it to me. "I was saving this for my grandson, but I think I'd prefer you have it right now. Pretty gal at the bank drive-thru gave it to me. You like lollipops?"

I nodded, then wiped my snotty nose with my forearm.

"Who doesn't?" he quipped, then chuckled. "You understand I'm just doing my job, right?"

I nodded.

"So, what's with the water works?"

"Well..." I started, then snuffled. "I guess I was trying to tell you he bullied me and my friends."

"Of course. Boys will be boys."

"And he beat us up behind the 7-Eleven after school one day when we were getting Slurpees."

"Boys be roughhousin' all the time."

I looked down at the lollipop in my hand. I twirled it between my thumb and forefinger, reading the brown lettering on the wrapper. It was root beer flavored: my favorite. I looked up at the sheriff who uncrossed his legs and sat back in the chair.

"You see, Billy Callahan is just a boy, just like you. And he got a mama that loves him, just like you. His mama is worried sick, just like yours would be if you went missin'. He's somebody's son. You understand, don't ya?"

"Yessir."

"Good."

We stared at each other for what seemed like forever, his gaze on me, steady as I imagined his shooting stance to be. His eyes penetrated my thin skin. I knew he knew something about me, but he didn't have to say anything. He just knew.

"Welp," he said, then stood up, lifting his cowboy hat slightly, tilting his head forward as a salutation. "Thanks for your time. I hope you enjoy that lollipop. I like strawberry, personally. Reminds me of when I was a boy. Good day."

He opened the door to my room and turned to me before leaving.

"You remind me of my grandson. Sensitive. Soft-hearted." He smiled. "Be good, ya hear? If you think of anything else, tell your mom to give me a call."

Then he left my room, closing the door behind him. I heard my mother chatting with him, even laughing at what I imagined were his cowpoke jokes. Heavy footsteps. The sound of a door closing. Light footsteps to my room. My mother slowly opened my door.

"You doing okay?" she said, looking somewhat concerned.

"Yeah."

"Do you want me to make you a microwave burrito?"

"No."

"Okay. I'll check on you in a bit after Steve gets home from work. I love you."

"I love you, too."

She closed the door.

I looked at the empty chair where the sheriff sat, the indention from his rump still in the vinyl seat. I could still smell him. His presence lingered in my room like a somber ghost or the dense haze from a smoldering cigar. I unwrapped the lollipop and placed it on my tongue, twirling it around in my mouth with my index finger and thumb. The saliva in my mouth took on the delicious flavor of the candy. I enjoyed receiving the unexpected treat, but not enough to forgive

Sheriff Hill for the way he treated me. And in my own room of all places! I became emboldened in his absence. I raised my profane middle finger in the air, aiming it defiantly to the universe.

"You're the dum dum!" I said, then wiped my wet nose with my forearm.

I picked up a piece of paper with a scene I had been coloring before Sheriff Hill came into my room. It was an elaborate fight scene I penciled between Spider-Man and my favorite nemesis to the teenaged web crawler: Doctor Octopus. I colored the scene late into the night, then went to bed without eating dinner.

29.

The rest of the summer ground along like beach sand in the seat of your bathing suit. Although sitting in my room and drawing comics was fun, its luster soon wore off. For some, routine can be stifling, even when that routine involves your favorite things in the world. I missed riding my bike around my neighborhood and just—you know—being outside. I missed my freedom that I took for granted before the misadventure, before experiencing real-life danger while stranded on an island without food or water. The funny thing was, once my parents brought me home from the Canyon Lake Marina and sentenced me to solitary confinement in my bedroom for the rest of the summer, they didn't mention my time on Sometimes Island again—for something like two decades. And even when they did mention it again much later when my wife and I were raising our own rascally children, they made it sound like I was off at summer camp somewhere, sleeping comfortably at night in air-conditioned cabins under the watchful eyes of camp counselors. So weird. But that summer when I was stuck in my room, that was a tough one.

And I missed my friends: all of them. I enjoyed the occasional clandestine visits from Brian, but they were few and far between. The letters from Miguel were much appreciated, but they didn't replace seeing his goofy face in person, and listening to the new things he learned about some ancient rulers who were supreme jerks to their lowly kingdoms. I hate to admit it, being that I loved all my friends, but I missed Randy the most. Maybe it was because he was in a different state that summer, rotting away at his grandmother's house in Louisiana. Or maybe it was because he almost died out there on Sometimes Island, and that was on me, since it was my idea to sneak away to the abandoned lake house. Sheriff Hill did a pretty damn good job of seeding my young mind with sinister doubts about my *motivations*. Maybe I was actually a bad kid after all, as he seemed to suggest, sitting in my room and intimidating a kid like me. Or I was just too stupid to understand the consequences of the choices I made in middle school. Who is wise enough in middle school to understand the choices they make, and how they affect others? Nobody.

Sitting in my room all summer with my guilty conscience did a number on me and, for the first time in my young life, I looked forward to the first day of school like it was Christmas morning. I couldn't wait to get out of my dreadful house, ride my BMX bike to school, and see my three friends again. On the morning of the first day of school, I met my friends in our usual meeting place at the front under the pecan tree. It's where we always met and I was pretty certain they would be there. At least two of them were there when I walked up: Brian and Miguel.

"Hey guys!" I blurted. I was so excited to see them. It was like no time had passed since seventh grade ended the previous spring.

"Hey dude!" Brian said. He was munching on a strawberry Pop Tart. Typical.

Miguel eyed him as he ate it. "You gonna eat both of them?"

"Yeah."

Miguel licked his lips. "You sure?"

"Where's Randy?" I said, looking around for my friend.

"He's trying out for foothh-ball. He'll be over in a bit-thh," Brian mumbled, his mouth full of pastry.

"Football?" I said. Something told me this was not good news.

"Yup," Miguel added. "He wants to be a jock and get all the chicks."

"You don't need to be a jock to get chicks," Brian retorted, visibly annoyed with Miguel's theory. "You just need to be smoooooth."

I burst into laughter. "*Oh, oh Sheila!*" I sang.

But Brian wasn't amused, returning a grim look. "I've moved on from Sheila."

"But—"

"Parents sent her to boarding school," Brian added. He wadded the Pop Tart wrapper into a tiny ball, then shoved it into his backpack. "And she's *not* coming back."

"What time does the assembly start?" Miguel said, looking at a brand new Casio digital wristwatch.

"Assembly?" I said.

"Nine o'clock. Get with the program," Brian quipped. "Jokers."

Just then, Randy trotted over, wearing practice football gear, a damp jersey without a number on it, and a football helmet in one hand. His skin glistened with sweat and his face flushed.

"Word up!" he said, happy to see us. "Anybody else trying out for the team?"

"Nah," Brian said. "I got more important things to do."

"Like what?"

"*Things.*"

Randy turned to me, still panting from tryouts. "You should try out for football. We can be on the same team."

"I'm not good at football, or sports in general," I said, looking down at the asphalt ground. I kicked a pebble with the toe of my canvas shoe. "Is there an art team?"

"That's funny!" Randy blurted, then guffawed.

"I'm starting a history club," Miguel said. "You should join my club."

"I don't know," I said.

"We could use an illustrator for our history reports," Miguel added.

"Hmmm. Sounds interesting."

Then the bell rang. All the kids outside, hundreds of them, shuffled slowly to the main building to go inside.

Randy put his helmet back on. "I'm going to change. I'll meet you at the assembly. Save me a seat!"

He ran to the gym while Miguel, Brian, and I slowly walked toward the school entrance.

"If he makes the football team, we'll never see him again," Brian said. "Stupid."

"Totally," I agreed.

Inside the school, we were corralled with all the students—some faces familiar, many new—through the halls to the auditorium / cafeteria. Most of the time, it was the cafeteria with row after row of eating tables. But this morning, rows of plastic chairs were configured to face the stage at the far end of the enormous room. On the stage sat a wooden podium—the school mascot (a shrieking eagle) emblazoned on the front—where the school principal would give his annual "state of the union" address to all the students and faculty. I could think of a million better ways to spend our morning than listening to Mr. David Roosevelt (no relation to our school namesake Franklin D. Roosevelt, just a weird coincidence) spew chunks about school spirit and shit like that, but we didn't have a choice in the matter. The three of us sat toward the back. Brian saved a seat for Randy, his backpack keeping the seat for him.

"I hope he shows up soon. I can't keep this seat for long."

"He'll be here," I assured Brian. "He wouldn't miss this exciting event."

"So exciting!" Miguel said. The three of us chuckled.

We watched the entirety of the school meander in while the principal manned the podium, waiting for all seats to be taken, rifling through index cards with copious notes on them. Randy appeared out of thin air, storming the row where we sat, almost tumbling our chairs over.

"Thanks for the seat, turd burglars!" He panted like an overheated Labrador Retriever, still sweaty even though he showered.

After a few more minutes, the principal turned on the microphone, then rapped it with a knuckle. The amplified knock reverberated through the auditorium, quieting the din of the students discussing who they made out with over the summer or if the cafeteria food would improve this year.

The principal roughly cleared his throat, then swept a loose clump of hair back onto his thinning pate. "Good morning students of F. D. R. Middle School. As you may or may not know, my name is Mr. Roosevelt—" The entirety of the student body sniggered, to the principal's consternation. "Still not sure why that's funny. Anyway, I would like to welcome you back for this glorious school year of 1986 – 87!"

A smattering of applause. Some whispering.

"And to all the incoming sixth graders: Welcome! I know you'll feel at home in no time and harness the eagle spirit. Go Eagles!"

More limp applause, accompanied by a whoop and a high-pitched whistle.

Randy leaned over to me. "I'm already bored!" he whispered through pursed lips.

"Me too!"

Mr. Roosevelt pressed on. "I have a lot of things to announce including information about cheerleader tryouts and an update on nuclear disaster drills. But before I get into all that, I have a quick announcement I'd like to make."

The din of the students' chatter returned and I could make out the collective curiosity.

The principal continued. "Over the summer, I was awestruck by a news story about four boys who were stranded out on an island in the middle of Canyon Lake..."

With the unexpected mention of the lake, I immediately felt a twist in my gut as if a mystical creature shoved its hand down my throat and gripped my stomach in its clenched fist. I looked to my three friends who obviously were accosted by the same mystical creature. Their faces were wide with surprise. And embarrassment.

"These four, brave boys were stranded on a little island for days on end without food or water. One of them was even bitten by a poisonous snake, until they were saved by a military helicopter. And I just wanted to acknowledge these four boys—your fellow students—and welcome them back to F. D. R. Middle School, safe and sound."

The auditorium erupted into applause, but I don't think most of the kids were aware of who he was referring to. Many heads swiveled on curious necks; many faces looked for the honored students.

"The four boys, please come up here on the stage with me. William Flynn, Randy Moss, Brian Johnson, and Miguel Gonzalez!"

And that's when all eyes turned to us, to the collective sound of plastic chair feet rubbing against cheap floor tile. We were no longer ghosts in that school. Everyone was looking at us. Us—of all people. The cheering began. Then hooting. Then clapping. We stood up, beaming red from the sudden attention. I made my way out of the aisle, sidestepping made difficult with my limp leg, my backside rubbing against other seated students. My three friends followed close behind. I limped down the middle of the auditorium with my friends behind me while the entire student body cheered and clapped, even called out our names. It was like we landed on the moon or discovered the cure for cancer. It was, I thought to myself, an odd thing for me and my friends to be praised for: our collective stupidity. We hopped on the stage and Mr. Roosevelt directed us with a stiff arm to stand in a line next to the podium, and motioned for us to look at our audience of peers.

"Let's give these boys a round of applause!"

And applaud they did, raucously for a couple of minutes, the entire school cheered for us, stomped their feet even, a seance for the ghostly seventh graders to emerge as revered eighth graders. Fellow classmates. Survivors. Heroes. Once Mr. Roosevelt felt we had enough of his allotted time, he commanded the kids to quiet down, pushing down the air in front of him to quell their enthusiasm.

He turned and smiled. "Welcome back, boys. Glad you're safe. You may return to your seats." He motioned again with a stiff arm for us to exit the stage.

We hopped down, then returned to our seats at the back of the auditorium, receiving high and low fives from seated students all along the length of the middle aisle.

Mr. Roosevelt roughly cleared his throat again, then leaned to the microphone. "Okay, where was I?" he started, rewinding in his mind the prepared outline for his assembly speech. "Oh, yes! Cheerleading tryouts."

Back at our seats, we gave each other fist bumps and hand slaps. I remember thinking to myself, amidst all the adulation that morning, that things would be different for us from that day forward. I couldn't have been more right about that.

***

Here's the thing about adulation for an introvert: it's kryptonite. After about an hour of stares from strange students and congratulatory handshakes from grinning teachers, I was ready to cover myself in the sheet of anonymity that a ghostly wallflower like me enjoyed so much. Being anonymous is only truly appreciated after it's gone. I guess if I learned anything that day, it was this: I didn't want to be famous. If that morning standing in front of the entire student body taught me anything, it was that being famous was for suckers. Privacy was where it was at. By the end of third period, I was ready to return to being a ghost at Franklin D. Roosevelt Middle School.

After school, I unlocked my bike, shoved the chain and combination lock in my new backpack (nylon, blue, water resistant), and waited for my friends at the bike rack, straddling my bike, ready to go home and eat a snack, maybe a Little Debbie chocolate cake or something salty. After a few minutes, Randy joined me, his football helmet under his arm, a large duffle bag slung over his shoulder, and sweat streaming down his face.

"You make the team?" I said.

He tossed the duffle bag on the ground and hung the helmet on one of the bike handles. "Yup. Varsity. Coach wants me as defensive tackle. He says I will destroy running backs."

"That's coooool!"

"Practice starts tomorrow morning at 6:30am."

"Six thirty?!" I said. "I don't even wakeup that early."

"You guys might be riding to school without me. Sorry."

"That'll be weird."

"I know," he said. He slung his duffle bag over his shoulder, then pulled his bike off the rack and parked it next to me. "We'll still eat lunch together, right?"

I nodded. "Definitely."

Brian and Miguel soon joined us.

"I got three girls' phone numbers today," Brian said. "That's radical!"

"Really?" I said.

"Yeah! Getting stuck on that island has boosted my popularity. Girls are throwing themselves at me!"

"Calm down, Romeo," Miguel said, rolling his eyes. "You gonna get crabs on your hairy beanbag."

The three of us cackled to Brian's dismay. He looked at his crotch, then whipped his head up defiantly.

"Nah!" he said. "Ain't gonna happen."

"Mmm hmm," Miguel replied. "Better wrap your love sausage so your meatballs don't get infested."

Brian and Miguel unlocked their bikes, then placed them next to me and Randy.

"Ready?" I said.

"Ready!" they all said.

I mounted my bike and pedaled as fast as I could. My friends followed.

We made our way down the sidewalk that wrapped around the two blacktop basketball courts and two tennis courts, until the sidewalk ended and turned into a gravel path. We followed the path into the wooded area behind F. D. R. until we came to the clearing where we always met, so we could hangout for a little while before going home. It was the same clearing where we were accosted by Bloody Billy and the Thousand Oaks Gang last spring. The set of bleachers was still there in what seemed like the same spot, sitting in patches of tall grass and sticker burrs, a few crushed beer cans strewn about. I rode around the left side of the bleachers, then jumped off my bike and watched it careen into the surrounding brush.

"Bullseye!" Randy cheered.

"Two points!" I belted out.

"That was awesome."

"Why didn't you jump off yours?"

"It's a new bike. I don't want it messed up."

"Ah," I replied, a little jealous of his new bike.

Brian, Miguel, and Randy dropped their bikes where they stood, and Randy jumped up on the bleachers to entertain us.

"Want to hear a joke?" he said, clapping his hands to encourage us to respond. "It's a dirty one!"

"Yeah!" the rest of us said.

"All right, all right! Gather round," he said, indicating for us to get closer. "I don't want to say it too loud cause it's really dirty."

Brian, Miguel, and I returned sadistic smiles.

Randy cleared his throat. "OK. What's lumpy, brown, and slimy all—"

Brian interrupted his comedy routine, pointing at something in the brush. "Hey! What's that?"

Randy turned to look. "What's what?"

"There in the bushes."

"Shit, I don't know," Randy said, then hopped off the bleachers and walked over to investigate.

We curiously followed him. He stepped into the tall grass, then leaned over. When he stood back up, he was holding a red backpack. It looked like it had been left outside for quite some time and been dowsed by a few thunderstorms, maybe peed on by a dog or two. He pulled it close to his face as if to sniff it, then jerked his arm stiff and as far from his face as possible.

"Eww! It stinks!" he said, then dropped the backpack.

The three of us stared at it for a moment or two. Dead silence. Not even the wind whistled. And I was certain we collectively thought of last spring, and the time we ran from the Thousand Oaks Gang, then hid in the culvert. We looked at each other, all our eyebrows lifting like repulsed caterpillars. It was clear we had all come to the same conclusion.

"I'm not picking it up!" I said, shaking my head.

"Me neither!" Brian said.

"Then leave it," Miguel suggested. "I gotta get home anyway. I have a lot to do for History Club."

"History Club? Did you get permission to start it?" I said, leading my friends away from the brush and back to our bikes.

"Yeah," Miguel said, mounting his bike. "The principal said it was cool. Better get your bike."

"Oh yeah!" I said, then ran back into the brush, where I released my bike. When I came back out with it, my friends were all waiting for me. "Hey Randy?!"

He turned to me. "Yeah?"

"Will you finish that joke tomorrow at lunch?"

"Yeah, dude!"

"Coooool," I said, then mounted my bike.

We rode away, leaving the stinky backpack behind for someone else to find. We had had enough adventure already for that year. For all of us, it was enough for a lifetime.

PART V.

Legacy of the Benevolent Lords of Sometimes Island

30.

I wish I had another crazy adventure from middle school to tell you about, but I don't. The rest of the eighth grade was pretty uneventful, kind of like watching an old dog take a nap. There were fits and starts of excitement, but nothing too crazy or dangerous happened. We weren't bullied by the Thousand Oaks Gang anymore. With the disappearance of Bloody Billy and Rogelio's nascent military career, that terror organization pretty much disbanded. All for the better, if I say so myself. The world was a much better place without the assholes that made up that gang of bullies. They never did find Bloody Billy's body in Canyon Lake. The Comal County Sheriff Department claimed to have trolled the body of the lake—using a team of scuba divers and the best sonar technology—but he wasn't to be found. My younger self imagined Sheriff Hill standing out on the pier by the Cabin of Seclusion, looking southwesterly as the team of divers brought up a whacky collection of sunken treasure like rubber boots covered in algae, rusty metal anchors, and slimy car tires. My older self knew their hunt was probably less comical and much more somber. Rogelio never returned to Converse, as the military shipped him off to Arizona, where he spent dozens of years as a mechanic for a variety of planes and trucks. The Thousand Oaks Gang simply disintegrated. But the disappearance of

Bloody Billy continued to haunt me for years to come. I'll get into that later.

Randy, Miguel, Brian, and I remained friends for the rest of the eighth grade, but "thick as thieves" did not describe us anymore by the end of middle school. Our personal obsessions kept all of us from being together all at once, and by the time high school came around, we got together less and less. That's the natural order of things as adolescents become full-blown teenagers. It wasn't anything personal between us, nor was it for a lack of effort. We simply became entrenched in our hobbies, school activities, and our own selves. Randy was the star defensive tackle on the varsity football team at Robert E. Lee High School. Miguel was the President of the History Club and Debate Team. Brian dropped out of the Boys Scouts and focused all his attention on girls. And me... well, I still wanted to be an artist, or a writer. And you know what that means? A lot of time alone. Being alone suited my introversion to the detriment of my friendships. Luckily for me, my friends didn't give up while I wasn't around. Good friends will do that—they stick with you.

As I said, Randy was the star defensive tackle at Lee High School and all his time was spent at practices—before and after school—as well as games on the weekends. That was just in the fall. In the spring, he attended football camps, morning and nights. Summers, too. He was a full-on athletic star, and I rarely ever saw him in person. Every once and a while, like a fool, I would attend a Friday night football game and watch my friend from the stands as he destroyed the opposing team's offensive players. Randy was a giant compared to almost everyone else and he used his size to his advantage. By the end of high school, he was a highly sought-after college recruit and eventually chose the University of Texas at Austin as his team and college of choice, although I'm certain he didn't study at all. Randy wasn't the greatest student in the world. C minus average, at best. *But boy!* He sure could crush running backs and wide receivers. He was unstoppable, mostly.

After two years in college, Randy was recruited by the Houston Oilers, a move I heard he appreciated since he got to stay in Texas, but his career was short-lived. During his first season, it was discovered that Randy had an aggressive case of testicular cancer that had already metastasized to his bladder and kidneys when doctors initially diagnosed the pain in his groin and the blood in his urine. A year later, Randy passed away. His mother (who never remarried) buried him at the Converse Memorial Cemetery, a concrete statue of a football player in a similar pose to the Heisman Trophy (on bent knee, one leg straight back, the football tucked in the nook of one arm, the other arm straight-out defiantly) atop a marble base as his headstone. It seemed like an odd choice. While I attended his funeral, neither Brian or Miguel could make it. They had busy lives like most people, so I was the stand-in for our middle school group. I can't even begin to tell you about the immense sadness I felt for the loss of my friend. I was unbearably depressed for well over a year after his untimely passing. I wanted to do something meaningful to memorialize our friendship, although I couldn't think of anything at the time. Grief does that to you; it paralyzes you for a brief period of time before you grow as a person, becoming stronger and wiser. I still miss Randy to this day. I think about him all the time.

As for Brian, he traded in Boy Scout discipline for unabashed skirt chasing. I truly feel this was his way of rebelling against his parents and the aggressive way they corralled him to be an overachiever and entrepreneur. They just wanted the best for him, but Brian took it as something more domineering, even fascist. It's funny how life can take a turn after middle school. I would've predicted Randy and Brian on opposite trajectories. In high school, Brian did work at various stores and restaurants near our hood, but only as a means of making quick money so he could spend it on girls. The only time I spent time with Brian was between girlfriends, those ill-advised relationships usually didn't last for more than a few weeks. He collected girlfriends like I collected colored pencils and drafting pens. He was obsessed. In some ways, I don't blame him. Love can be intoxicating, although I think he was afflicted with a case of sex addiction. That's the insight my generation learned in the 80s and 90s. Men weren't cads anymore like in the 50s and 60s; they were addicted to sex. Semantics. Go figure.

Brian's girl problems followed him to the University of North Texas where he majored in liberal arts, a suggestion from his mother as a useful bachelor's degree as a leadup to law school. Brian quickly discovered he was as interested in liberal arts as a squirrel was interested in rocket science. He preferred getting his "nut" and incessantly chased female undergraduates, sometimes having three or four girlfriends at a time. But after a series of drunken hookups, venereal diseases, and bad breakups, Brian fled U. N. T., and went back to the confines of his parents' home. To Brian's surprise, his folks were kind and supportive. His father suggested Brian enlist in the Army—a thoughtful suggestion based on his understanding that Brian craved discipline, even though he hated to admit it—and to consider using his G. I. Bill entitlement to pursue a nursing degree. "Registered nurses are in high demand, they can fill prescriptions, and get paid a boatload of money," his father quipped. "You could be making six figures when you get out of the Army."

Brian ruminated over the suggestion for a few days, then agreed. The following week, he was off to boot camp. Looking back, that was one of the best decisions Brian made in his young adult life. He stayed in the Army longer than originally intended, convinced an Army commander to station him at Fort Sam Houston in San Antonio, Texas, and he worked at Brook Army Medical Center, the very hospital where Randy was flown to after we were rescued, so he could receive antivenom for his snake bite. Crazy, huh? Life can take a turn.

As for Miguel, his life worked out as predictably as you can imagine. He followed his passion for history and debate from middle school all the way through high school, where he captained the Robert E. Lee High School debate team and presided over the History Club all four years. He attended the University of Texas at Austin where he studied history on the Plan II track—another name for an honors degree—and even wrote an honors thesis on benevolent rulers throughout history. What else would you expect this particular benevolent lord to do? Miguel eventually found his way to Rice University, where he received his masters and his doctorate in history. And after all these years in academia, where did Miguel eventually land a tenure position to teach history? Harvard? Stanford? Nope. Trinity University in San Antonio, Texas, fourteen miles from our hometown of Converse. He wanted to teach Texas history to young Texans. Makes sense, right? The turns we take lead some of us back home.

And unlike Randy's unfortunate early demise or Brian's rough road to stability, Miguel's life was remarkable and unremarkable in equal measures. He got through all levels of school with honors, married his college sweetheart (I was his best man at the wedding), then settled down to start a career and a family at the same time. Nothing unseemly about my friend to report. Not that Randy or Brian's lives were uncouth, just more difficult, I guess. But that's the way it goes sometimes, as they say.

I even tried to keep up with Tony and Victoria over the years. I occasionally saw them the following summer, but not out at Canyon Lake. (Are you kidding me? My parents didn't *knowingly* allow me near the lake.) Sometimes, Tony would call me to see how I was doing, and give me the latest scoop on he and Victoria's future plans. I liked hearing him talk about her as she was my secret crush, but the more and more he talked about his true feelings for her, my crush eventually disintegrated. It's hard pining over someone when someone else you care about loves them. They would sometimes drive into town and I'd meet them at the arcade or ice cream shop or something like that. I enjoyed spending time with them. They had *plans*, man.

Their most precious plan was to get married right after high school and run away to Europe, far from the family businesses where they worked as indentured servants. Their parents insisted they run the respective businesses as soon as they graduated from high school so they could retire, but that just wasn't in Tony and Victoria's plans. The day after they graduated, they slipped away to the Bexar County Justice of the Peace to secretly be married. They could do that since they were both 18-years old. And the day after that, they drove to the San Antonio International Airport to catch a one-way flight to Ireland: their first stop in Europe. They had been saving money for a year to afford to go, all the while submitting the proper forms and identifications for their passports. Their clandestine plan worked perfectly; their parents had no idea. I wouldn't see them again for years, although I would occasionally receive postcards from them from various European countries, usually with Tony's favorite salutation scrawled in ballpoint ink. "What's up, ass bandit?" That always made me laugh.

I'm often asked if I had friends later on like the ones I had in middle school, and I find this question difficult to answer without sounding glib or hokey. I love my friends from middle school, just like I love the ones from high school, or college, or from my raging 20s, or the other parents I befriended when my wife and I had our own kids. I do look back on my time in middle school with fondness, and a bit of wonder, mostly at the amount of freedom we were given at the time. No devices to track us meant more freedom. It's a generational thing, I guess. But what I've learned as I've grown older is this: the best friends you'll ever have are the ones you have right now at this moment in time. That's the most solid piece of wisdom I can impart to you. Not that old friendships aren't more fun or more valuable or more important. They are important. But the friends who are with you right now—supporting you, cheering for you, loving you right now—those are the most important friends you'll ever have.

It just so happens, Brian and Miguel are still two of mine. And Tony and Victoria are another two. When I find good friends, I like to keep them, at least to the best of my abilities. Sometimes, your friends just leave you. I miss Randy. I have no doubt that we would still be friends today if he had survived cancer. I truly believe that.

31.

After middle school, I went on to Lee High School along with my friends and—while they had hobbies they pursued—I immersed myself in art and literature. I dreamed that one day I would be an artist, or maybe a writer, pouring my love for comic books and stories into my studies. The holy grail would have been living a life as both together, but I would've been happy doing either one. An artist's or writer's life was the one for me but, as is all too common, it just didn't happen. Don't get me wrong. I tried my damnedest to make it happen; it just didn't. Fizzled out may be a better way of putting it, because of other more pressing priorities. You see, I graduated from high school and went on to study art and literature at the University of North Texas—the same school as Brian, but I rarely ever saw him. Who I did see a lot of during my time there was my future wife—Melissa.

I met Melissa my freshman year at a local art show in downtown Denton, Texas. We hit it off pretty fast after we learned that we were both art students at U. N. T. My major was Graphic Design with an English minor. Hers was Ceramics with an Art History minor. Neither of us were destined to make loads of money. But we fell in love and were inseparable. On the day we graduated with big dreams of storming the creative world, Melissa learned we were pregnant. As careful as we tried to be, neither of us were to blame for our mutual lust for each other, and its possible biological outcome. We rolled the dice and came up with a baby. We discussed having the pregnancy aborted, but in the end, neither of us wanted that. Our love for each other made a baby and the baby won out. I'm glad we kept that baby. We moved to the city closest to both of our families: San Antonio, Texas. And eventually, we got married in the La Villita Historic Arts District next to the Riverwalk in downtown San Antonio. It was a magical day. Like I've said, sometimes life can take a turn and, with that turn, my dreams of an artsy work life were dashed.

I did my best to find meaningful work that paid well, but it was a slog. Many of the gigs were contract jobs without the benefits that come with full-time employment. Melissa had a girlfriend—Samantha was her name—whose husband was a government employee for Bexar County (the county where both San Antonio and Converse reside) in their tax appraisal unit. Samantha often bragged about the benefits he had and offered to put in a good word for me with her husband, if a position ever opened up. The spot that finally became available was nothing even remotely close to my college education: property tax compliance. But Samantha's husband—Bob was his name—promised me that all the position required was a college degree (*Any ol' degree will do*, he said at the time) and I would get trained on the job. *Easy peasy*, he said. The benefits were so good that I couldn't refuse. Melissa and I would soon be parents to a newborn. I had to do what was best for my new family. Plus, Bob and I became fast friends. That's a twofer, as they say. My life as an artist or writer soon took a backseat to my fledgling career as a government employee.

That was my life for many years. Eight to five, Monday through Friday. Weekly work routine set on repeat. But one thing I could never forget—no matter how the years rolled along or what new obstacles were put in our way—was my time at the Cabin of Seclusion with my friends and our misadventure being stuck on Sometimes Island. I would often daydream about our nights in the lake house or our time—

hungry and dirty as we were, at the brink of death—on the island, and found that as time went on, my time there became more precious. Isn't that strange? For anyone who has lived through a tough time in their life, those trying moments we survived delineate who we are as we grow older into the full beings we are to become. My wife has often told me, as I recount the strange yet dangerous adventure that me, Brian, Miguel, and Randy experienced out on Canyon Lake, that the biggest smile on my face accompanies my story, as if I'm telling her about the most wonderful time in my life. Oh, the things our bodies unconsciously reveal to our family and friends. And I guess that was true; it was a wonderful time in my life. I couldn't stop thinking about that damned lake house.

One day while I was sitting at a table in the break room during lunch—listening to Bob dissect the squares he bought for the previous weekend's football games and where he went wrong with his gambling strategy—I was eating a ham sandwich and I realized that an amicable agreement between Texas counties would allow me to lookup property tax records for other counties in addition to Bexar County. An example would be Comal County, the county where Canyon Lake resided, as well as the old Meyer lake house. A quick search on the internet provided me the address of the lake house, which I put into our tax records system. And *voila!* I had insight into years of tax records, who owned the property, if the taxes were paid or not, etc. I could voyeuristically watch an aspect of the Meyer family's life through electronic tax records. The property had multiple owners, probably the children or grandchildren of Griffin and Mary Meyer, and the property taxes had been promptly paid for decades. I could flag the property as one to watch for any changes or discrepancies, so I did. Whenever I was bored at work, I would login to the tax records system and read about the old Meyer lake house. Some people at work farted around by playing games of Solitaire on their computers, instead of actually working; I read about that lake house during my free time.

Some months later, my grandmother on my mother's side passed away. Well, I won't say that it was unexpected. She was rather old. But her death was a tragedy to our family nonetheless. She was a kooky woman with eccentric tendencies. She smoked cigarettes for 80 years and drank whiskey on the rocks every afternoon starting at 3:00 pm. She used to always tell me—while pinching my cheek or my butt—that I was her favorite. I didn't understand why she would tell me that because my mother was an only child and I was the only grandchild, so I must have been her favorite between me and my mother, which was weird. But a few weeks after her funeral, I learned that I inherited $500,000 from my eccentric grandmother, a sum of money that shocked me. My wife was ecstatic. My mother was irritated as her inheritance was much smaller, but our relationship fortunately wasn't tainted by my grandmother's unusual gift. Upon receiving advice from friends and financial advisors, it seemed the best place to invest my inheritance was either the stock market or real estate. I had experience investing in neither. There was a part of me that wanted to heed the advice of the smart ones around me, and another part of me that hoped for a sign—a mystical tap on the shoulder from the great beyond—that would inform me what to do. And, believe it or not, a mystical tap came in the form of a notification from the tax records system: the old Meyer lake house was available to purchase through a sheriff's sale.

Now, I know you may be thinking (or may even be skeptical that this happened in this fashion, but life is funny this way), *What the hell is a sheriff's sale?* You see, if multiple people own a property and they have a disagreement, like what to do with it or if to sell it, and they can't come to an agreement about what to do, then one of the owners can request a sheriff's sale. Let's say nine ungrateful children own a lake house that they all inherited from their kind parents. After years of disrepair and grief, four of the children want to sell it and five do not. Well, owning property isn't necessarily a democracy in the eyes of the government and the ones who want to sell don't simply lose out as the minority. All they have to do is call a sheriff's sale and the sheriff of the county will lock up the house and sell it at auction. So, if I was waiting for a mystical tap on the shoulder from the universe, then this was it. I did some quick research on how to win a property through an auction, informed my wife of the wise investment I was planning on making (she was onboard with it, fortunately), and arrived at the auction ten minutes early. I wasn't in any way, shape, or form going to lose this auction. I had my trusty checkbook and ballpoint pen ready. Property auctions require cash and my kind and generous grandmother (bless her smoky and pickled soul) provided just that. My only worry was being outbid by a richer investor, but that didn't happen. I was the only one to show up for the auction and bought the property for not much over the starting bid: $199,999. It was a done deal. The old Meyer lake house was mine. And good ol' Sheriff "Sam" Hill was nowhere to be found, because he died years before (natural causes, no big deal). I would know; I asked. One of the deputies told me, "Sheriff Hill. Good man. God bless him." So, there you go.

They say you can never go back to your youth. And I say, they're wrong. You can always go back to your youth—the places, the friends, the retraced adventures—but it really is never the same. Things change. That's the natural order of things. Maybe that's why they say you can never go back: the changing part. There's something to be said for that, I guess. The marina and the campground were gone. Tony and Victoria's parents sold them soon after they skipped town for their European elopement. The Canyon Lake Marina is now a Mexican restaurant / margarita bar (decent enchiladas, overpriced margaritas) and the land where the KOA campground sat nestled in trees is now a parking garage for the restaurant. Progress, they say. Bullshit, I say. The only thing in the whole area that had not changed one bit was the abandoned Meyer lake house, except it wasn't abandoned anymore. It was mine. I even christened the lake house with a new name: Cabin of Seclusion. I had the moniker cast in iron and installed above the entrance gate at the end of the drive out to the farm road. Now, that's what I call progress.

The first summer I owned the place, my wife and I didn't do much to it. We did stay there one night, roughing it as there was no water or electricity to it. I did have those utilities turned on, but they still didn't work. I would later learn that the main power line had been eaten by squirrels and the main water line burst underground years before. The water company plugged the line, so it wouldn't dump thousands of gallons of fresh water underground. It would cost a pretty penny to fix all that—in time. The one night we stayed—a blowup mattress in the middle of the living room with several blankets on top for me, my wife, and our young son—I searched for signs of our time in the lake house that summer after the seventh grade, but I couldn't find a single trace of our visit. I stood in front of the bay windows with my wife and my son—my left arm around her, my right arm cradling my boy—the same windows my friends and I had huddled in front of, cowering from Bloody Billy and the fear of his wrath. I pointed out to my wife that the island we were staring at, the one out in the middle of the water with the rocky base and the spiky cedar trees, was the one where me and my friends were stranded.

She gasped. "You could've died out there."

I sighed. "Yep. We were so stupid."

The second summer I owned the cabin, my wife and I started to make it our own. That summer was dedicated to demolition and foundation repair. The third summer was for remodeling. By the fourth summer, it was practically a livable cabin. By the fifth summer, it was officially our second home. The summer time became our time at the lake, where we'd take our boy and spend quality time as a family in the out of doors.

I taught my boy things like fishing and how to use a pocket knife to whittle a stick. You know? Outdoorsy stuff. I loved showing him how to do these things, and I continued to spend time with my boy every summer as much as I could, even as he grew into a somewhat ornery teenager. Certain aspects of his personality curdled once he started high school. And as I shook my head and wondered how my wife and I could raise a kid that at times seemed like Dr. Jekyll and Mr. Hyde (depression, anxiety, bi-polar), I often thought about what Sheriff "Sam" Hill said to me, slouched on the chair in my bedroom, looking through me with those dirty, brown eyes of his.

"Billy Callahan is just a boy, just like you. And he got a mama that loves him, just like you," he said to me. "He's somebody's son."

Ain't that the damned truth?

I did one last thing before I considered the Cabin of Seclusion complete. I had two bronze, commemorative plaques made. The first one was for my friend Randy. I had his name put on it along with the important dates to demark his life as well as the professions he probably would have excelled in: football star and comedian. He was really good at both. He was also my best friend. I mounted the bronze plaque on the tallest pecan tree that sat across the driveway to the cabin. It's trunk was solid like concrete and seemed like a fitting place to mount the plaque. It was tall and solid, just like Randy.

The second one was for Billy Callahan. And I know what you're thinking. I must be crazy, right? Maybe you could say that. It's your opinion, I guess. But here's the thing. I thought a lot about my visit from Sheriff "Sam" Hill. What he said to me about Billy—the bully we all called Bloody Billy—it stuck in my mind. Then it got stuck in my craw, that place where you ruminate on things. And I couldn't help but wonder why he told me that. It wasn't until years later when my own son's behavior and issues initiated a mantra that I often repeated over and over. *A boy, just like you. He's somebody's son.* That's when I realized that Billy's parents must have loved him unconditionally, just like I loved my own troubled son unconditionally. And with that unconditional love is the hope that whenever someone you love does something bad, they will hopefully one day have an opportunity for redemption.

Hope.

Redemption.

A boy, just like you. He's somebody's son.

So, on this second bronze plaque, it said this:

Billy Callahan
Somebody's Son

I had it mounted on the last wood plank at the end of the pier, probably the last place his feet touched something earthly before he disappeared into the water forever. I look at the plaque every time I stand on the end of that pier, peering out across the dark water at Sometimes Island, the desolate place where I experienced real, life-threatening danger for the first time in the seventh grade, along with my best friends, surrounded by the murky water that took somebody's son.

Afterword

When I was a boy, I loved comic books, just like William. Wait! Let me rephrase that. I fucking loved comic books. That's more like it. I didn't fall in love with literature until I was in college. Stupid me. It took an excellent English professor, Margaret Downs-Gamble, to blow my mind with literature. As a boy, most literature did not capture my imagination. I don't know why. Maybe it was my short, attention span. Comic books satisfied that quickly (Frank Miller, Alan Moore, John Byrne—to name a few—were on the newsstand when I was in junior high). Maybe it was the long list of bored school teachers I had in junior high and high school (underpaid, overworked, unenthused). But there was one novel that captured my imagination as a young reader: *Lord of the Flies*. It was—for me—the perfect book for boys. It had action, violence, insolence, and—most importantly—an amazing premise. What would happen if some boys were trapped on a deserted island without domineering parents around? In short, they would destroy each other, of course. It's simply what humans would do. Right? Right?! Well, I don't know. It made sense to me as a boy.

I first read *Lord of the Flies* in high school and was drawn to that intriguing premise. Being a teen short on empathy and wisdom, but long on rebelliousness and energy, the premise that these boys would destroy each other in the absence of rules or grown-ups resonated with me. *That's exactly what would happen*, I thought in high school. Reading the novel again in college—not much wiser, but just as rebellious—the premise still held true to me. *That's exactly what would happen*, I thought in college. And that was it concerning that book for a very long time. I had read the novel twice and I thought I knew what it was all about. Case closed. Book on the shelf. Done.

Many years later, having read hundreds of novels and written six novels myself (so far), as well as two books of short stories, and published hundreds of cartoons and a dozen poems for good measure (during my angsty 20s), I still thought the same thing whenever I noticed *Lord of the Flies* on the Amazon bestseller lists. As of this very moment (2:48pm on Sunday, December 8, 2019), *Lord of the Flies* is #11 on the Young Adult Classics list as well as #1,285 in Books overall in Amazon's Book Store, which carries millions of books, by the way. And this is a novel that was first published in 1954—for gods sakes. What. the. Hell?! This premise must still have a hold on our collective imaginations. *That's exactly what would happen?* I thought last year. *Wouldn't it? Right?!* My curiosity was piqued.

I decided to do what every modern human would do. I fell into an internet vortex which started with a simple Google search of *Lord of the Flies*, that led to summaries of various websites with articles about or dissecting the novel, that led to a link to a Wikipedia page about William Golding, which instigated my revigorated interest as a full-grown adult in *Lord of the Flies*. One of the things I learned about *Lord of the Flies* was that it was William Golding's response to another novel titled *The Coral Island*, which was a novel written by Scottish author R. M. Ballantyne in 1857, and was one of the first works of juvenile fiction to feature exclusively juvenile heroes. The story relates the adventures of three boys named Ralph, Jack, and Peterkin marooned on a South Pacific island (sound familiar?), the only survivors of a shipwreck. (I lifted this summary off the Wikipedia page. FYI.) I had already decided at this point that I was going to reread *Lord of the Flies* for a third time, but since I hadn't heard of *The Coral Island* before and since it was the novel that *Lord of the Flies* was written in response to, I decided—right then and there—to read it first. Boy, was I in for a treat. Reading an adventure book from 1857 that I had never heard of before in my spare time? Seemed like the right thing to do.

The Coral Island is an "adventure story for young folks" as described by the author, one similar to Daniel Defoe's *Robinson Crusoe*. It is told by Ralph Rover, one of the boys, in first-person as an adult, reminiscing about his time stranded in the South Pacific. The book is steeped in Christian morality and is somewhat hindered by the narrator and author's limited worldview. The first 60% of the book is about the boys' time on the pristine island and they encounter few dangers except for a shark that happens into their favorite swimming bay. When the boys encounter cannibals that land on their island, then Ralph is kidnapped by pirates soon after, the plot finally revs up, at the behest of losing the presence of two of the boys since they remained on the island. Ultimately, the novel is bogged down by the Christian moralizing, where as the pirates and cannibals are the salacious counterpoint to the Christian crusaders that convert the heathen cannibals and offer an assist to the boys when they needed it most. I found this novel to be more of a historical document than a fun read. Although the relationship between the boys was sweet and realistic, the rest of the book left little to be desired in this modern reader.

In contrast, *Lord of the Flies* is a well-crafted allegory with beautifully descriptive passages about Ralph, Jack (sound familiar?), Piggy, Simon, and a group of British boys stranded on an uninhabited island and their disastrous attempt to govern themselves. The narrator of *Lord of the Flies* tells the lost boys' story vividly and, at times, poetically, yet keeps an emotional distance from the boys, never eliciting empathy or affection for them or their dilemma. Golding explains before starting his story that these boys represent scaled-down society and, if left to their own devices, would reduce their company to all-out anarchy. This is where Golding's genius lies: creating a premise to contemplate where evil instigates. Golding demonstrates that the disregard of rules and order is what nurtures evil, and it's hard not to disagree with Golding because of the way he structures his story with these three fetid protagonists.

Ralph is not an empathetic character, as demonstrated by his disregard of Piggy's feelings throughout the novel, only to have the tiniest bit of remorse for Piggy when it's too late. Jack's self-esteem is so low that he props up his toxic masculinity with bold promises of hunt kills and other threats of violence. Even Piggy's sniveling and hurt feelings are tossed to the side because of his brazen toadiness. It was plain to see from the start of the novel where it was going with these three malcontents leading the stranded children. There was no chance for a positive coexistence on the island without the moral compass of grownups or adults around to steer them right.

But unlike *The Coral Island's* slow first half of pastoral observations of the island (there were a couple of natural disasters those three boys easily overcame), Golding wastes no time after the first chapter wallowing in detailed observations of nature. He quickly jumps into the meat of his narrative, dissecting the boys' interactions with his keen eye, their one-upmanship on full display, their decisions based on hurt feelings and wounded pride. The economy of Golding's storytelling is a marvel and his ability to create some truly beautiful sentences is astounding. By the time the story abruptly ended, my mind raced with the possibility of redemption for these terrible boys, these little lords of corruption.

These terrible boys.

That's it. That's the key to the premise right there. That marvelous premise.

With these terrible boys.

Of course, these four boys—these terrible boys—were going to fuck each other over in the end. That was plain to see from the start, from the very first two pages. And because of that, Golding's premise teeters. This is not a scaled-down society, as he posits. This is four damaged, *White* boys infecting the lot with their toxic masculinity, their low self-esteem, and their desire to be the leader. Evil germinates within these four boys because this is fertile ground for evil to grow. Maybe I could see this more plainly on my third reading because I'm older, wiser, a more experienced reader and writer, a father, a good friend, and... well, a full-fledged human being. I started thinking.

That's not exactly what would happen.

What if the boys were friends from the start instead of bastards?

What if the friends were like the kids I knew in junior high or middle school?

Would they fuck each other over?

No, they wouldn't.

I am certain of this.

And this, everybody, is how the mind of a writer works. Well, this writer at least. This was the genesis of my new story, the story that would become *The Benevolent Lords of Sometimes Island.* What would happen if four friends of diverse backgrounds were stranded somewhere in the middle of Texas during the time when I was their age, circa mid-1980s? Sounded interesting to me. I'd never written something in response to an already published story before, let alone a famous story like *Lord of the Flies.* But if William Golding did it, then why couldn't I?

Why couldn't I?

I began outlining a story with characters based on the boys I knew when I was in junior high—kind and funny boys of different races and different economic backgrounds. Where would they get stranded in the middle of Texas? How would they get there? What would they do once they were stranded? How would they treat each other? What kind of danger would they encounter? Would they be able to survive? Besides, I loved this era of the 1980s. It was a formidable time for me with great music, movies, comic books, video games—you name it! This was working itself out to be a great idea for me, not only as a writer, but as a fan of great literature.

My response.

My addition to this literary conversation.

This is exactly what would happen.

There was one more story added to this mix. A novella, actually. While in my *Lord of the Flies* internet vortex, I remembered seeing a list of famous authors who loved *Lord of the Flies*. Stephen King was one of them. Turns out he references *Lord of the Flies* quite a bit in his own work. His fictional town in Maine called Castle Rock is named after the mountain of rocks on the island in *Lord of the Flies* where Jack claims the beast resides. And my favorite story of King's, *The Body*, is about four boys from Castle Rock who go on an adventure to find the dead body of Roy Brower. And even though the four boys in this story—Gordie, Chris, Teddy, and Vern—are not stranded on a deserted island, it is clear that their adventure is inspired by Golding's take on feral boys in the wilderness. I decided to read this novella again for the third time. Here's what I discovered.

Structurally, this novella is flawed. There are some things about it that I do not like at all and detracts from the overall plot and narrative. But even with its flaws, it is an amazing story with literary flourishes and fully-formed characters. It has a touch of nostalgia and reveals an endearing remembrance of a friendship whose power is not diminished over time. It's an affecting depiction of the power of friendship. "The most important things are the hardest things to say…" is the mantra of this story. Stephen King repeats this mantra a few times, even parses it at one point, then admits to the irony of an author declaring that words diminish the important things in our lives.

Here's the brief book description: It's 1960 in the fictional town of Castle Rock, Maine. Ray Brower, a boy from a nearby town, has disappeared, and twelve-year-old Gordie Lachance and his three friends set out on a quest to find his body along the railroad tracks. During the course of their journey, Gordie, Chris Chambers, Teddy Duchamp, and Vern Tessio come to terms with death and the harsh truths of growing up in a small factory town that doesn't offer much in the way of a future. This novella is the basis for the classic movie *Stand by Me* which was released in 1986 (the year *The Benevolent Lords of Sometimes Island* takes place), although the story itself takes place in 1960.

King shows great descriptive flair and the dialogue is snappy and true to life. Gordie (the narrator and one of the boys as an adult) is likeable and an effective storyteller who reveals the goodness beneath the hard exterior that is beginning to form during this formidable time in their lives. The story is both an adventure and a coming-of-age tale with a bit of mystery. We, the readers, never find out how or why exactly Ray Brower is killed, neither at the time or in hindsight. But the initial spookiness of his death and the morbid desire of the boys to see his body eventually turns into a meditation on life, what Ray Brower will be missing, and what the four friends unintentionally have to look forward to in their own lives. The connection between the four friends is palpable, particularly between Gordie and Chris. They eventually find the wherewithal to do better in school, so they can escape the oppressive blue-collar life of the town of Castle Rock. And the connection they have begins with this adventure to find Ray Brower.

Structurally, I feel the novella fails in a couple of areas. First, two short stories were included—in full—within the novella that are examples of what Gordie publishes as an adult when he becomes a professional writer. Unfortunately, they do not add anything to the story of the four, young friends; and the "pie eating contest" could have more effectively been told by young Gordie as a campfire tale within the main narrative. Second, the ending is a letdown. It feels—to me—like King didn't know what to do with a story like this, as it was way outside of his wheelhouse at the time of its original publication. The morbid Ch 33 and deflated Ch 34 (the last two chapters) seem as if King decided to "right the ship" and steer the plot to an ending that would ultimately satisfy his horror-loving readership, rather than find meaning in the things he is exploring in this story: friendship, camaraderie, and many of the important things in one's life. "The most important things are the hardest things to say…" And as we are reminded of this time and time again in the story, King chooses not to say them, or even to try to attempt to say what he really wants to say. A period of great friendship in a person's life can have a lasting effect, one that resonates long after the friendship is over, as is evident in a story like this. In the end, King was and still is known as a horror writer, and there was no way he was going to end this story on a positive note.

But again, even with these flaws, I *love* this novella. The friendship between the boys is the heart of the story and I love their adventure and the way they look out (mostly) for each other. I love that an adventure like this can be known only to its principal actors, as no one in Castle Rock is aware of what they are doing during their time looking for Ray Brower, and it is a secret we share with the boys. And I love being reminded that any preconceptions you can have about a writer can be shattered with a curveball like this. King summarizes the story best at the end of Ch 11, right in the middle of the novella. "I never had any friends later on like the ones I had when I was twelve. Jesus, did you?"

Why yes, Mr. King. I did.

I was very fond of them.

They were the inspiration for William, Randy, Miguel, and Brian.

And I wasn't going to let what happened to Chris, Teddy, and Vern happen to William, Randy, Miguel, and Brian.

They deserved better.

So, as I reread and analyzed these great stories by Ballantyne, Golding, and King, I wasn't in the position to write my own story about four friends who escaped to an abandoned house by a lake in the middle of Texas, then become stranded on a rocky island out in the middle of the lake after being chased by their worst enemies—Bloody Billy and Rogelio from the Thousand Oaks Gang. I was writing my novel *To Squeeze a Prairie Dog* at the time. Since I was busy with that project, I did what many writers would do. I ruminated about this beautiful nugget of an idea for a story. And a year after finishing *To Squeeze a Prairie Dog*, then publishing it, then promoting it, I begin writing *The Benevolent Lords of Sometimes Island* in June 2019 and finished writing in December of 2019.

I hope you enjoyed reading it as much as I enjoyed writing it.

And thank you R. M. Ballantyne, William Golding, and Stephen King for your stories. I hope that my story is a worthy addition to this literary discussion.

Author's Note and Acknowledgments

If you could, then please indulge me a few more minutes so I can acknowledge the folks who helped me with this novel and give credit where credit is due. Writing novels is a long and difficult journey, although a very satisfying one for me. But I have discovered after taking this journey quite a few times that it is a much more pleasant experience when I have a great team to assist with the journey. So, I would like to acknowledge the folks who have helped me so much along the way.

Brandon Wood for your editing.

Lori Hoadley for your editing.

Charlotte Gullick for your editing.

Andrew Leeper for your cover design.

My kids—Ryan, Sophia, Ahnika, and Colin—for your support.

My sister, Sheryl Russell, and brother-in-law, Chris Russell, and niece Haley Nicole, for your support.

My mother-in-law, Cora Hoadley, for your support and readership.

My father-in-law, Ed Hoadley, for your storytelling. Rest in Peace.

My Uncle Barry Semegran and Aunt Jody for your support and readership.

My parents—Mike and Eloise Semegran—for everything. Rest in peace.

My friends—Dave Holmes and Michelle Zweede—for your friendship, and for just listening.

To all my beta readers—John Morgan, Anthony Marks, Jeff Loftin, James Grayson, Cora Hoadley, and so many more—thank you for your insight and kind words.

My literary brethren—Larry Brill, Heather Harper Ellett, Charlotte Gullick, Brian Kendall, Selraybob, J. Reeder Archuleta, Owen Egerton, Jacqui Castle, Michelle Rene, S. Usher Evans, and all the other great writers I've met along the way—that are kicking ass and taking names with their great books. Huzzah!

But most importantly—my wife, Lori Hoadley, for her love and support. For her editing. For her kind spirit. For help with creating a home and a family life conducive for me to be a productive, creative person. For that, I am truly and forever grateful. She is a gift to me. And without her, this novel wouldn't have been completed.

Take care, Scott.

About the Author

Scott Semegran is an award-winning writer of eight books. *BlueInk Review* described him best as "a gifted writer, with a wry sense of humor." His latest novel, *The Benevolent Lords of Sometimes Island*, is about four middle school friends who sneak away to an abandoned lake house to evade the wrath of high school bullies, only to become stranded on the lake's desolate island. His previous novel, *To Squeeze a Prairie Dog: An American Novel*, was the 2019 Readers' Favorite International Book Award Winner: Silver Medal for Fiction - Humor/Comedy, the 2019 Texas Author Project Winner for Adult Fiction, and the 2020 IBPA Benjamin Franklin Award Gold Medal Winner for Humor. His book *Sammie & Budgie* was the first place winner for Fiction in the 2018 Texas Authors Book Awards. His book *BOYS* was the 2018 IndieReader Discovery Awards winner for Short Stories. He lives in Austin,

Texas with his wife, four kids, two cats, and a dog. He graduated from the University of Texas at Austin with a degree in English.

Books by Scott Semegran

To Squeeze a Prairie Dog is the story of J. D. Wiswall, a sincere young man from a small town, who joins a state government agency in a data entry department comprised of quirky clerks. Quickly endearing himself to the diverse group in Unit 3, J. D. learns his coworkers have a pact to share the $10,000 prize if they win a cost-savings program for a suggestion that could save the government money, in turn helping them rise above their own personal struggles. A multimillion-dollar cost-savings suggestion is accidentally discovered by J. D.'s supervisor, the goof-off alcoholic Brent Baker. This lucrative discovery catches the attention of crotchety Governor Dwayne Bennett, a media-hungry demagogue, who turns the coworkers of Unit 3 into props for his selfish political reasons. The publicity surrounding the clerks piques the interest of a newspaper reporter, Esther Jean Stinson, whose investigative reporting threatens to reveal the governor's career-ending secret, as well as jeopardizes the prize that the clerks so desperately desire.

Along with J. D. and Brent, the lives of the amiable coworkers in Unit 3 are revealed. There is Rita Jackson, the kind matriarch of her large brood, who spends her time outside of work caring for her five struggling children and thirteen wily grandchildren. Then there's Deborah Martinez, a single mother to a felonious son, who struggles to keep her head above her sinking financial woes. There's also Conchino Gonzalez, a quiescent giant of Mexican and Japanese descent, who street races at night to relieve worries about his ailing grandfather in Japan. Finally, J. D. has dreams bigger than his small hometown can provide, and Brent wants nothing more than to drop the bureaucratic routine to become a rock star with his bar band.

A few blocks away from the agency that houses Unit 3, Governor Bennett, a smarmy politician who whizzes around the Governor's Mansion on a gold-plated wheelchair, parades the unwitting clerks in front of the local media in an attempt to raise his sagging poll numbers. But reporter Esther Jean sees through the governor's bald-faced motives and uncovers secrets not meant to be revealed. Will her revelations keep Unit 3 from receiving their elusive prize?

From award-winning writer Scott Semegran, *To Squeeze a Prairie Dog* is an American, modern-day tale with working-class folks—part fable, part satire, and part comedy—revealing that camaraderie amongst kind-hearted friends wins the day over evil intentions.

"An amusing yet heartwarming romp... *To Squeeze a Prairie Dog* is an entertaining slice-of-life story that's humorous yet uplifting at the same time. By the novel's last page, readers will be longing for more." — *BlueInk Review* (Starred Review)

"A comic sendup of state government that remains lighthearted, deadpan, and full of affection for both urban and rural Texas." — *Kirkus Reviews*

"*To Squeeze a Prairie Dog* paints a rollicking story that careens through the office structure to delve into the motivations, lives, and connections between ordinary individuals... an uplifting, fun story." — *Midwest Book Review*

"An accomplished tale... a recommended read for fans of humor, drama, and office politics." — *Readers' Favorite Book Reviews.* 5 stars.

"Fascinating and heartfelt." — *IndieReader*

"Semegran is at the top of his game as he crafts this thoroughly engaging read. Written in a crisp, clear prose, this fast-paced novel will delight fans of literary fiction." — *The Prairies Book Review.* 5 stars.

"Semegran lures you in with a combination of sardonic wit and slapstick comedy, but before you know it, you're contemplating issues of money, class, media, politics, the social contract, and the many possible definitions of success... *To Squeeze a Prairie Dog* concludes on just the right note and contains depths you won't expect." — *Lone Star Literary Life*

***

Sammie & Budgie is a quirky, mystical tale of a self-doubting IT nerd and his young son, who possesses the gift of foresight. The boy's special ability propels his family on a road trip to visit his ailing grandfather, a prickly man who left an indelible stamp on the father and son. The three are connected through more than genetics, their lives intertwined through dreams, imagination, and longing.

Simon works as a network administrator for a state government agency, a consolation after a promising career as a novelist flounders. He finds himself a single parent of two small children following the mysterious death of his adulterous wife. From the ashes of his failed marriage emerges a tight-knit family of three: a creative, special needs son, a hyperactive, butt-kicking daughter, and the caring, sensitive father. But when his son's special ability reveals itself, Simon struggles to keep his little family together in the face of adversity and uncertainty.

Sammie is a creative third-grader that draws adventures in his sketchbook with his imaginary friend, Budgie, a parakeet that protects him from the monsters inhabiting his dreams. Sammie is also a special needs child but is special in more ways than one. He can see the future. Sammie seemingly can predict events both mundane and catastrophic in equal measure. But when he envisions the suffering of his grandfather, the family embarks on a road trip to San Antonio with the nanny to visit the ailing patriarch.

Sammie & Budgie is an illustrated novel brought to you from the quirky mind of writer and cartoonist Scott Semegran. The novel explores the bond between a caring father and his children, one affected by his own thorny relationship with his surly father, and the connection he has with his sweet son is thicker than blood, going to the place where dreams are conceived and realized.

2018 Texas Authors Book Awards: First Place Winner for General Fiction

2018 Texas Authors Book Cover Awards: First Place Winner for Fiction

"Illustrated throughout by Semegran, this book is the author's best... An unconventional, beguiling, and endearing family tale." — *Kirkus Reviews*

"The novel's delights abound... Semegran is a gifted writer, with a wry sense of humor." — *BlueInk Review* (Starred Review)

"The writing quality is excellent and the dialogue between Simon and Sammie is immersive." — *Foreword* Clarion Reviews. Clarion Rating: 4 out of 5.

***

Other Books by Scott Semegran

Boys
The Spectacular Simon Burchwood
The Meteoric Rise of Simon Burchwood
Modicum
Mr. Grieves

For more information, go to:
https://scottsemegran.com/books.html

***

Find Scott Semegran Online:
https://scottsemegran.com
https://www.goodreads.com/scottsemegran
https://www.twitter.com/scottsemegran
https://www.facebook.com/scottsemegran.writer/
https://www.instagram.com/scott_semegran
https://www.amazon.com/author/scottsemegran
https://www.smashwords.com/profile/view/scottsemegran

Mutt Press:
https://muttpress.com

Bildungsromans

Suspense Fiction

A positive "spin"/"take" on William Golding's bleak novel Lord of the Flies (1986 TX island vs. Golding's 1950s island in the Pacific).

CPSIA information can be obtained
at www.ICGtesting.com
Printed in the USA
BVHW031704301220
596760BV00001B/19

9 781087 8786